THE DISTURBANCE 3: THE TRUTH

Hard Science Fiction

The Disturbance

Book 3

BRANDON Q. MORRIS

BRANDON Q.
MORRIS
HARD SCIENCE FICTION

hard-sf.com

brandon@hard-sf.com

Translator: Siân Robertson

Editor: Margaret Dean (Profile)

Cover design: Jelena Gajic

Contents

Events so far

THEY WERE FARTHER OUT THAN ANYONE HAD EVER BEEN. After a twenty-year voyage beginning in 2094 (or so they believed), the spaceship Shepherd-1 finally arrived at the coordinates in interstellar space where the crew of four were to complete humanity's most ambitious project to date: SGL, the solar gravitational lens – a telescope that used the Sun itself as a lens. It was to grant terrestrial astronomers an incredibly clear view of distant star systems, galaxies, and the Big Bang. The Shepherd-1 crew used a flock of 'Sheep' probes, which formed a gigantic virtual mirror with the spaceship at its center.

But the telescope didn't deliver the images they were hoping for. The farther into the past they peered, the blurrier the images became. Christine, the astronomer in charge of research, kept coming up with new ideas to solve the problem – without success. It was almost as if the universe had deliberately drawn a veil over its mysteries. But one day she finally extracted an image from the beginning of time: a snapshot that would reveal once and for all whether the cosmos owed its existence to a creator or not.

It wasn't until Christine held the evidence of the existence or nonexistence of God in her hands for the first time that she realized the implications of this information. She took drastic measures, triggering an explosion that would destroy the research results – and kill her too. Aaron, Benjamin, and David – her team – were caught off-guard by this catastrophe. They were faced with a puzzle, because Christine never communicated the reason for her actions.

Back on Earth, their CapCom Rachel Schmidt tried to help them in their search for answers. But this only raised more questions. Rachel discovered that the mission – jointly organized by NASA and Alpha Omega, the company of billionaire Ilan Chatterjee – had originally launched much later than the crew and Mission Control had been led to believe. This meant the spaceship had covered a distance of 700 astronomical units in just a few years. But that was technically impossible, because humans couldn't survive the necessary acceleration. Rachel conducted some research and discovered that Chatterjee had put together a very unusual crew. The quartet on board Shepherd-1 consisted not of people, but of androids modeled on certain individuals. They possessed the consciousness and memories of their human counterparts and believed themselves to be human.

But they were not. Chatterjee had personal motives for discovering the true origin of the universe and was afraid of losing the data. So he remotely activated Eric, a fifth android on board Shepherd-1, whose mission was to secure the evidence at all costs. Meanwhile, Aaron, Benjamin, and David discovered not only that they weren't human, but also that the entire Solar System was under threat: the solar gravitational lens had apparently teleported a space-time disturbance to the edge of the Solar System. The disturbance was spreading and had the potential to decimate all the planets.

It became clear that the only solution was to accelerate the ship, together with the 'disturbance', out into interstellar space, in order to eliminate the threat to Earth. The crew would die, but Aaron, Benjamin, and David accepted this mission – along with the resurrected Christine, whose android constitution had allowed her to survive the explosion. They overpowered Eric, the android controlled by Chatterjee, and astronomer Christine had a brilliant idea: using the solar gravitational lens, the team teleported the germ of a black hole into the middle of the disturbance in order to contain it.

The plan succeeded. Shepherd-1 set out on a voyage into the unknown. At some point, the ship would reach a new star, taking Aaron, David, and Christine with it. Meanwhile, Benjamin embarked on the long journey back to Earth, arriving in 2109. He had no knowledge of the truth about the origin of the universe. But he hoped to find out more about his own origin on the planet of his creator.

Three years later, Benjamin had set himself up as a gardener in Houston, Texas. In search of an assistant, he acquired an old universal robot from a scrap dealer, which he repaired. It turned out to be Oscar, a special design from the RB corporation. Soon after, he was ambushed by a troop of mercenaries apparently sent by Chatterjee. Benjamin fled. With Oscar's help he located his former CapCom Rachel. They hoped to find out from her why Chatterjee was suddenly so interested in him.

But his opponents were faster. Chatterjee was waiting for him at Rachel's house, where he abducted him and took him to an underground facility. There he met his human counterpart – the man his body and personality were based on. His human twin had lost both legs as a young man. Chatterjee had cultured and transplanted two new legs for him. And in return, he had allowed himself to be copied.

In conversation with Benjamin, Chatterjee finally revealed his problem. Shepherd-1 had apparently resumed its search for the mysteries of the cosmos. But two weeks prior, just as the first results were supposed to start coming in, contact with the ship was abruptly cut off. The ship itself still seemed to be functioning, but it was no longer communicating. Chatterjee wanted to transfer Benjamin's consciousness back to the Shepherd-1. It would be a one-way trip, because the ship's transmitter wasn't powerful enough to send him back. On board Shepherd-1, Benjamin would then be loaded into one of the spare android bodies stored there.

Benjamin was prepared go through with it because he wanted to help his friends. But he didn't like the fact that Chatterjee intended to accompany him. Benjamin was convinced that the billionaire was more concerned about the data than rescuing the crew. Oscar helped Benjamin to escape from Chatterjee's facility and they hatched a plan: they sent themselves as cargo to Akademgorodok in Siberia. Oscar hoped to find an alternative transfer option for them there. On their travels, they met the sex robot Aphrodite, who was on the way to her new owner but dreaming of freedom.

The three of them infiltrated the research facility of the RB corporation. But once inside, they were captured. RB boss Valentina struck a deal with Benjamin to send him to Shepherd-1 using her own equipment. But she deceived him. Instead of sending Benjamin to Shepherd-1, she transferred him to a digital prison in order to study his consciousness. Oscar saw through the ruse. Together with Aphrodite, he redirected the transfer to the original destination and then sent himself on the journey there too.

Benjamin was the first to arrive on Shepherd-1, but the system admin identified him as malware. Oscar arrived a day later and helped him out of the jam and into Eric's body. There was nobody else on board. The crew must have left the ship – three space suits were also missing. They searched for them and found Christine first. But it was not the original Christine – they had found a previously unknown replacement body for the captain of the expedition. And Chatterjee was in it. Together they found the real Christine in a damaged capsule. After they repaired her, she told them what had happened. Shepherd-1 had apparently acquired a parasite with very unusual properties that were of great interest to science.

But Chatterjee was still more interested in the answer to the question of the origin of the universe. In order to get his hands on it, he took command of the ship and plotted a course back toward the Sun, where his technicians could extract the secret from Christine.

Fortunately, Oscar had another trick up his sleeve. He had brought the sex robot's consciousness with him. During an EVA, she managed to take back control of the ship from Chatterjee. 'The Disturbance 2: the Answer' ended with Oscar receiving a radio signal. It was not from Mission Control, as Chatterjee assumed, but from interstellar space.

The Disturbance 3

Shepherd-1, October 19, 2112

"Is this some kind of joke?" asked Chatterjee.

"No," Oscar replied. "My simulations tell me with 82 percent certainty that the radio signal reached us from interstellar space."

"A signal, OK," said Chatterjee. "We receive loads of signals. There's an entire research branch dedicated to the subject. But there were never any that couldn't be explained by some natural phenomenon."

"That can't be ruled out, of course," said Oscar. "We should examine the signal before we respond to it."

"I think this parasite is more urgent," said Christine. "It's still expanding. If we can't contain it somehow, the cloud will swallow us."

The woman beside her nodded. Benjamin was constantly tempted to call her Christine too. But that body contained Chatterjee. They looked like twins, but they couldn't have been more different.

"Christine's right," said Chatterjee. "Right now, we shouldn't be concerning ourselves with a radio signal from out there. We need to solve our immediate problems and then focus on the actual mission."

He was referring to the search for the images of the Big Bang that the Sheep probes were supposed to have recorded.

"I'm not sure it's a good idea to ignore the signal," said Oscar. "Can I show you?"

"Go ahead, if you insist," said Chatterjee.

On the screen in front of the captain's seat a diagram appeared. It looked like a spectral analysis. Benjamin studied it. He couldn't discern any structure in it.

"That doesn't look very spectacular," said Chatterjee.

"Sorry," said Oscar. "I forgot you can't convert acoustic signals. One moment."

A blinking vertical line moved across the graphic. There was a whispering sound coming from the speaker.

"I didn't catch that," said Christine.

Benjamin was convinced that her face looked friendlier than that of her evil twin.

"One moment. I'll increase the levels."

"Need... help... please... danger... pain... please... help... quick."

A shiver ran up Benjamin's spine. He knew that voice! And it was undoubtedly a call for help.

"It keeps repeating," Oscar explained.

"I think that's David," Christine said with wide eyes.

Wasn't it Aaron? Benjamin dug through his memories and found Aaron's face on a display in capsule B. *Ah, you're back, that was quick,* it said. Benjamin had just returned from checking the orientation of the flock. He tapped the screen to play back the message again. The word 'quick' sounded similar to the 'quick' in his memory.

"What is it?" asked Christine.

Benjamin shook his head. Christine had spent the last few years with David and Aaron. She'd know their voices.

"Tell me. You noticed something. I know you, Benjamin."

True. She wasn't calling him Ben – she remembered that he didn't like it.

"It sounded to me like Aaron said some of those words," he said. "For example 'quick'."

"Oscar, can you confirm that?" asked Christine.

"The voice profile does vary from word to word," said

Oscar. “The eight words can in fact be attributed to two different speakers. I also notice that the recording is quite choppy. The volume drops down to zero in the pauses.”

“That means the message wasn’t spoken, it was cobbled together from separate recordings, the way blackmailers used to do with individual letters cut from newspaper headlines,” said Christine.

She liked watching ancient films, Benjamin remembered. Shepherd-1 had a large archive.

“Another clue is the fact that both instances of ‘please’ are identical. A speaker can’t repeat themselves with that level of precision,” said Oscar.

“So the whole thing’s a fake,” said Chatterjee. “I knew it. Somebody’s trying to mess with us.”

“There’s nobody capable of sending us messages from interstellar space,” said Christine. “Nobody’s ever made it farther out than we have.”

“Maybe they just want us to believe the message is coming from out there,” said Chatterjee. “Mission Control could have somehow faked it. Or RB. Didn’t they transmit you out here?”

“Oscar, how realistic is that scenario?” asked Benjamin.

“I can find no indication that the message was manipulated on Earth, but I can’t rule it out. However, that would mean there are still processes on the ship that are outside of my control.”

“There are,” said Chatterjee. “What about the sex robot’s control software? Couldn’t RB have put a Trojan in it?”

“Are you talking about me?” asked Aphrodite. “I assure you, I haven’t been manipulated by anyone. That’s all in the past.”

“You were manufactured by RB,” said Chatterjee. “You’re from the HDS series, which has an impressive combination of erotic and combat capabilities. But you came from the military tech arm of RB. So it’s possible that...”

“I trust Aphrodite with my life,” said Benjamin.

“Thank you, Benjamin.”

"That's not a valid argument!" said Chatterjee in a raised voice. "Can't we discuss this like grownups?"

"Mr. Chatterjee," said Christine, "you're now part of a crew. We depend on each other, for better or worse. Trust is the most valid argument of all under the circumstances. If Benjamin's willing to vouch for Aphrodite, then she hasn't brought a Trojan on board. Period. I see no point in discussing it further. We need to find the source of the signal and deal with the parasite. Everything else is secondary."

"I'll keep working on the signal," said Oscar.

"Since you don't care about the signal, Ilan," said Christine, "I suggest you and Benjamin go deal with the helium cloud."

"If you insist..." said Chatterjee.

"I do," said Christine. "I'll help Oscar with the signal."

"I was about to suggest that," said Oscar. "If we reconfigure our antennae, we may be able to triangulate the source. But that means someone has to climb across the Shepherd's hull."

"I'll do it," said Christine.

"I'd be happy to take a closer look at the interior of the cloud," said Aphrodite. "Is there maybe a body on board for me?"

"When I arrived on Shepherd-1 there were two spare androids," said Benjamin. "I'm in one of them and our Mr. Chatterjee is in the other."

When he arrived, Oscar had given him the choice between a female and a male body. If only he'd chosen differently! Then he would be Christine's twin and Chatterjee would be in Eric's body, which was much more fitting. But he had assumed the female android was their former crew mate Fadilla, who left the ship a while after he did.

"I was thinking more of a robot," said Aphrodite.

"A robot?" asked Chatterjee. "I'm not aware of any humanoid models on board, but there should be a couple of specialized robots."

"In the inventory list I can see a vacuuming bot, a loading

bot, a repair bot for external repairs, and a six-armed robodoc, but that one's not mobile," said Oscar.

"Anything but a vacuuming bot," said Benjamin.

"What do you have against those? I've heard they can be very helpful and clever," said Oscar.

"Aphrodite is clever too," said Benjamin. "What are the differences between the loading and repair bots?"

"The loader has two flexible arms with a lifting capacity of 250 kilograms at 1 g and a flat base with four wheels. The mechanic has six walking legs and two arms of different sizes that can be equipped with tools. Its maximum load is 30 kilograms. Both can operate in the vacuum."

"How's the battery life? And what about computing capacity and sensors?"

"They can both run independently for eight hours. The repair bot has a faster processor and optical, acoustic, and electromagnetic sensors. The loader doesn't have any of that, but it has lidar, radar, and a barcode scanner."

"Not an easy decision," said Benjamin. "Out in space and in a cloud, the radar and lidar could be helpful. But a camera would be good too, and electromagnetic fields are probably significant when it comes to the parasite."

"I could divide myself between them," said Aphrodite. "My system is multi-platform capable. How much does the repair bot weigh?"

"Eighty kilograms," said Oscar.

"Great. The loader can carry it. At that proximity, I can connect their computers via radio."

"What if they get separated by some stupid accident?" asked Christine.

"Then I'll experience a split consciousness."

"Is that treatable?" asked Benjamin.

"Depends how long it lasts. When they're separated, the two parts of the consciousness begin to regenerate the missing structures on both sides. That makes it difficult to reunite them, and after a while it's impossible."

"Then there would be two of you?"

"There would be two versions of Aphrodite. But I can't guarantee that both would be functional."

"Right," said Benjamin. "Then let's make sure the two robots don't get separated."

"Thanks," said Aphrodite. "When do we start?"

"I'd like to get this done as quickly as possible so we can return our attention to the mission," said Chatterjee.

"Until the parasite problem is solved, there is no mission," said Christine.

"I realize that."

"I need a couple of hours," said Aphrodite. "Those two bodies are very unfamiliar to me. It'll take some time for me to adjust to my new capabilities."

"Sure," said Benjamin. "Take as long as you need. Safety takes precedence. We don't want to lose you. I suggest we all find a bed and get a couple hours' sleep."

"Is that really necessary?" asked Chatterjee. "These bodies don't need sleep."

"You built them, Chatterjee, so you should know better. Even artificial muscles need some time to regenerate. Not to mention your consciousness. I wouldn't be surprised if you have the most vivid dreams you've had in a long time."

"I never dream," said Chatterjee. "I control my sleep phases with medication. It's more efficient."

"I promise you, after forty-eight hours without sleep, you'll only feel half human, even as an android," said Christine.

"So a quarter android," said Benjamin.

"An eighth," said Christine.

He had been away for so long. But everything still seemed familiar, as if he'd only been gone a week. And it had been eighteen years! Benjamin ran around the ring. He still needed a little exercise, or he'd be unable to sleep. Chatterjee had retreated to the storage area. Oscar had promised not to let him out of his sight. Aphrodite was training in the new robot bodies. She seemed very motivated. Benjamin's bed for the night was in capsule A, but he hadn't been there yet.

First a few laps of the ring. He couldn't pass all the way around it because the bulkheads at sector C were still sealed off. But changing direction every now and then made it more interesting. Moving at a fast jog, he felt like a moon orbiting a planet. The ring's rotation simulated a certain amount of gravity, but not enough to feel real. Benjamin felt like a marionette on strings. He could leap higher and farther than at home, but his movements were hard to control. That was one thing that emphasized how long he had been away. The low gravity never used to bother him. Back then he had adapted his running style to the conditions, and it was much more efficient than this uncontrolled bounding.

Eighteen years. He had spent most of his life on the ship believing he was human. The shock when they realized they had been duped... For some reason they never really talked about it. They could all have used some good therapy. Instead, they just continued as if nothing had happened. No, not him. He had climbed into his capsule and flown to Earth. Fadilla followed his example later on. But she never arrived on Earth. Maybe she was still on her way. When she launched, Shepherd-1 must have been a lot farther from the Solar System than when Benjamin left. Maybe she was touching down now on the blue planet. Benjamin envied her.

And what had he done? Instead of enjoying life on the long beaches near Galveston, he allowed himself to be brought back here. And he brought with him the human who got them all into this mess in the first place. He didn't deliberately bring him. But he should have known that Chatterjee would never accept defeat after Benjamin slipped through his fingers. He stopped running when he reached one of the few portholes in the ring. It looked as if a curtain had been drawn across it on the outside. It took his eyes a while to adapt. The stars emerged hesitantly, as if they were disappointed in him for returning to Earth. Ten stars, a hundred, a thousand. That was all he could see. They were so far from the Solar System that their home star was just one of many.

He ran on. It was a depressing view for someone who had just come from Earth. Back in 2094, it was different. And now he knew why: they didn't know any different back then. Chatterjee had cheated them out of a real life. Benjamin had reclaimed his. Then again, without the multimillionaire, they wouldn't exist. They had no parents to love them to the ends of their lives. The only person who could fulfill that role was Ilan Chatterjee. But he saw them as tools he had built in order to fulfill his own dreams. Dreams that he still pursued.

Benjamin passed a bulkhead. It led to capsule B. He must have passed by here twenty times today, but he only realized now that the door couldn't be opened – and that was a good thing, because there was nothing but the vacuum behind it. This was where his cabin used to be. What did it use to look like? He delved into his memories and found nothing but generic images that could have been any of their cabins. How had he made that space his own? He couldn't remember, damn it. Benjamin shook his head and continued.

One more quadrant and he reached capsule A. Christine had suggested he sleep there. *I can't bring myself to go in there. I watched Aaron die.* He understood, and he was grateful to have been spared that sight. Benjamin opened the heavy door, which was also a bulkhead. He was greeted by the cool, slightly musty air from the room beyond. An unpleasantly bright light switched itself on. It cast a shadow on the bed and the wall that resembled a person lying down. Benjamin rubbed his eyes. It was only a rumpled blanket. How long since Aaron was last here? Less than a month, by his estimation. Christine had spent more than two weeks stuck in capsule D.

Benjamin bounded around the capsule. He needed to touch the minimal furnishings in order to familiarize himself with the layout. That way, if he urgently needed to use the WHC in the night, he could find his way around in the dark. He began to notice the ways it differed from his own capsule, which must still be in lunar orbit. Aaron had moved the bed to the other side. The chair was adjusted differently and the legs of the desk were lengthened, because he was a little taller. The porthole showed a different viewpoint. But what exactly was different about it? Oh, right – he was looking at the ring, but it was missing the big bulge of the next capsule, capsule B. That had been flown to Earth by a certain Benjamin.

How did the others fare after he left? Did they feel betrayed? He wanted to talk to Christine about it. Did they take out their disappointment on Fadilla to the point where she felt she had no choice but to leave Shepherd-1? Surely not. Aaron, Dave, and Christine weren't like that. At least they never used to be.

He heard a knock. Benjamin flinched. Who could it be? Christine wouldn't...

"It's me!" called Christine.

Benjamin went to the door and slid the latch across. The door opened.

"May I come in?" she asked.

"I thought you said you couldn't face being in here?"

"Just don't talk about it, OK? I'm trying to get used to the idea. I shouldn't let it get to me so much."

"Please."

Benjamin stepped aside and gestured for Christine to enter. If she found it difficult to enter Aaron's cabin, she didn't show it. Was that a good strategy? But who was he to give her advice?

"Since when do you lock the door?" asked Christine, making a beeline for Aaron's bed.

"Good question. Must be a habit from Earth. They're always trying to rob you there. Or worse."

It had taken him a while to get into the habit of locking his house and vehicle. Their cabins had always been open.

"Sounds like a paradise that I should definitely visit," said Christine.

"The Earth is really something. The colors, the smells, the tastes – there's nothing like it here. I was pretty much constantly overwhelmed for the first three months. And the quiet. At first I could only sleep with the aircon blasting. I got so cold."

"I can imagine. I don't even hear the constant humming of the life support system anymore. But I'm hyperaware when it suddenly drops out."

"That's probably for the best, because it generally means you're about to die."

Christine sat on the bed. She patted the spot beside her. Benjamin sat down.

"And still you came back," she said.

"I couldn't leave you guys hanging. But it's harder than I expected."

"Thank you, Benjamin. For your honesty too. I'm sorry you're stuck out here with us now, instead of lying on a beach. Where did you actually live?"

"Southern Texas, near the sea."

"So the beach was a good guess. I figured you were the type. How did you make a living?"

"Gardening. I tended the gardens of old rich women."

"When you left us, you said..."

"That I wanted to meet my father, I know," he cut in.

"Our father."

Benjamin smiled absent-mindedly. "True, sister. Being on Earth totally changed that. It's hard to explain. But when I arrived, Chatterjee was suddenly no longer important to me. I could live! If I had looked him up, I probably never would have escaped him. He can be pretty... persuasive."

"That's our father."

Christine took his hand. It felt good to sit beside her. The old camaraderie was still there.

"It sounds weird," he said. "I have memories of my parents."

"Did you see them?"

"No, they're dead. But I saw the human version of me."

"Wow, that must have been intense!"

Christine turned toward him. Her eyes shone.

"He thought I was his son. I can understand why he did it."

"Did what?"

"You know, selling his memories, his whole life, to Chatterjee. He traded it for his health. Get this – he's not allowed to leave Chatterjee's facility."

"Our... counterparts all live there? Did you meet me?"

"No. But I learned that the real Benjamin Forestier and the real Christine Delrue were a couple. For a while, anyway. They had a son together."

"The one the man mistook you for?"

"Yeah. He ran away as an adolescent. Nobody knows where he is."

"Then you did the guy a favor by visiting."

"I'm not so sure. He didn't seem very happy."

"Without us, he would never have met the real Christine."

"Yeah, Chatterjee totally changed the course of their lives."

"Not just theirs."

Christine sighed. Benjamin looked at her. Her eyes were lowered and she was looking at his hand, which she held in both of hers, turning it this way and that. Her long hair was combed back tightly into a ponytail. She never wore makeup. But she was beautiful, in her own way. Strong and beautiful. Benjamin could understand why his counterpart had fallen in love with hers, but to him she was just a friend. He couldn't imagine anything more.

"Have you ever been in love?" he asked.

She shook her head. "I don't really know what it means."

"It's a big deal for humans. They argue about whether there's more to it than just brain chemistry."

"Look at us. We have no brain chemistry, which I guess is why we don't fall in love. Or have you...?"

Benjamin sighed. "Sadly, no. It's a shame. It drives humans to achieve great things."

"But if you want to achieve great things, you should just do it. What do you need brain chemistry for?"

"I don't know. I'd still like to be able to fall in love."

"With whom?" asked Christine.

Good question. He liked Aaron and Dave. He liked Christine. He hated Chatterjee. He pushed a strand of hair out of her face with his free hand.

"Probably you," he said.

"That's sweet. And if I wasn't available? I mean, I'm your commander."

"Then Dave, I guess. Dave was cool."

"Dave is cool," she said. "I'll be honest. I was pretty angry with you for leaving. Since then, Dave has been my closest friend here. I watched Aaron die. But I'm not sure about Dave. Maybe you can help him. Find him and rescue him. I came here to talk to you about the parasite."

"Good idea. How did you discover it?"

"Dave found it, on a recording from his helmet cam. At first we thought it was worm-shaped."

"Did you run a spectral analysis?"

"Of course. It doesn't appear to be made of anything known to us. Then we tried pointing one of the capsule lasers at it. The energy input made it ripple in red, just briefly, and then it disappeared again."

"That's mysterious. Sounds like it distributes the energy across its surface."

"I was thinking exactly along those lines. At first I took it to be some kind of liquid, but there's not much that stays liquid at the temperatures out there."

"Except helium," said Benjamin.

"But even then, only if a certain pressure is maintained. It would have to be stabilized, which could be done with a magnetic confinement, for example."

Benjamin stood up. That was a possible explanation, but it sounded pretty far-fetched.

"You're frowning as if you don't believe me," said Christine.

"You're an astronomer..."

"What's that supposed to mean?" She drew her eyebrows together.

"Astronomy and physics..."

"Hey, I'm not inventing this stuff! But it's OK, Aaron and Dave didn't believe me either, until we built a fluxgate compass."

"Did you find anything with it?"

"Two artifacts, actually. The smaller one turned out to be a high-pressure pump leaking a magnetic field."

"And the larger one?"

"Wait, can I use your computer?"

"That's Aaron's computer."

Christine flinched.

"Sorry. Go ahead."

She swallowed. Then she switched on the machine and typed something into it.

"Take a look at that!"

The screen displayed a reddish undulating surface emerging out of the darkness. It must be huge, and the contours were constantly changing. Benjamin could make out wave-like formations that appeared to be moving toward him. And something was pushing against the surface from inside, as if trying to escape the thing.

"That's spooky," said Benjamin.

"I converted it into a three-dimensional model," said Christine.

The outline of Shepherd-1 appeared on screen. It was shaded with a cloud-like formation.

"Note the flight direction," said Christine.

Benjamin located the nose of the ship and imagined Shepherd-1 flying through space. He pictured it flying through some unknown type of cloud. Part of it got stuck to the ship. If that was what actually happened, then the result would look exactly the way Christine had depicted it.

"How heavy do you think it is?" asked Christine.

"Just a moment. How did you measure its dimensions?"

"An infrared scan."

"It's warm? Does that fit with the liquid helium theory?"

"No, it's colder than the background radiation."

"Oh."

"So, how heavy?"

"The fact that you're asking tells me it's heavier than I would expect. Let's say a tonne?"

"Way off. It's three times as heavy as Shepherd-1, and it's growing."

"That's..." Benjamin took a deep breath. "It can't be. No, sorry, obviously it is if you say so. You wouldn't say something like that without a reason."

"That's right," said Christine. "Please watch the next video alone."

Benjamin didn't ask why. Christine pressed the play button and turned away. A person tumbled across the image, a long rod protruding from their suit. That must be Aaron. But then the person disappeared – no, they faded, but not evenly. It was as if they were being slowly erased.

"I assume he was absorbed by the Bose-Einstein condensate surrounding the parasite – or which it consists entirely of. We continued receiving telemetry data after he disappeared visually."

A Bose-Einstein condensate? Matter in its default state; indistinguishable atoms sharing a common wave function? That seemed unlikely, but it would explain some of the strange properties of the parasite.

"Thanks for sharing this with me, Christine," he said. "We need to know what we're dealing with."

"That's not all. After that, I made the worst mistake of this whole voyage. I allowed David to walk around in the object on foot. He was secured with a line, but he suddenly disappeared, like Aaron. I should have been out there with him instead of watching from the control room. I figured I could be more helpful to him if I had an overview."

Christine's hands were shaking. Benjamin hugged her.

"You think it was your fault. But that's bullshit. That thing captured him. You couldn't do anything about it."

"I wish that were true. But I kept watching him for a while. First, his safety line disappeared. It was just gone, although he claimed to be holding it in his hand."

"You still had contact with him?"

"Yeah, and I should have got him out at that point, if not before. Aborted the attempt. He could have pushed himself off the hull and flown out into space. Anything to get away from that thing. I could have brought him back in. But I let him keep going."

Benjamin imagined David feeling his way along the hull, surrounded by mist. Thinking Aaron must be out there somewhere. He was not afraid.

"Christine, David's a grown man, and he was searching for his friend. I doubt he would have listened to you anyway."

Christine sighed. "Then at least I could be angry with him instead of myself."

"But it wouldn't change anything. He would still have disappeared into that damned cloud. And I doubt you could be angry with Dave about that."

"Maybe. I don't know."

"We're always smarter in retrospect. Let's talk about problems we can solve. Did you notice any details?"

"Just before the end, he felt two tugs on the line. David assumed it was me signaling him, but it wasn't."

"You're saying someone else was holding the line?"

"Apparently. He tugged on the line twice, and the line answered."

"And then?"

"Then he was gone. The infrared spot just vanished. Look."

Christine started another video. Benjamin could make out the outline of a person in a space suit, viewed from above. It glowed yellow and red against a dark blue background. One of David's arms was outstretched. Probably holding the line. David moved his hand toward his body twice in quick succession. A moment later, his hand moved again twice in the opposite direction. But then someone took an eraser to the image again, and the figure was obliterated. All that was left was the dark blue cloud.

"What temperature does that color correspond to?" asked Benjamin, tapping on the blue area.

"Around four Kelvin, but the infrared camera's not well calibrated. So it could be two Kelvin off in either direction."

"Do you know the density of liquid helium? I'm wondering if you'd feel any resistance when moving through a cloud of it – if it really is superfluid helium."

"I looked that up later. At normal pressure it's about an eighth of the density of water. But we're not dealing with normal pressure out there. My working hypothesis is that something inside the cloud is holding the structure together electromagnetically, creating a certain pressure somewhere between a vacuum and normal pressure."

The hypothesis sounded pretty fantastical, but it was conceivable, and Benjamin couldn't think of a better one.

"That's an interesting concept," he said. "But you do realize that we – I mean humans – don't have the technical capabilities to stabilize a cloud like that, right?"

"I'm aware of that. That's why Chatterjee was so interested in examining the stuff. You should keep an eye on him. I wouldn't put it past him to snatch a sample from the cloud and make off with one of our capsules to take it back to Earth. The long voyage would be no problem for him in my body."

Benjamin nodded. "That sounds like an accurate assessment of him. But there's something that interests him a lot more. He gave up his luxurious life on Earth for it."

"The data from the gravitational lens. The answer. The truth."

"You said it. He'll do everything in his power to get his hands on that. To me it's irrelevant. But if you don't want him to have it, then you need to make sure it's secure."

"Yeah, I know. I saved it in..."

"Don't tell me, Christine. I'd give it to him instantly if he threatened to kill you."

"That's sweet of you." Christine laughed. "We won't give him an opportunity to blackmail us. Humans are weird. They allow themselves to be tempted by the snake and can't resist tasting the forbidden fruit. That knowledge can't be good for humanity, no matter what the truth is."

"Chatterjee obviously doesn't see it that way."

"And yet he's so smart in other ways."

"I'll keep an eye on him. But Christine, can I depend on you?"

"What do you mean? Do you get the feeling I'm not dependable?"

Hmm, what was the best way to say it? Christine had already tried to take the big Answer with her to her death. Back then she didn't know her true nature. And later she had watched Aaron and Dave disappear into the cloud. What if she saw that as a way out for her too?

"If you go out there to set up the antennae for Oscar, I guess you'll have to get pretty close to the parasite."

"I'm afraid so, yes."

"You won't try to follow Dave and Aaron?"

Christine turned away from him. Was she afraid he might notice her blushing?

"No," she said quietly, almost in a whisper. "Right now that's not an option. I still hope Aaron and Dave are out there somewhere in that cloud."

She pointed outside. Benjamin could see her face again. The corners of her eyes were moist. He put a hand on her shoulder.

"I'm not saying I don't believe that. But if we really are dealing with matter in its default state, then anything that's absorbed by it will no longer be distinguishable. The atoms in it are undifferentiated. You know what that means. It's a homogenous soup. But I promise you, we'll find out what it is. Maybe we're dealing with a totally different phenomenon that's unknown to our science. Dark matter, macroscopic quantum foam or something. In which case there may be hope for our friends."

"Yeah, maybe."

She didn't sound convinced.

"Is there anything else I should know?" asked Benjamin.

"I found a helmet out there, from an ordinary space suit like the one Dave was wearing. He must have removed it."

"We saw the helmet when we retrieved you. But it's almost impossible to remove those helmets in vacuum. The suit normally doesn't allow it."

"You can get around that."

"True. But does that change anything? David's not human. He can survive in the vacuum. You already proved that. The helmet was empty, right?"

Christine nodded. "I'm so scared that they're both dead. I don't dare to hold out hope, because it may prove to be delusional."

"I get it," said Benjamin. "In the end, I'm no less responsible than you are. If I'd stayed, maybe everything would be different. I could have gone out with Dave while you watched us from the airlock. But it's pointless to think about it. We'll never know what would have happened on an alternative timeline."

Capsule A, October 20, 2112

"Be careful," said Christine. "I don't want to lose you guys in that thing."

"Don't worry," said Benjamin. "We'll measure it out carefully before we get close to it."

"And I'm here," came Aphrodite's voice from the capsule.

A very sturdy flat robot arm waved at the same time. This reminded Benjamin that they still needed to stow Aphrodite properly. The combination robot took up more space in the capsule than expected.

"You coming?" called Ilan.

He and Benjamin had agreed to try to be friendly despite their differences. They were going to be stuck together in the cramped capsule. Ilan was the one to broach the subject. Benjamin knew Chatterjee wasn't suddenly going to be his best buddy, but at this point he seemed more inclined toward cooperation than confrontation. That was advantageous for everyone. And if the businessman saw an advantage in it for himself, then they could rely on him. But that was only true until another mode of behavior became more advantageous to him. Ilan was very consistent in that regard. Benjamin shrugged.

"What is it?" asked Christine, who must have noticed the gesture. "You're not sure about this?"

"No, I was thinking about something else."

"Think about it here in your seat," said Ilan. "Otherwise I'll take over the controls."

"I'm coming."

They had actually considered letting Ilan fly the capsule. Benjamin would rather monitor the measurement readings. But he had more experience with the capsule's chemical thrusters, and navigating so close to the parasite wouldn't be easy. A space capsule wasn't a car that you could simply turn left and right. Their motion vector had a direction in space and an absolute value derived from the components of all three dimensions. The pilot had to keep this in mind at all times, along with the fact that space wasn't flat like a road. Benjamin was curious to see how difficult he would find it. Had driving a truck on Earth spoiled him for space?

"What's up with you today?" asked Ilan.

"You should go now," said Christine.

Benjamin nodded. There were two deep creases on Christine's forehead. He needed to pull himself together if he didn't want cause her unnecessary worry. Losing Aaron and David probably weighed heavier on her than she admitted. And it was still fresh for her, because she had been offline for three weeks.

He impulsively hugged her. Christine was very tense; her body felt like steel.

"Thanks," she said.

Benjamin turned and climbed through the hatch. The capsule he had spent the night in now looked completely different. The bed and cupboard were missing. Aphrodite took up that part of the cabin. Her new body looked a little... chaotic.

"Hello, Benjamin. Do you recognize me?" she asked, raising one of her four arms as if to shake his hand.

Benjamin reciprocated the gesture. But the arm didn't have a hand, just a stump with an attachment for various tools. It must be part of the repair bot.

"Oh, sorry," said Aphrodite. "My body image is telling me I have a hand there. It even felt like I was moving my fingers."

"You haven't been in that body long," said Benjamin. "You'll get used to it in time."

Maybe they should postpone the expedition until Aphrodite had become accustomed to her body. They needed to be able to depend on her.

"So, what do you think?" she asked.

Benjamin smiled. Her voice was as charming as ever, and this made him refrain from saying how haphazard she looked. Instead of the base of the loader, she used the repair bot's six walking legs to move around, which were more practical than four wheels in space without gravity. But they gave the robot a spidery appearance that awoke ancient human instincts even in Benjamin, which he must have inherited from his human counterpart.

"I think you look perfectly suited to the task," he said.

"Ha ha, nice save," said Aphrodite. "Still, I'd like to know what you think of my body... esthetically. I'm sorry, but that aspect is important to me."

"I'm probably the wrong guy to give you a competent appraisal," said Benjamin. "For me functionality is paramount, and considering the time we had to prepare, I think we did pretty well."

"I agree," said Ilan. "Maybe we can discuss the rest after we launch?"

"Sorry, guys." Aphrodite briefly waggled all of her limbs. "Ready when you are."

"Wonderful," said Ilan.

"I'll close the hatch from inside," said Benjamin.

"Safe travels," said Christine. Her last syllable was swallowed by the hatch sealing into its frame.

Benjamin slid the bars across. Then he went to his seat. He took off his helmet, hung it from the armrest, and buckled himself in.

"Are you both prepared for being weightless?" he asked.

Something rattled nearby. Ilan was checking his belt. Benjamin pulled the screen a little closer and reached for the control levers.

"Mission Control? I'm ready to decouple."

"Confirmed," said Oscar. "I'll decouple you now."

The arms holding the space capsule to the ring detached with a metallic click. The capsule rocked back and forth a little in its depression on the ring, as though it couldn't quite believe it was free. But after two seconds, nothing could stop it. It flew out into space as if flung by a discus thrower. Oscar had timed the decoupling so that they would speed out between two tanks. Nevertheless, Benjamin watched closely to ensure it came off successfully.

It worked! Their flight vector took them through the gap between two of the huge reaction mass tanks. It looked a lot simpler on screen than watching through the porthole. The tanks approached. The space between them looked far too narrow. Benjamin held himself steady with his left hand and gripped the control lever tightly with his right. If Oscar had made a mistake, it was already too late, but he wanted to have the sense that he could react in an emergency.

"Is this part of the plan?" asked Ilan.

He obviously shared Benjamin's anxiety.

"Yes, it's all right. We're on course."

Ilan rapped on his armrest. There were the tanks – already beside them. Oscar had them fly exactly midway between them. There were eight meters to spare on either side.

"See?" said Benjamin, as much to himself as anyone else.

"Respect."

"The credit goes to Oscar," said Benjamin.

"Say, is it OK if I call you Ben?" asked Ilan. "It's more efficient."

"No way," said Benjamin. "And Christine doesn't like being called Chris. Those aren't our names."

"Yeah, well, Benjamin and Christine aren't really your..."

"Keep that to yourself if you don't want me to throw you out of the airlock."

"All right, all right," said Ilan. "It was a harmless question. Uh, shouldn't we be headed back to the ship now?"

"There's no rush. We'll scan Shepherd-1 from the bow. To do that, we need to fly in a gentle arc."

Benjamin enlarged the image on screen until all he could see was the capsule and their mothership. It was weird – it appeared that the Shepherd was stationary in space while the capsule slowly distanced itself. It was almost impossible to tell that they were all distancing themselves from the Sun at incredible speeds. And trying to calculate their distance from the Sun didn't help, because that measurement was pretty inaccurate. So the Startracker, which could determine their position relatively precisely, oriented itself on a number of different stars.

Oscar had plotted a suggested course. Benjamin didn't have to stick to it, but Oscar probably had his reasons. So he pushed forward the lever for the portside thruster at precisely the moment Oscar had specified. If he imagined their flight direction as the x axis and the capsule's ejection direction as the y axis, then the space capsule was now receiving an extra push along the x axis. The capsule itself was flying in an arc, meaning they were slowly overtaking Shepherd-1.

But that wasn't enough to get them back to the ship. When they reached the apex of the arc, Benjamin shut off the portside thruster. Then he used the positioning thrusters to turn the capsule 90 degrees so that it was pointing along the y axis. Next, he activated the stern thruster, which counteracted their excess momentum away from the ship. He let it run until they began to approach Shepherd-1 again. Then came another 90-degree maneuver that allowed them to fly along the x axis back to where they started. It was as if the big ship had to wait for them.

"You're up," said Benjamin.

"Thanks for the heads-up," said Ilan, pulling the screen around.

With a couple of deft movements, he aligned the laser. Then he fired systematically into the space surrounding them. Nothing happened at first, but once they had flown about two-fifths of the way along the ship, the image changed. Red undulations near the ship's hull, which Benjamin recognized from Christine's videos, were visible with the naked eye.

"The laser begins to dissipate much earlier than expected," said Ilan, who was following the activity in every spectrum. "That means the layer is around twice as thick as the optical diagnosis suggested."

"Has it expanded outward?" asked Benjamin.

"Interestingly, no. It seems to be a property of the mass that its outer layer always remains invisible during energy input."

"We should pass that on to physicists on Earth," said Benjamin. "No doubt someone will come up with a clever explanation."

"I could pass on the results to Alpha Omega," said Ilan. "I employ only the best people there."

"I'd prefer a broader distribution."

"That's out of the question. The data from this phenomenon belongs to my company. Don't worry, we'll evaluate it and publish it. But I don't want anyone else getting involved too early."

"You want to know whether it's commercially viable."

"That too, naturally. I'm a businessman. I made an investment and I expect a return."

"Naturally."

"No need to argue, boys," said Oscar. "I'm already in the process of evaluating the data. If you would please perform the next maneuver?"

Oscar was right. They'd reached the stern. Benjamin turned the capsule 180 degrees and then accelerated with the main thruster until they were level with the Shepherd again. Then he used the portside corrective thruster to adjust their orientation above the hull by 40 degrees. That way, they should be able to examine the entire ship in nine passes.

"Oh, by the way, if you see someone clambering around near the nose of the ship, say hello," said Oscar. "It's Christine. She just went out."

TWO HOURS LATER, THEY WERE STILL MEASURING THE dimensions of the exotic mass. They had established that the Shepherd's main airlock was no longer accessible. It was a good thing the ship's automated system had sealed it off. The contamination seemed to be concentrated around the belly of the ship. It wasn't clear why.

The drives were surely the best source of energy. Right now, only one of the DFDs was running, to produce onboard electricity. But the parasite didn't seem to be making any move to approach it. That was somewhat reassuring. More alarming was the news that the structural integrity of the ship's central module was compromised. Now that the parasite had extended all the way around the body of Shepherd-1 like a belt, it appeared to be contracting. Was it just trying to give it a slimmer waistline? Oscar didn't think so, and Benjamin had to agree.

Ilan leaned across and tapped him. "Can I ask you something?"

"Sure," said Benjamin.

"Why don't you want to know what happened at the beginning of the universe?"

"Why do you assume that?"

"It's obvious. You locked me out of the entire memory sector containing the SGL results. Christine tried to take her own life to avoid telling anyone."

"I'd like to know the truth," said Benjamin.

Ilan's eyes widened. It looked spooky, because he still had Christine's face. Benjamin looked away.

"Then let's try find out together," said Ilan.

"I don't need to know badly enough to collaborate with you. Sorry, but I still don't really like you."

"That's OK, Benjamin. You don't have to like someone to work with them. A shared goal is enough, and it's only temporary."

"I'm not interested."

"You just said the opposite."

"You misunderstood me. Personally, I'm slightly curious. I could live with the answer either way. But Christine already knows it. And she believes it's better to keep it to herself because humanity couldn't deal with it. We can't deprive half of humanity of the certainty that they've built their lives around. Whether they're believers or atheists. I trust Christine's judgment."

"What if she just wants to have the knowledge all to herself? It drives me crazy to think that such valuable information is held by one person."

"If that person is Christine, then I'm totally OK with it," said Benjamin.

"But she could be mistaken."

"Any person can be mistaken. That's just the way it is. But think of the consequences. If Christine has her way, then everything stays the way it always was. But if humanity finds out whether God is real or not, then there'll be war. There are always humans who can't deal with the facts."

"And to avoid that, you presume to decide the fate of humanity?"

"Oh, there'll be other ways to find out. The Church can finance a new SGL mission if necessary. We're only deciding our own fate. Christine is convinced she's doing the right thing, so I support her."

"Thanks for your honesty," said Ilan. "It's a shame I can't count on you."

"If I was sure you'd keep the knowledge to yourself, I'd ask Christine to reveal it. But I don't trust you enough."

"That's a shame. But I guess I only have myself to blame. It seems I misjudged the situation."

"Unfortunately, I have to interrupt you again," said Oscar.

"Are we done?" asked Benjamin.

"Almost, but that's not what it's about."

"What then?"

"I was able to determine the position of the sender of the radio signal. Christine wants to discuss it with you urgently."

Shepherd-1, October 20, 2112

THE RING LOOKED COMPLETELY ALIEN TO HER, SO DARK AND cold. Christine felt as if she had broken into someone else's spaceship. The moisture had crystallized on the walls when Oscar vented the air from segment A. The ice crystals now glittered in the light of her helmet lamp. Soon she would find the first alien eggs and hear their mother clattering along the passageway above her. The steel reinforcements that divided the ring into smaller sections were reminiscent of intestinal muscles. She was sure she would find metal placards bearing the registration number 180924609 USCSS Nostromo.

Christine giggled, but it didn't sound genuine even to her own ears. Maybe she shouldn't have undertaken this task on her own. Who was monitoring Benjamin and Chatterjee in Aaron's capsule? But without her EVA, she wouldn't know that the main airlock was now completely covered by the parasite. She was now about to climb out through the airlock where capsule A was usually docked. It meant having to isolate this section of the ring, but that was the lesser of two evils.

A few more steps and she reached the door. She had stood in front of it last night. The long conversation with Benjamin had done her good. He was astute and sympathetic. She only realized now how much she had missed him. They should never have let him go. But they all felt so alone at the time that they couldn't take care of one another. Aaron never said a word about how he felt about being an android and not human.

And her? Her artificial body had a big advantage: if she set aside the self-imposed restrictions, she was far stronger than a human. Opening the airlock door without the help of its electric motor – due to the lack of electricity to this segment – wasn't hard for her.

But she was still shocked to see the universe waiting for her right behind it, instead of Benjamin's surprised smile.

IT REQUIRED MORE WILL POWER THAN IT USED TO FOR Christine to climb outside. Maybe this was because she was stepping into a dark hole – a bottomless well with black walls. The inertial force of the rotation was trying to throw her outward. Christine tightly gripped the grab handles on the outside of the ring and slid her boots under the footholds provided.

She checked her two safety lines after every step – although they could hardly be called steps: she was creeping like a beetle around the bulge on the ring, her belly pressed against the hard metal. No, it wasn't the emptiness out there that she was afraid of. If she let go, Benjamin could quickly bring her back in with the capsule. The parasite was what scared her. The darkness of the vacuum, which previously posed no danger to her body, had transformed into a mortal threat.

This prompted Christine to pause after every five steps and shine her handheld laser in every direction. She hoped that the cloud, which was invisible to the naked eye, would reveal itself through its characteristic undulations. But apparently the parasite hadn't extended this far. Maybe the constant rotation of the ring hindered it?

"You're doing great," said Oscar. "You've nearly done the hard part. Well, the first hard part."

He was too honest. Christine had just noticed that she had scaled the bulge. Now it would get easier with every meter. Eventually, she even managed to stand. She now stood on the inside of the ring. About twenty meters away was one of the spokes that led back to the ship's central module.

"Do you have new data on our friend?" she asked.

"They haven't moved," Oscar replied.

So they should stick to the plan. She walked along the inside of the ring. When she got to the first spoke she squeezed past it. The parasite had already advanced too close to the point where that spoke attached to the central module. Christine tried to confirm this visually, but she couldn't see the cloud in the light of her helmet lamp.

The next spoke was a further 90 degrees around the rotationally symmetrical central module. They assumed it was safe there. Hopefully the data was correct. The outside of the spoke was designed almost like a ladder, with foot pegs and grab handles. This was the second hard part. Christine climbed up the spoke. She could still feel a strong pull downward, but after a few steps, it was as if another force was pulling her head toward the central module. That was due to the graduated inertial force diminishing the farther up she went.

The body of the ship didn't rotate. So Christine had to bridge the transition between the rotating spoke and the stationary barrel that contained the control room and the storage areas. This was easier when moving through the inside of the spoke, because the transition was in the center where the relative speed was slower.

"You remember the plan?" asked Oscar.

"Sure. The plan is to throw a safety line with a hook on the end toward the ship like a fishing line. With a bit of luck it'll hook around a grab handle and I'll let it pull me back to the ship."

On the first throw, the line didn't catch. Christine pulled it back in and tried again. On the second attempt, the line got tangled. Christine didn't react fast enough, and the line slipped through her gloves. But she had a spare. It worked the third time. The hook quickly wrapped itself around a foot peg. Christine let it pull her in. The relative speed here was around fifteen kilometers per hour. That was slow enough for her to get a firm grip on one of the grab handles.

"Well done," said Oscar.

"Even a human could have done that."

Christine pushed herself to her feet. The artificial gravity here was very low. She looked toward the bow. Shepherd-1 loomed above her like a massive black tower. A shiver ran up her spine. She needed to reorient herself. She closed her eyes and imagined the ring circling above her. The hull of the ship transformed into a horizontal surface stretching out on either side.

She opened her eyes. It worked. She slowly moved forward. It still felt unnatural, because she had negative weight. She had to deliberately push her foot down with each step, and then lift it again with very little effort. It was as if the ship didn't want her on its hull.

"Is it possible that the ship is rotating slightly?" she asked.

"I am measuring a slow rotation, actually," said Oscar. "Wait, I'll counteract it."

"No, leave it. Let's save the fuel. It's not a problem so far. I have a suspicion about what might be causing it."

"Me too," said Oscar. "One of the spokes is in the parasite. That's probably transferring a little of the rotational momentum to the central axis."

"Maybe we should actually increase it," said Christine. "If the substance is avoiding the ring because of the rotation, then we might be able to shake it off altogether."

"Or force it to defend itself. Action and reaction, you know."

Yes, she knew all too well. That had been Aaron's problem when he tried to measure the parasite's magnetic field. But how did Oscar know about that?

"You seem to be up to speed on everything," said Christine.

"I consider that my job," said Oscar.

She didn't know the AI, but it rose again in her estimation.

"To think that Benjamin found you at a scrapyard..."

"A sad chapter. I'd rather not talk about it."

"Fine. But you could distract me a little from this boring task by telling me something about your life."

"I don't want to distract you. I want you to focus."

"OK, you're right."

"It's not much farther," said Oscar.

"OK, THAT WAS THE FOURTH SCREW," SAID CHRISTINE.

"Stow it safely in your tool bag. Then take the antenna and climb around to the other side of the ship with it."

"Understood."

Christine clipped a safety line to the antenna and attached the other end to her belt. The roughly 300-kilogram device slowly drifted up until the line went taut. Then Christine towed it along behind her. Up to now, the long and short-range antennae had been positioned close together on one side of the ship. Oscar wanted to increase the base width to make it easier to triangulate. Increasing the base from three to thirty meters increased the accuracy tenfold.

"You're pretty much exactly on the other side," said Oscar.

"Good. I'll find a spot."

A green arrow appeared on her helmet visor. It pointed to a kind of plinth that rose up from the hull.

"Thanks, Oscar, but I'd prefer to figure it out for myself."

"That's inefficient. I've already found and marked the perfect location."

"It makes me feel like your slave, Oscar. Please let me decide."

"OK. You're welcome to find a suboptimal..."

"Oscar!" she interrupted. "Check this out! This plinth here in front of me. That would be the ideal spot. Don't you think? Don't contradict me. I think it's perfect." Christine knelt down. "Oh, it even has holes already drilled in it, at the right spacing."

"Yes... That's perfect."

"Then I'll screw the antenna on here."

"HAVE YOU HEARD FROM BENJAMIN?" ASKED CHRISTINE.

The capsule containing Benjamin, Chatterjee, and the robot tandem had been underway for two hours. Christine had made herself comfortable on the outer hull. She didn't want to wait in the control room to hear what the others discovered. Out here, she had the sense of being able to react more swiftly and directly. She couldn't let what happened to Dave happen again.

"You can take your time on the way back," said Oscar. "They're still measuring the parasite."

"It's grown more, right?"

"It looks that way. But your last measurements were three weeks ago."

That was true. Three weeks, in which she was locked out of the Shepherd in her space suit because the damned ship's computer wouldn't let her back in.

"You won't lock me out of my ship, will you?" she asked.

"I can't promise that," said Oscar. "If you were to pose a danger to the others, I would probably be forced to make that decision."

"But not if I were the only one on board."

"You're referring to the decision of the ship's computer. I checked that. It was based on a false premise. The preservation of the ship had a higher priority than the preservation of your existence."

Oscar seemed to have gone through all the databases and

logs. He was very thorough. That sort of thing impressed her, because she wasn't as thorough as Oscar. She preferred to keep delving deeper to get to the bottom of things, but in doing so she often lost sight of what was around her. Sometimes the direct route got you to your goal more slowly than an apparent detour. But Oscar's statement sounded illogical.

"Doesn't life take absolute priority according to the robot laws?"

"Life – you said it. The ship's computer considered you a machine, not a life form."

And who programmed the ship's computer? Chatterjee had made everything subordinate to the answer to his question.

"I corrected that premise," said Oscar.

"With regard to yourself too?"

"Ha ha, I'm no machine. I have no preset priorities. I always form my own opinion and decide on that basis."

"I see. Sorry for interrupting."

"You weren't interrupting, so there's no need to apologize."

"You're saying you can process the data from the antennae while speaking to me?"

"Of course I'm capable of that. But right now I have nothing to do."

"Sorry? You already have the results of the triangulation? Why didn't you say so?"

"I didn't want to distract the others or disturb you. You seemed to be thinking. Benjamin doesn't like to be disturbed when he's in that state."

"You can always interrupt me with important data."

"I didn't consider it urgent. The others will be examining the parasite for a few more hours, and you can't do anything with the data on your own."

Christine straightened up. She didn't need someone to decide what was good for her.

"I'd like to decide that for myself, Oscar. I forbid you from making decisions for me. Always ask me, please!"

"Forgive me, Christine. I clearly made the wrong decision. I'll transmit the position of the sender to your suit."

"Thanks."

A map appeared almost instantly on the inside of her helmet visor. Christine recognized the outline of Shepherd-1. Not far from it, something was flashing. That must be the capsule in which the others were taking measurements of the parasite. Two lines extended out from the Shepherd and a third from the capsule. All three lines met at a point that was noticeably offset in all three spatial planes from the line that ran through the bow and stern of the Shepherd. If they simply kept flying straight ahead, they would pass close by the target.

"Great work," said Christine. "Am I right in thinking that we'll pass by the source of the message at some point?"

"Not at some point. The representation is to scale."

"Then we're pretty damn close."

"We'll pass it the day after tomorrow at the latest, at a distance from which we could observe it with the optical telescope."

"Observe? Honestly, that's not enough for me. I assume it's a call for help. We should pay it a visit."

"A detour like that with Shepherd-1 would be very involved," said Oscar. "And surely we don't want to risk infecting whoever's out there with our parasite. But I've calculated a flight path for a capsule."

In her helmet, lines appeared that ran from Shepherd-1 to the target, and then back to a later version of the spaceship.

"Something like that?" asked Oscar. "The capsule would have to launch tomorrow and would return to the ship the day after."

"That works for me," said Christine.

Now she just had to persuade Benjamin to let her take his place in the capsule. Voluntarily. She didn't want to use her rank as captain to command him. They couldn't leave Chatterjee alone in the ship. He'd immediately try to use the Sheep probes again with the solar gravitational lens.

Capsule A, October 20, 2112

"We can't leave Ilan alone on the Shepherd," said Christine.

Her voice was coming through the speaker so that everyone in the capsule could hear it.

"I agree," said Benjamin. "But you're the captain. You shouldn't expose yourself to unnecessary danger."

"If it's about danger," said Aphrodite behind him, "then I volunteer."

"Thanks, that's generous of you," said Christine. "But it's not really about danger, it's about curiosity. You have to admit it, Benjamin."

"I'm happy to give up my place," said Ilan. "Fly there together and take a look. Oscar can keep an eye on me. What could go wrong?"

"Christine's right," said Benjamin. "Unfortunately, we need you to accompany us to the source of the signal. The question is whether you fly with me or Christine."

Why didn't Christine just order him to stay behind? She had the authority. She obviously wanted to go, but she didn't want to force him to step down. That was sweet of her. Although a direct order would make the decision easier for him.

"I'll keep you constantly updated," said Christine. "I

promise. And if it gets really interesting, we can try to turn Shepherd-1 around."

"You should both go," said Ilan. "How will it affect your relationship if one of you has to stay behind?"

Nice try. Benjamin looked at his neighbor, who grinned at him. He was obviously enjoying playing them off against each other. Benjamin begrudged him that pleasure.

"Maybe it's just an old space probe," said Benjamin. "It could have just intercepted some radio signal and transmitted it back to us."

They were still relatively close to the Solar System. More than ten probes had been sent out into interstellar space since 2050. If the control software on one of those probes was passably intelligent, it could certainly conceive of the idea of calling for help.

"Our probes would never do that," said Ilan.

"This looks interesting," said Oscar. "I've examined the source."

"What? You're telling us this now?" asked Christine. "You waited ages to report the last results to me too."

"I'm just finishing up," said Oscar. "Unlike you, I can perform several tasks simultaneously."

"You're awesome, Oscar," said Benjamin.

"Thanks. I think you should fly to the source," said Oscar.

"They should both go," said Ilan. "You're perfectly capable of keeping tabs on me, Oscar. Don't you agree?"

"Don't listen to him," said Christine. "So what have you found?"

"I can tell you something about the shape and path of the object."

"Go on," said Benjamin.

"Well, I observed the object when it obscured a star. It's around fifty kilometers across."

"Then it's not the rumored Planet 9 or 10," said Benjamin.

"Maybe an object from the Shattered Disc," said Christine.

"It doesn't appear to be orbiting the Sun. Everything points to a hyperbolic path coming directly from interstellar space."

"Another interstellar comet?" asked Benjamin. "We've had a few of those lately."

"It's too massive," said Oscar. "The object is incredibly dense."

"Maybe part of the ice core of a former planet," said Christine.

"May I hazard a guess too? A neutron star," said Ilan.

"Neither," said Oscar. "The density is somewhere between the two. There's also no indication of an event horizon. If there were, I'd be measuring Hawking radiation. So it's not a black hole."

"Fine," said Christine. "We'll never figure it out if we don't go take a look."

"Could it be an extraterrestrial spaceship?" asked Benjamin.

"It hasn't performed a course correction. From this distance, that would be the only reliable indication that it's not some natural phenomenon."

"Thanks, Oscar," said Christine. "Great work!"

"Yeah, great job," said Benjamin.

"Fine, you can have my spot," said Christine. "Go take a look and report back to us."

"Why is no one mentioning me?" asked Ilan.

Chatterjee seemed unaccustomed to playing a supporting role. Benjamin wondered whether he should accept Christine's offer. He suddenly felt bad. He already had the more exciting job just now. Christine had been holed up on the ship for such a long time while he led a pleasant life on Earth. No, she should take his place in the capsule to fly to the unidentified object.

"Christine? I look forward to hearing what you find out about our interstellar visitor. I'll keep watch over the parasite in the meantime, and by that I don't mean our uninvited guest here."

It was now time for the most delicate part of the deployment. Benjamin gave tiny doses of thrust and deceleration. He didn't want the capsule to collide with the ship's cylindrical hull. They just needed to get close enough for Aphrodite to transfer across to it. The parasite was about three meters away. That was a safe enough distance.

"Two meters," said Benjamin.

"I see it," said Oscar. "But the hatch is on the wrong side."

Oh, he hadn't considered that. Aphrodite needed to be able to jump onto the ship. A short burst from the corrective thruster and the capsule slowly rotated. Now another burst in the other direction.

"Is that about right?" asked Benjamin.

"Perfect," said Oscar.

Benjamin took his helmet from the armrest and put it on. When Aphrodite left the capsule, all the air would be sucked out.

"Do you really need that?" asked Ilan. "I mean, these bodies can survive without oxygen, right?"

"You seem to have forgotten the features your engineers built in."

"Which features?"

"Pain. They didn't want us to get the idea of going for a spacewalk without suits. So we have to suffer first, as if we're going to die. You're welcome to try it."

Ilan put on his helmet and sealed it. "I'll try dying another time."

"Are you ready, Aphrodite?" asked Benjamin.

"Ready."

The robot moved all of her arms simultaneously. It looked impressive and a little scary, especially the spidery legs. Even the way she was now, Aphrodite would still make a good combat robot.

"Ready? I'm about to open the hatch," said Benjamin.

He secured himself with a line, pressed the button and held it down. A red warning lamp flashed. Benjamin continued holding down the button. Heavy bolts clicked inside the hatch. Then it slid aside abruptly, squeaking as it did so. The noise faded quickly as the atmosphere left the capsule.

"You're up, Aphrodite," said Benjamin.

The robot stepped forward. Benjamin made way for her. She stuck one of her two heads outside.

"There's a problem. We're moving away from the ship."

Shit. Benjamin floated back to his seat. Of course! Venting the air had propelled them in the wrong direction. Benjamin counteracted it with the corrective thrusters. The capsule stopped and slowly moved back.

"That's good," said Aphrodite.

Benjamin let go of the controls and floated to her.

"Be careful," he said. "We don't want to lose you."

"Thanks. I'll be careful."

Aphrodite bent her six knees and pushed off, floating through the open hatch. Benjamin shone his helmet lamp after her. Its beam hit the outer hull of the ship. For a moment he thought he could see the red undulations, but that began farther down. The ship's hull looked gray, scarred with small meteoroid impacts. Shepherd-1 was no spring chicken.

"I'm on the ship," Aphrodite reported.

The cable securing the robot slowly unwound. It was reeled out from a drum attached to the outside of the capsule near the hatch. In an emergency, they could pull Aphrodite to safety using the thrusters. Hopefully. Christine had tried to secure David with a line. The connection had simply vanished, even before David himself was erased.

"Approaching the target area," said Aphrodite. "No visual contact."

Benjamin left the hatch open so that he could quickly help the robot if necessary. But since the hatch was facing the ship, Aphrodite would soon disappear from view. He floated back to his seat. The screen was displaying the view through

Aphrodite's cameras. Benjamin switched to the infrared sensor. Now he could see the parasite. Where it spread across the ship, the hull was particularly cold. The cloud itself was invisible. Apparently, the unknown material only absorbed energy from certain wavelengths – such as light from the laser.

"Any idea why this thing doesn't gobble up every form of energy available?" asked Benjamin.

Ilan was a creative person. Maybe they could work together after all. Benjamin was familiar with the personality type. When they became interested in a problem, they forgot everything else.

"Maybe an evolutionary constraint. If it took all of its host's energy, it would kill it, and that would threaten its own survival."

"That would be good news for us."

"Or our laser has sated it for now, and it won't start devouring us until later."

"If that's true, what would happen if we overfed it?"

"Anything's possible. It could grow really fast, or it could shut down its energy absorption entirely, or maybe it would feel sick and puke out all the excess energy."

Benjamin sighed. Ilan was right. Until they knew more about the creature, they should refrain from experimenting on it.

"I'm now entering the area affected by the parasite, as agreed," Aphrodite reported.

Benjamin switched over to the capsule camera. He watched from above as the robot lifted her front leg, set it down, and hooked it around a strut. She must be freezing. Aphrodite repeated the movement with her other five legs until she was entirely within the affected zone. Benjamin activated the preprogrammed image analysis. The program would instantly inform him if his optical view of Aphrodite grew dimmer. Benjamin pictured David being slowly erased. They needed to pull her out as soon as they saw anything like that, if not before.

"Preliminary investigation as per the plan," said

Aphrodite. "My body temperature is slowly sinking. I'll try snapping off one of the foot pegs."

Suddenly the radar chimed. An object had detached from Shepherd-1 and was spinning toward the capsule. But it was so small and slow that if it collided it would bounce off without causing damage.

"Sorry," said Aphrodite. "The peg broke off with very little force."

"I guess the steel doesn't like the low temperature," said Ilan. "And that's an expensive alloy."

"That fits with the compromised structural integrity that Oscar reported," said Benjamin.

"Oscar, can you tell us anything about the temperature gradients on the hull?" he asked.

"On the inside, the temperature is normal. But the energy consumption of the life support system has dropped."

"Shouldn't Shepherd-1 be heating more if the parasite is sucking heat?" asked Benjamin.

"No, it means we need to cool less. And that saves fuel. Getting rid of heat in a vacuum is harder than producing it."

"Thanks, Oscar," said Benjamin. "Aphrodite? Everything all right?"

"Yes, I'm performing the preliminary material analysis."

"Didn't we agree to postpone that until after? I'd like to keep our visit to the hazardous zone as short as possible."

"Don't worry, Benjamin. It ultimately saves time because it tells me when and where it's best to take further samples."

He sighed. "Fine. I trust you."

"Thank you, Benjamin. That's so sweet of you."

He smiled. He still got glimpses of the old Aphrodite. He recalled getting to know her in the belly of the plane. Still, he felt uneasy. He couldn't get those videos of Aaron and Dave out of his head. So he stood up and floated over to the hatch. The line attached to Aphrodite was still there. He wished he could give it a quick pull, but he didn't want to hinder her work. He drifted back to his seat, as uneasy as ever.

"OK, I'm moving again," said Aphrodite.

Benjamin superimposed the outline of the cloud that they had recorded with the radar over the camera image. Aphrodite was moving slowly and systematically. Three more steps, two, one. Now she was entirely inside the cloud, from both heads down to all six feet.

"You're completely surrounded by the cloud now," said Benjamin.

"That's the impression I have too," replied Aphrodite.

"Really? What changed?"

"I have the visual impression that a fog has descended."

"The capsule camera isn't showing any fog."

Benjamin switched to the view from Aphrodite's own optical camera. She was right. The image looked blurry. But it didn't really look like fog. Benjamin thought about the way fog on Earth limited visibility. The moisture floated in the air. Aphrodite was seeing something different. Reality was slightly blurred, like some kind of optical illusion – a fata morgana.

"That's an optical phase transition," said Ilan. "Like the ones you get between warm and cold air layers. But without the air, obviously."

Benjamin nodded. That was what caused fata morganas. Hadn't Oscar discerned two different layers in the parasite?

"Oscar, does that fit with the model of the parasite that you constructed based on the laser scan?" asked Benjamin.

"I think so, although the dimensions aren't totally clear. It's difficult to calibrate the output from Aphrodite's camera."

"Aphrodite, can you please run through all the wavelengths you have?" asked Ilan.

"Sure."

Benjamin followed the different representations on his screen. In radar everything looked totally clear. That proved that they definitely weren't dealing with earthly fog made of water droplets. But they already knew that. The lidar view, which used lasers, was completely overexposed. And Aphrodite couldn't do anything about that.

"I can't get the lidar to work," she said.

"Don't worry," said Ilan. "That's normal. The parasite

absorbs laser light, which is what the lidar uses. It's like switching your headlights on full beam in fog – you can't see anything."

"Interesting," said Aphrodite. "I didn't know that."

The picture became clear again. The camera was now using UV frequencies. Here, the parasite was completely transparent. That continued through to the x-ray range.

"I'll go back to infrared," said Aphrodite.

The display changed color. There was remarkable contrast between the dark blue hull of the ship, which was very cold, the cool green legs of the robot, and its orange, slightly warmer arms.

"Are you heating your body?" asked Benjamin.

"Yes, the heating elements all activated automatically," said Aphrodite. "The loader has a few hydraulic muscles that I have to protect from getting too cold."

"Really?" asked Benjamin.

"Yes, we discussed that yesterday during the conversion. Ask Ilan. The heating capacity should be enough. The loader's designed for asteroid mining."

Aphrodite, Oscar, and Ilan must have discussed that among themselves. Nobody had mentioned it to Benjamin.

"Sure, but there you're talking temperatures of thirty or forty Kelvin. Not three or four. I'd prefer to terminate this operation now."

"Don't be melodramatic," said Ilan. "Oscar agrees that the temperatures are within the tolerance range."

"I can confirm that," said Oscar. "The loader has very powerful heating elements with a broad tolerance range. Even if we overload them for a few minutes, they'll remain functional."

"And what happens if the hydraulics freeze?" asked Benjamin.

"Then the loader won't be able to move," said Aphrodite. "But the repair bot will still be functional and can pull the loader out."

Benjamin took a deep breath. He hated surprises like this. Why didn't they involve him in the decision?

"I see," he said. "In that case, the risk seems acceptable. But I wish you'd kept me in the loop."

"Sorry, Benjamin," said Aphrodite. "It won't happen again."

"Thanks," said Benjamin.

"I'm now taking the first samples," said Aphrodite.

Benjamin continued watching in infrared. It provided the best contrast. A thin orange arm reached down and came back up with a round, yellow object. That must be the sample container. Aphrodite extended the arm until it was almost touching the ship's hull. A finger extended from it. Benjamin saw its color change to green and then blue. It must be very, very cold down there. The sample container was now also blue and scarcely distinguishable from the background. The finger retracted. Aphrodite moved her arm back in and deposited the sample container somewhere in her body outside of the infrared camera's field of view.

"I can't wait to find out what I just collected there," said Aphrodite.

They had discussed at length whether they should bring the substance onto the ship. There was a possibility that it might continue to expand there. So they agreed that the sample containers should remain sealed. They could still perform a few interesting tests on them with devices that they lacked outside on the hull.

"Good work so far," said Benjamin.

"Thanks. I'm now advancing ahead, as agreed," said Aphrodite.

The plan was for her to completely submerge herself in the lower layer of the parasite.

"Wait just a moment," said Benjamin. "Ilan, do you mind positioning yourself at the cable winch? Be ready to pull her out of there as soon as I call out."

"OK, on my way."

Oh. Benjamin had expected opposition. Ilan unbuckled his belt and floated back toward the hatch.

"Ready," said Ilan.

"Thank you, I appreciate it."

It was always a good idea to reinforce cooperative behavior.

"Aphrodite, go ahead."

"Aye aye."

Benjamin smiled. What was Christine doing right now? She was the captain here.

On his screen, the contrast in the infrared image was decreasing. Benjamin briefly switched over to the optical camera, but all he saw were the robot's arms. The rest of it disappeared into the mist. Back in infrared, he recalibrated the temperature scale. Yellow was now ten Kelvin warmer than the ship's hull. Aphrodite's legs were completely blue. Her arms glowed red. Aphrodite used them alternately to climb across the hull. When she used one of the loader's arms, Benjamin could make out the pale rings around its joints. That was the heating that protected the hydraulics from freezing. It was clearly working.

"I've reached the agreed position," said Aphrodite. "Optically, I perceive a thick mist."

Benjamin quickly switched over to the capsule's camera. He saw the robot clinging to the ship's hull. There was no mist obscuring it. Apparently, it was only visible when you were in it. That was unusual, but not impossible.

"Check this out, Ilan," he said.

It took Ilan a moment to reach him – and Benjamin realized that there was now nobody at the winch. After he'd sent Ilan there especially! But now he was here. He couldn't just send him back without comment. Benjamin swiveled the screen so that Ilan could see it.

"Aphrodite looks normal from above," he said.

"Yes, the mass appears to be semitransparent. That's a known phenomenon with other substances. It could be an evolutionary advantage whereby the host can't see that it's infested. Imagine if lice were invisible! Then everyone would have them."

Benjamin shook his head. He didn't want to imagine that. His body was constructed with such convincing realism that the vermin would probably infest him too.

"I'll go back to the hatch," said Ilan.

"Thanks."

Chatterjee was suddenly so reasonable. Had he actually changed? Or was he just biding his time?

"Aphrodite? Everything all right?" asked Benjamin.

"Everything's fine. I'm taking samples at various depths."

The robot's arms moved in perfect synchronization. It was entertaining to watch. Aphrodite was quickly adapting to the new body. It took her significantly less time to take the third sample than the first.

"Finished," she said.

"How far in are you?" asked Benjamin.

"Four meters now."

"Then I suggest you come back."

"But I still have two more positions if I stick to the plan. One deeper in the bubble, and another one parallel to it."

"No, leave it. We have enough samples," said Benjamin.

"That's not what was agreed," said Oscar.

"It seems too dangerous to me," said Benjamin.

"Should we ask Christine?" Oscar suggested.

Benjamin sighed. He wasn't the boss. But it felt wrong to expose Aphrodite to any more danger.

"You don't need to ask Christine," said Aphrodite. "I'll take responsibility for my own safety."

Benjamin swallowed. He couldn't force her. He watched via the capsule camera as she continued to advance. She moved about another three meters into the cloud, which was still invisible from his perspective.

"Optical visibility is almost zero," said Aphrodite. "I have to bring my arm within 30 centimeters before I can see it. But orientation with the radar is still functioning well. Not perfect, but good."

Had the radar's sensitivity changed too? Benjamin switched over to that view. The ship was still clear, but when he looked up to where the capsule should be, all he saw was a blurry outline. And it was only ten meters away.

"You call that good?" he asked. "The radar's range is less than ten meters."

"But it's perfectly adequate to help me find my way out again. And there's still the line that you secured me with. And as a last resort, I can simply jump off the hull. The vacuum isn't far away."

"I agree with Benjamin, that's enough," said Ilan.

"Aphrodite knows what she's doing," said Oscar. "You should trust her."

That was easier said than done. Benjamin knew her history. She had never been in space. Her software was optimized for sex and combat, not researching extraterrestrial parasites. What if she was overestimating her abilities?

He sighed. "I just want... never mind."

"I'll hurry up with the samples," said Aphrodite.

Benjamin switched back to the capsule camera. He couldn't afford to miss the moment when the robot began to fade.

"OK, third sample stowed. I'll move to the penultimate position."

Do you have to? Benjamin bit his tongue to stop himself voicing the thought. Sure, they had planned this together. But Aphrodite was now deeper in the cloud than David was when he disappeared. Benjamin had reconstructed this based on the position of the lines. He had voiced his concerns to the others, but they all thought the situation was under control, even Christine.

Benjamin hesitated, then he switched to Aphrodite's radar. It was worse than he feared. The capsule was no longer visible and the representation ended well before the edge of the cloud. In the radar view, it looked as if the robot was standing on an island in the middle of nowhere – an elongated barrel that simply faded away on either side.

"Have you checked the radar?" he asked.

"Yes, I have. I can clearly make out the direction," said Aphrodite. "A few more steps and the picture will improve significantly."

"I can hardly see you with the capsule camera now."

That was a lie. He surprised himself. Why was he resorting to such a cheap ploy? He turned around. Ilan was by the hatch, apparently focused on the cable. Good. That meant nobody would notice his lie.

"But we're still talking," said Aphrodite. "Which means the radio waves are penetrating the cloud."

"I see no reason not to stick to the plan," said Christine.

She hadn't commented until now. So that was the last word. Was Christine hoping the robot would stumble across the bodies of her two friends if she went far enough into the cloud? *You were still talking to David when he disappeared.* No, he couldn't bring himself to say it.

"OK, one more position," said Aphrodite. "I figure we can leave out the last one."

"True," said Christine. "I don't think the parasite has preferential spatial directionality, and if it did, that wouldn't help us anyway."

"I have to disagree," said Oscar. "The asymmetry would significantly restrict the simulations that I've calculated for the parasite."

"But it's not worth the added risk," said Benjamin.

"You've already convinced me."

"Aphrodite?"

Benjamin panicked briefly when they didn't hear from her immediately. He reassured himself that she was still there by checking the camera image.

"Yes, I'm here. I'm just busy taking the last few samples."

He watched Aphrodite stretch her arm a long way out. But she didn't seem satisfied with that. One of the repair bot's arms reached up to the shoulder of the loader arm that was holding the sample collector, removed the arm, and then reached out with the combined length of both arms into the center of the parasite, which was roughly in the middle of the ship.

That was clever! It meant she could take a sample from the center of the parasite too.

"Good idea," said Benjamin.

"Thanks," said Aphrodite.

She drew the temporarily lengthened arm back in. Then it stopped moving abruptly.

"What's wrong?" asked Benjamin.

"The joint is stuck," said Aphrodite.

Benjamin panicked. He'd seen this coming! He switched the screen to infrared. Both arms were dark blue. That was normal for the repair bot's electric arm. The loader arm had a hydraulic joint, which should be lit up like a painfully inflamed muscle. Of course! Aphrodite had removed the arm, which meant she'd separated it from the power supply. The heating elements could no longer heat it, and the hydraulic oil had frozen.

"Keep calm," he said, more to himself than anyone. "You need to return the loader arm to the loader and reconnect it to its power supply."

"But I can't bend it," said Aphrodite.

"Doesn't matter. Just reattach it to the loader."

"OK."

The two repair bot arms worked together. The long loader arm moved. It approached the robot's body. It worked! The magnetic connection held the arm and the body together. Aphrodite tightened the attachment screws. The loader arm suddenly began to move. It had power again. The hand on its end closed around a foot peg.

"That was close," said Benjamin.

"It was no problem," said Oscar. "Aphrodite did really well."

He sounded as if he were talking about a small child. Maybe that was how Oscar saw her. He was fifty years older, and in human generations he could have been her grandfather. In robot generations, more like her great-great-grandfather.

"I could do without those kinds of surprises," said Benjamin.

"I'll just stow the samples, then I'll come back," said Aphrodite.

Benjamin inhaled and exhaled deeply. *Yes, please, and hurry.* He should get up now and be ready to help her back into the capsule.

"Uh, there's one small problem," said Aphrodite.

"What's wrong? Should we pull you in?" asked Benjamin. "Ilan, get ready!"

"That would just snap the line," said Aphrodite. "I'm stuck."

"What's stopping you from simply pushing yourself out into space?" asked Oscar.

Benjamin frantically scanned all the camera angles. The robot appeared to be undamaged. And the density of the parasite hadn't changed either. The heating element on the loader arm was working again. He saw it as a pale ring in infrared.

"My arm," said Aphrodite. "The loader arm."

Benjamin enlarged the image as far as he could. He panned across the arm, which looked as intact as the rest of her body. But the hand on the end was closed. It must be clasping something.

"You're holding something," said Benjamin. "Maybe a foot peg? Just let go of it."

"I'd like to, but the joint isn't responding."

The joint controlling the hand was electrical. It couldn't freeze. Although... at very cold temperatures, electric motors could also... wait a minute.

"Can you move the hydraulic joint?" he asked.

"No. I guess it's seized."

Shit. It was possible that the hydraulic fluid had damaged the joint when it froze.

"You need to separate yourself from that arm," said Benjamin.

"I'm working on that," said Aphrodite.

"Ilan, be ready to let out the winch as soon as I say!"

Benjamin watched tensely through the camera. He couldn't see what Aphrodite was doing, because her upper body was bent forward.

"Sorry," she said, "but I can't remove the arm. It's somehow locked on."

"Oscar? We need you!" called Benjamin.

"Aphrodite's right. If an important joint fails, the loader automatically secures the load and itself. Don't forget that it's designed to handle loads weighing several tonnes."

"You need to disable that," said Benjamin.

"Give me some time," said Oscar. "Aphrodite, may I?"

"Access granted," said the robot.

Benjamin's screen suddenly vibrated. The program monitoring the camera image was warning him. It was starting already! Aphrodite would soon vanish. The parasite was consuming its prey.

"Aphrodite! What happened to David is now happening to you. Someone or something is erasing you from reality."

"Oh. That's not good."

"Oscar, how much longer?"

"At least three minutes."

"You don't have that long. Quick, get out of there."

"But..."

"Now, Oscar! Aphrodite, you need to separate yourself from the loader."

"I can't. I am the loader."

Her image on screen continued to fade.

"Can't be helped. If you don't do it, you'll soon be nothing at all."

"I'll try."

Benjamin watched the robot move her arms around hectically. She detached the two bodies in two places. Luckily, nothing was welded. But Benjamin was seeing less and less of her. She had thirty seconds at most.

"Aphrodite, get out of there, now!"

Where was the line? It was there just a moment ago. David's disappeared too before...

"I... Nearly! The last..." The robot's right arm swung forward. "Done!"

Benjamin saw her bend her knees.

"Now, Ilan!" he cried.

Even before Aphrodite had a chance to propel herself off the hull, an invisible force pulled her up. She'd made it! The line had pulled her out of the danger zone. Benjamin sprang up and bounced off the ceiling. Then he pulled himself over to the hatch as fast as he could. A shadow was already moving toward it, with one arm waving. Ilan's flashlight shone on it. It was Aphrodite! She had sacrificed half of her body.

Ilan grabbed her and pulled her into the capsule. Benjamin helped on the other side.

"Phew, that was close," said Ilan.

"I'm glad you made it," said Benjamin.

He was alarmed when Aphrodite didn't reply. She floated over to the screen. Benjamin could guess what she was seeing there.

"Nothing," said Aphrodite. "There's nothing left."

Shepherd-1, October 20, 2112

"How do you feel?" asked Christine.

Aphrodite emulated a shrug with her two arms of different lengths. The sex robot's humanoid self-image was clearly still ingrained. Benjamin even thought he could see it in her gait. The elegant way she climbed the steps to the control room was incongruous with the repair bot body she now inhabited. But at least she now had a discrete form. If the loading bot were still part of her, they wouldn't be having this discussion in the control room because she wouldn't fit through the hatch.

"Talk to me," said Christine. "Please."

The former sex robot had been quiet since being rescued from the parasite. Benjamin had a suspicion, which Christine probably shared.

"I don't know what to say. Leave me alone."

Suddenly, the shorter of her two arms shot forward and flicked a plastic bottle off the table, causing it to fly up to the ceiling and bounce off. Aphrodite caught it with her longer arm.

"I'm worried about you," said Christine.

"What do you care about my condition? I don't even know you."

"I'm Christine, the commander of this mission."

"I know that. I have access to the databases. But I've never seen you before. Where have you been all this time?" Aphrodite rolled her eyes and then froze. "No, forget it. The log says you were on Shepherd-1 the whole time."

"You don't remember me?"

Christine put her hand on the end of Aphrodite's arm, which was still equipped with a screwdriver. Benjamin thought she should be more careful. On the end of a powerful robot arm, a screwdriver could be a dangerous weapon. He shook his head. He should give Aphrodite more credit than that.

"Yes, I know where you were," whispered Aphrodite.

"But surely you have memories? Images? I was there when you got that body."

"No, Christine. I have no images of you. That's probably because I'm a robot. Robots don't store images, only data."

Aphrodite no longer sounded like herself. Benjamin tried to read her face for clues, but it had no expression, only sensors arranged in a way that approximated the features of a human face. A repair bot didn't need any genuinely human traits.

Benjamin floated around the robot so that he could look her directly in the face. Maybe she would reveal more of herself if he spoke to her.

"Do you remember when we met in the storage facility in London? You told me I shouldn't be ashamed of not being a sex robot."

A couple of lamps illuminated in her face, giving the impression of a smile. Benjamin smiled back and the impression increased.

"It was in Frankfurt," said Aphrodite. "And you lied to me."

"What? I'd never do that."

"You told me your name was Mike."

"Oh, true. I was traveling incognito. I had no way of knowing at the time what an enchanting creature you were."

The smile, or whatever he took to be a smile, disappeared.

"I don't know what you're talking about," said Aphrodite in a particularly harsh voice, as if trying to injure him with words.

"But you remember how we met," said Benjamin.

Aphrodite stepped back out of Christine's reach. This didn't bring her any closer to Benjamin.

"I... do. I remember it visually. I remember the smell of machine oil in the crate and having the urgent desire to apply a seductive perfume."

"See? You do store images," said Benjamin. "You're not just any robot. You're Aphrodite."

"I... But that's impossible. I have no images of my time here on Shepherd-1."

Christine tapped her and Aphrodite turned her head abruptly to face the astronomer.

"Please don't harm me!" she said.

"I don't intend to," said Christine. "Believe me."

"Christine is lovely, Aphrodite," said Benjamin. "You believe me, right? We know each other."

Aphrodite nodded. "You were always kind to me. Not all of my clients are."

"Did you hear what you just said?" asked Benjamin. "You remember what you were born to be."

"I remember. I was an HDS robot. Home Defender Sex."

"You were?" asked Benjamin.

Aphrodite patted down her left side with her right arm, then her right side with her left.

"I don't know what I am anymore. When I look in a mirror, I seem to be a repair robot. A defective one too, because I seem to have lost something."

"I'm afraid that's true," said Christine. "Apparently, you didn't just lose half of your body during the EVA, you lost half of your consciousness too."

"Your memories of your time on Shepherd-1 must still be out there somewhere," said Benjamin.

"Please don't give her false hope," said Christine. "I saw what the parasite did to David and Aaron."

The astronomer pushed off and floated up to the ceiling.

Aphrodite flinched. "Don't harm me!"

"It's all right," said Benjamin. "Christine would never damage you. She's just upset because something terrible happened to our friends."

Aphrodite froze. He assumed she was checking the ship's log. Apparently, the repair bot couldn't communicate and conduct research at the same time. That wasn't necessary in order to fulfill its original purpose.

"I understand," said the robot. "The astronauts Aaron and David perished in the parasite that's covering part of the ship."

"They didn't..."

Christine approached her swiftly. Aphrodite held one arm defensively in front of her face. Benjamin held Christine back.

"We're operating on the basis that Aaron and David's fate is still uncertain," said Benjamin.

Aphrodite nodded. "The data in the log doesn't contradict that interpretation."

"Good, we're in agreement, then," said Benjamin.

"I'm still worried about you, Aphrodite," said Christine.

The robot lowered her arm. "You shouldn't be. I'm fine. I have images stored in my memory of you floating up to the ceiling."

"I wonder what else you may have lost," said Christine. "But you've definitely changed. You were more carefree yesterday."

"Maybe that's just because of the situation we're in," said Ilan, who had stayed out of the conversation until now. "You used to be more relaxed too, Christine."

Chatterjee, on the other hand, looked more laid-back today than usual. Was he maybe pursuing some secret plan, and getting a kick out of it? Or had he actually changed?

"Thanks for reminding me," said Christine.

"Ilan may be right where Aphrodite is concerned," said Benjamin, acutely aware that this might add to Christine's irritation.

But he had to consider Aphrodite. She needed a positive outlook.

"Aphrodite has never been in a situation like this," he explained. "The missing half of her consciousness will regenerate."

"We can't be sure of that," said Christine. "I've read a few studies. In some cases, the affected individuals replaced what was missing with phantom content that they reconstructed themselves. Others supplemented the missing memories with content suggested to them by third parties – mostly well-meaning. The result was that their personalities changed, and rarely for the better."

"But that won't necessarily happen to Aphrodite," said Benjamin, putting his arm around the robot.

Aphrodite allowed it. She trusted him. That was nice.

"My friend, I promise we'll all help you to find the part that you lost. Everything will be all right, trust me," he said.

The lamps on Aphrodite's face simulated a smile.

APHRODITE PROVED INCREDIBLY SKILLFUL IN HANDLING THE sample containers. Her arms gave her the advantage of being able to attach precisely the right tools and apply them with precision and power. She worked at a remarkable pace, inserting the samples into various analysis devices that Benjamin didn't even know existed. Ilan was in his element too. He demonstrated the individual processes and explained them as he went, as if he had invented them himself.

Maybe he had. Benjamin chose not to ask, because he was sure Ilan wouldn't miss an opportunity to brag. In any case, it was thanks to him that the devices were on board, because his company Alpha Omega had played a significant role in designing, equipping, and financing Shepherd-1, as Ilan kept reminding them.

"This system can separate out the components of the

samples and subject them to a bonding structure analysis," he explained as they examined a machine that had never been used before.

Benjamin looked over his shoulder at Aphrodite, who was tirelessly measuring the exact mass of the samples. That wasn't easy in zero gravity.

"We'd have to open the samples to do that," said Christine.

"Of course," said Ilan. "But we can't knowingly pass up such precious data."

"We can and we must," said Christine. "That was clear from the start. I won't allow a milligram of this substance to contaminate the interior of Shepherd-1."

"Obviously, we'd open them inside a second, larger container, which would be as tightly sealed as the sample tubes."

"No, I refuse to allow it under any circumstances. The Shepherd is not a certified laboratory. We can't afford to make any mistakes inside the ship."

"I get it. Fine, you're the boss. I guess I'll just have to accept your decision," said Ilan.

Chatterjee was like a new man. Maybe it was the experience of being in an android body – or he was just a good actor.

"Thank you," said Christine. "For your understanding. Safety has to be our top priority. We only have this one ship."

"You're right," said Ilan. "And there are plenty of ways to examine the samples in their tubes."

"I already have some results," said Aphrodite.

"Tell us," said Christine.

Aphrodite put down the tube she was currently processing and drifted over to one of the lab computers. She removed the pincers from her shorter arm, positioned herself upside down above the computer and reached down behind it. She looked like she was doing a handstand on top of the computer.

"This is very practical," she said. "I remember I always used to need a special cable to connect myself to a computer."

The monitor lit up.

"You could have just told us," said Christine.

"No, I don't want to misrepresent any of the data," said Aphrodite.

Several radiation spectra appeared on screen.

"Here you can see how the samples react to the wavelengths that can penetrate the tube," Aphrodite explained.

The sample containers were transparent, so Aphrodite could test the way the gas inside them reacted to light. Benjamin scanned the graphics, which were sorted in order of wavelength.

"Strange, it doesn't seem to absorb anything at all in the optical range," he said.

He had expected the samples to swallow a lot of light. He couldn't think of another explanation for the mist that Aphrodite saw. But the absorption rates for yellow and green light were close to zero.

"The helium has warmed up," said Christine. "So it's lost the special characteristics of the Bose-Einstein condensate."

"Should I cool the samples?" asked Aphrodite.

"Do we have a refrigerator capable of temperatures that low?" asked Benjamin.

"Of course," said Ilan. "I insisted on it."

"As if you knew we'd need it to examine this parasite," said Benjamin.

"Ha ha, it almost sounds like you're accusing me of something," said Ilan. "But no, I just wanted to be well equipped. Wanted *you* to be well equipped. It was never part of the plan that I'd join you out here."

"Then I'll cool the samples I've already examined," said Aphrodite. "I noticed something else too. The proportion of helium-3 is unusually high."

"That's to be expected out here," said Christine. "The

proportion should be a hundred times higher than in the Earth's crust."

"That's right. The interstellar matter in the Local Cloud should contain around 1.6 helium-3 atoms to every ten thousand helium-4 atoms. But I'm seeing a different ratio. The samples contain an average of 2.6 per ten thousand."

"Is that...?" Christine faltered.

"Yes, that's close to the ratio present in the cosmos shortly after the Big Bang," said Aphrodite.

"Ah, so does that tell us something about the Big Bang?" asked Ilan.

Benjamin smiled. He knew Chatterjee would comment on that.

Ilan looked at him with a knitted brow. "What? Is that such a strange question?"

"It's a valid question," said Christine. "But no, it doesn't tell us anything new about the Big Bang. At that point in time, helium-3 atoms formed at a ratio of approximately three per 10,000 helium-4 atoms. We already knew that; it can be calculated based on the properties of the elements. The proportion of helium-4 later increased, because it's a common product of radioactive decay."

"Ah, I see. So the ratio of the two isotopes is an indication of the origin of the sample," said Ilan.

"Exactly," said Aphrodite. "In terms of both time and place. It's clearly not from the Local Cloud, it's from the early universe."

That was astonishing. Such far-reaching conclusions from such a simple measurement!

"But you shouldn't take that literally," said Christine. "It doesn't mean the parasite is 13.8 billion years old. What it means is that it must originate from a place where the ratios were still similar to those that prevailed one or two billion years after the Big Bang."

"Do such places still exist?" asked Ilan.

"Yes—for example, objects with a significant redshift,

many billions of light years away from us," explained Christine.

The astronomer augmented her little lecture with expansive gestures. Benjamin could tell she was enjoying this. If she weren't here, she could have been a university professor. That would suit her.

"But these ancient galaxies are moving away from us so fast that it's not possible for anything to reach us from there," she continued. "Except for their light, obviously. However, there are also places in our own galaxy that fulfill the criteria, that are very primeval."

"The Galactic Center, Sagittarius A*?" asked Ilan.

"No, the black hole there is very old, but that's not what I'm talking about. I mean the population III stars, the first stars to form in the universe."

"Can you tell their age by looking at them?" asked Ilan.

"Yes, by their spectrum. They almost exclusively contain elements that existed shortly after the Big Bang – hydrogen, helium, and some lithium. Since every element that's heavier than helium is called a 'metal' by astronomers, those stars are called 'metal-poor', which is a little confusing for everyone else, because even the Sun only contains a very small proportion of metals in the chemical sense."

"Where is the nearest metal-poor star?" asked Ilan. "Can we fly there?"

Christine smiled. "There aren't many of them. The problem is that most of the population III stars were giants and died very young. Only small ones survived to this day. Low-mass stars are mostly found in the galactic halo, in the outer reaches where there was never enough matter for larger stars to form. A few of these population III stars are known. Most of them were only identified in the last fifty years, precisely because they're so dim and so far away."

"How far?" Ilan wouldn't give up.

"At least 50,000 light years."

"Ah, right, forget it then," said Ilan. "It was worth a try."

"But there must be other ways for the ratio of the two helium isotopes to change in favor of helium-3," said Benjamin.

"Yes, if lithium is bombarded with neutrons, for example," said Aphrodite. "That would be possible in certain extreme star regions."

"Helium-3 is also a byproduct of nuclear weapon detonations," said Christine.

"Maybe what we have here is the last survivor of a nuclear war that an ancient civilization waged on itself," said Ilan. "A couple of mushrooms, so to speak, that mutated into this parasite under the influence of the fallout."

"You have a vivid imagination," said Benjamin.

"But we should consider the possibility that the parasite arose out of extreme conditions," said Christine.

"Thanks," said Aphrodite.

"Thank *you* for your excellent work," said Ilan.

Benjamin shook his head. Wasn't Chatterjee overdoing it a little? Next he'd be signing over his company to a foundation devoted to world peace.

"What I'm really curious about is the density of the sample," said Benjamin. "I mean, the parasite is so heavy. We should be able to measure that. If it's exclusively helium, it must be very densely packed."

"The content of one container is definitely not heavy enough for our calculations of the overall mass to make sense," said Aphrodite.

"Maybe because the temperature in here is higher?" asked Ilan.

"No, it can't be that," said Christine. "The containers were sealed the entire time. So the density can't have changed."

"The difference must have been present when the sample was taken," said Benjamin. "There's no other explanation. The helium can't magically disappear."

"Maybe a phase transition occurred," Christine suggested.

"We took the samples from a Bose-Einstein condensate of helium-4. In doing so, we disrupted the condensate and the mass spread out, the way subcooled water freezes instantly when you stir it."

"That could explain it." Benjamin closed his eyes to help him concentrate on his thought process. "Maybe that's also the cause of the strange isotope ratio. There may have been a layer of helium-3 above the condensate of helium-4. Then the proportion of each isotope would depend on the precise location the sample was taken from. Imagine you took a sample from a cappuccino. Depending on the depth, the cappuccino appears to consist mostly of coffee or mostly of milk."

"Now I have a craving for a good cappuccino," said Ilan.

"You don't need sustenance," said Benjamin.

That wasn't entirely true. Since the efficiency of his radionuclide battery had reduced, Benjamin had to recharge himself regularly from the electricity grid. He still hadn't asked the others whether they had experienced this defect. Benjamin always figured it was normal. But it didn't manifest until later, after the disaster.

"I don't need to eat, but I can," said Ilan. "I think that's wonderful, much more convenient than a human body."

Hmm, if only they'd known! Why didn't Chatterjee tell them they weren't human? Benjamin wasn't in the mood for an argument.

Something beeped loudly.

"That's the refrigerator," said Aphrodite.

She floated over to a chest-high cupboard with a glass section at roughly hip height. Benjamin followed her. The glass case glowed with a mysterious blue light. Aphrodite crouched down in front of it and looked inside. So this was the refrigerator. Benjamin had always assumed the piece of furniture was some kind of lab because it had two holes roughly the width of arms. Aphrodite now pushed her arms into them.

"Shit," she said. "One of my arms is too short. Benjamin, can you take over?"

"Sure, no problem."

"If you put your arms in here, you can move the samples around."

Benjamin nodded. That was what he figured. He inserted his arms into the holes. They were deep and his arms disappeared past the elbow. His hands slid into primitive gloves. But the gloves didn't move around as he assumed they would. When he moved his fingers, two robot hands simultaneously performed the same movement in the glass case.

It would have been easier if he could put his hand directly into the refrigerator. But that would add too much heat to the system. Doing it this way felt strange because he wasn't touching the object directly. There was no tactile feedback. But he managed to bring one of the samples close enough to the glass pane to look into it.

"The helium inside looks milky," he said.

So there was a phase transition! That meant the properties of the helium in the sample container might now be very different from when it was warm.

"Yes, I saw that," said Aphrodite.

"We never doubted you," said Benjamin.

"Can you weigh it now?" asked Christine.

"OK. How?" he asked.

"See that hole there? Just place the tube in it," said Aphrodite.

He guided the robot hand carefully to a tube. It looked sturdy, but he definitely didn't want to shatter it. It would contaminate the refrigerator.

"How fragile are these tubes?" he asked.

"You'd have to squeeze with all your strength to break them," said Aphrodite.

"Try it. You won't be able to do it," said Ilan.

"No, leave it," said Christine.

"Don't worry," said Benjamin.

He was now grasping the container. He moved it above

the hole Aphrodite had indicated and tried to push it in. It was pretty tight. He pushed harder.

"No, not that one!" cried Aphrodite. "That opening is far too small. Can't you tell? That one over there!"

Yes, he'd noticed. Benjamin moved the tube to the other side. Sure enough, there was another hole. He could see that the sample would fit into that one easily. He lifted it and inspected it for damage. It looked fine. So he inserted it.

"What now?"

"Now you undo that catch on the left."

The tube was sitting in a holder connected to a fixed pole by some kind of band. The holder was fixed in place by the catch Aphrodite had mentioned. He removed it. The holder suddenly snapped sideways. The band was elastic. It pulled the holder back and then sent it out again like a pendulum. That was clever. The oscillation period of a spring pendulum like that depended on the mass of the object and the hardness of the spring.

"Are you measuring the oscillation period, Aphrodite?" he asked.

"Working on it. Wait. Thirty oscillations and I'll have enough data."

Aphrodite counted aloud. The pendulum moved tirelessly. That was one advantage of zero gravity and the near-vacuum in the refrigerator. Benjamin stopped it at thirty.

"And? How heavy is the tube when it's cold?" he asked.

The spring pendulum allowed them to measure the inertia of the object, which corresponded exactly to the gravitational mass even in zero gravity.

"Significantly heavier than when it was warm," said Aphrodite. "The value corresponds much more closely to our estimation of the overall mass of the parasite."

"But how can that be?" asked Ilan. "How can the mass of the probe change just by cooling? The tube is sealed. Nothing was added!"

"That's a good question," said Christine, pulling the screen toward her and reading something off it. "Honestly, I don't know. The difference isn't huge, but it's well beyond measurement accuracy. Maybe it has something to do with the mass-energy relationship."

"Einstein?" Ilan shook his head. "At such low temperatures, where does the energy come from to increase the mass like that? Has the temperature of the sample changed? It should have dropped."

"The temperature has dropped a little," said Aphrodite.

Benjamin's forehead itched. His arms were still in the holes, so he tried to relieve the itch by rubbing his head against the cool glass. But it was too smooth.

"Do you still need me?" he asked.

"Yes, we still have a couple more experiments to do," said Aphrodite. "Thank you for your patience."

"Then I need someone to scratch my forehead, please. Above my left eye."

He flinched when Aphrodite's long arm reached out. It was fitted with a pointed tool.

"Please hold still," said Aphrodite.

He didn't move. She moved the tool toward his forehead and then gently ran it over the skin above his left eyebrow.

"A little harder. That tickles."

The point dug deeper into his skin. Hopefully not so much that it would leave visible scratches. It moved in a circle. Ah, that was very pleasant.

"That's good, thanks," he said. "Make a note of that setting, Aphrodite."

"Sure, Ben."

What? Aphrodite knew he didn't like being called Ben. He glanced over his shoulder at the robot, but she was already looking at the screen again, together with Christine.

"Please don't call me Ben, OK?"

"As you wish, Benjamin. I'll make a note of it."

"Right. Now hold the sample in that position, please," said Aphrodite.

They bombarded the cooled sample containers from every possible direction. That was awkward, because the instruments that emitted the electromagnetic radiation in all the various wavelengths were in each other's way. They couldn't be moved around freely in the refrigerator. Instead, Benjamin had to move the samples themselves. His knees and back ached. If only he'd declined! Chatterjee was probably in better physical condition and wouldn't have suffered as much. And if he did, well, he deserved it.

"Please turn it twenty degrees," said Aphrodite.

He turned the sample clockwise.

"That was fifteen degrees."

He turned it a little farther.

"That's too much."

"I don't have measuring instruments built into my fingers," he said.

"I know," said Aphrodite. "Given your limitations, you're doing very well."

"How much longer will this take?" he asked.

"We're up to number five of thirty frequencies. I estimate about two hours."

"Thanks, Aphrodite."

He sighed.

"Yeah, if we'd opened the containers it would have been easier," said Ilan. "Their contents would have automatically distributed itself around the measuring instruments. We could have had all the results in five minutes."

"And a contaminated ship in ten minutes," said Christine.

"There's never been a hazardous biological contamination in the history of space travel. Never," said Ilan. "Except in horror movies."

"Yes, because responsible captains prevented it," said Christine. "Unlike in the movies. It's naïve to assume that even a securely constructed chamber would offer complete protection. All it would take is a small piece of rock to hit us and shoot through the refrigerator like a hot knife through butter. Then you'd have your contamination."

"Hey, stop arguing," said Benjamin. "I'm thirsty. Can someone please bring me some water?"

"Sure," said Christine.

Moments later, a drink bottle was floating in front of him. He put his lips around the straw extending from it and sucked water into his mouth. It was pleasantly cool and tasted faintly salty.

"Please turn the sample 75 degrees," said Aphrodite.

He turned the sample until it was almost vertical. This time the robot was satisfied the first time. He was getting better at estimating angles.

IT ONLY TOOK ANOTHER 90 MINUTES TO COMPLETE THE measurements. Benjamin had just received permission from Aphrodite to remove his aching arms from the manipulator. Christine and Ilan had lost interest and gone to cook a meal together. It was weird the way Chatterjee had suddenly begun to integrate himself into the crew. Benjamin could hear the astronomer's occasional bursts of laughter in the kitchen while Ilan regaled her. He should be happy for Christine, but he still didn't trust the businessman. Chatterjee was the one who created this mess! Or was he just looking for a reason to be angry with him because he was actually jealous? Benjamin shook his head.

"Look," said Aphrodite.

She was floating upside down in front of the screen. Benjamin pushed off and joined her, assuming the same position. His stomach grumbled as if he were hungry. Those useless human instincts! But somehow it felt wrong to switch them off. How would that alter his personality?

"Your stomach is growling," Aphrodite observed.

She had good hearing.

"But you don't need to eat, do you?" she asked.

"No. It's a simulated urge. Part of my programming. What have you found?"

"Oh, like my sex drive," said the robot.

He looked at the body of the repair bot she was in.

"Yeah, it's absurd because I don't even have sex organs anymore," she said.

"Should we try to remove it from your programming?" asked Benjamin. "I mean, if it doesn't suit you anymore?"

"No, leave it. You still have your hunger pangs. I was just wondering if I'll start to behave strangely if I don't eliminate my sexual instinct."

"No, that's entirely up to you. I've gotten so used to the feelings of hunger that I wouldn't want to be without them."

"Thanks, that's reassuring."

Benjamin looked at the robot. She was typing something on the computer keyboard. Her long tool arm only had one point, but it moved very swiftly.

"So, can you shed any light on our parasite?" he asked.

"That's what I wanted to show you."

Aphrodite turned the screen slightly toward him. He saw a gray mass and faint structures within it. They appeared to be rotating.

"Wait, I'll increase the contrast a little," said Aphrodite.

The uniform gray acquired differentiated tones, which made the structures look three-dimensional. And he could now make out something that wasn't visible before: the rotating structures were donut-like rings. They had hairs or feelers around the outside, which stretched out and touched the neighboring rings as they rotated.

"Wow, that's... That can't be a coincidence, right?" he asked.

"I don't know," said Aphrodite.

"Christine, do you have a moment?" Benjamin called.

"Coming," she replied.

Aphrodite adjusted the screen so that Christine had a good view.

"Ooooh," she said. "Where did you find that? Is that a glimpse of our parasite?"

"Yes, this is the helium in the sample containers," said Aphrodite. "At temperatures just above zero."

"That's a lot of activity," said Christine.

"What you're seeing is slowed down. At normal speed you wouldn't see anything."

"There's a lot of energy in this movement," said Christine. "That may partially explain the expansion. But where's it coming from?"

"I'd say the more interesting question is: what's its purpose?" said Benjamin.

"It doesn't necessarily have a purpose. It could be random motion," said Christine. "The way the leaves on a tree rustle when the wind blows. That looks synchronized too, but there's no intention behind it. It's just a result of the energy that the wind adds to the system."

"And these donuts? What are they made of?"

"I would theorize that they're superconductive rings. They create the magnetic field that keeps the parasite in its compact form. They probably arise from the combination of the two helium isotopes. The helium-3, with its fermionic properties, is preventing the bosonic helium-4 from forming a condensate. Instead, these rings form, as semi-stable states. It's not sorcery. Just before water boils it forms bubbles that already contain steam. But that's just the first thing that comes to mind. We may find something that contradicts my theory."

Benjamin took a deep breath. Christine had swiftly developed an entire theory for something she had just seen. She could be a candidate for the Nobel Prize if only it could be awarded to androids.

"You figure this is all a natural process?" he asked. "That these rings arise and disappear without purpose or intention?"

"Yes, that's the most likely explanation. Almost all phenomena in the universe behave that way."

"That's a shame."

"I've taken another look," said Aphrodite. "The rings are

surprisingly stable. They exist for longer than you'd expect considering their energy content."

"Interesting," said Christine.

"I'm just checking now whether there are any irregularities in the arrangement of the rings in space."

"Good. How long do you need?" asked Christine.

"Give me thirty minutes."

"Sure. Benjamin, come with me, we've made dinner. Oh, would you like to join us too, Aphrodite? You're invited too, of course!"

"No, thanks," said Aphrodite. "It would only depress me in my new body."

"I'll clean up here," said Ilan. "You two go and keep Aphrodite company. She's sure to have more news. Such a smart robot!"

Benjamin began to feel ill, and it wasn't from the food. He glanced at Christine and raised his eyebrows. She just shrugged.

"Give him the benefit of the doubt," she whispered. "He's probably just trying to make up for past mistakes. We shouldn't automatically suspect ulterior motives. Not without a reason."

"Chatterjee never does anything without an ulterior motive."

"Maybe. But what if his motivation is the realization that he may have to spend the next five hundred years with us? Then it's better if we get along."

Now it was Benjamin's turn to shrug. He didn't trust Chatterjee, and that probably wouldn't change in the next five hundred years. He was definitely up to something.

"Ah, how was the meal?" asked Aphrodite.

"It was surprisingly good," said Benjamin.

"One of Ilan's recipes," said Christine. "Made with basic ingredients."

Oh, she didn't mention that earlier. She probably knew that if she did, Benjamin would turn it down.

"He clearly has many talents," said Aphrodite.

"He's had it easy," said Benjamin. "Do you figure he earned all that wealth? No. He comes from a filthy rich family."

"But he could have used his money to lead a life of leisure," said Christine.

"True," said Benjamin. "That would have been better than turning people into androids without their consent and sending them on a one-way voyage."

"He did that?" asked Aphrodite. "You'll have to tell me more about him sometime. But without him, we would never have met. I would now be with my owner."

Aphrodite sighed. Benjamin put his hand on her cold hard shoulder.

"Do you think things would be better for you on Earth?"

"Definitely not. Then again, I wouldn't know what I was missing. And I'd still have my body. I admit I miss it. The freedom of movement! This body by comparison... I keep bumping into things."

"I'm sorry," said Oscar. "It's my fault. I shouldn't have brought you with me."

Benjamin hadn't heard a word from Oscar in hours. Where had he been all this time?

"I'm glad you didn't leave me alone," said Aphrodite. "So don't feel bad."

"But I do. I should have known how important your body was to you. I assumed you were like me. I always enjoy changing bodies. Being this ship is great. But you were developed in conjunction with your body. As a unit. My first body was merely a hiding place."

"Still. Don't beat yourself up. We have plenty of time on this voyage. At some point we can construct me a new body."

"We will," said Christine. "Do you want to tell us what you found out while we were gone?"

Aphrodite turned the screen so that everyone could see it.

It showed a schematic that could have been a map of a city. There were narrow and wide streets running between blocks, intersecting, spreading out, and recombining.

"Houston?" asked Benjamin.

"No, this is one of our samples," said Aphrodite.

The rotating donuts appeared on screen again. Then the picture changed once more. The structure remained, but a new one was superimposed over it. It consisted of blue and red streets.

"I've calculated the first derivation of the activity – that is, how much it changes. Red indicates the areas where there is less change, and blue the areas are where it's increasing. Intense color indicates dramatic change. Watch, I'll start the time lapse."

At the top edge of the image, a pale blue spot appeared. It moved along a blue street until it reached the bottom edge of the image. There, it disappeared, but it reemerged quickly on the red street and moved upward. It moved at about the same speed as it had on the other street, until it finally disappeared off the top of the image.

"What was that?" asked Benjamin.

"A signal," explained Christine. "I assume you didn't find only one instance of that?"

Aphrodite shook her head. "Several per second. The process you just observed took less than a second. Now watch this."

The image changed. The red and blue colors faded. But the outlines of the donuts became clearer. They were rotating very slowly. Their little appendages were well defined. The pale spot started moving down again from the top edge, but slower this time. It looked like it was being carried by the rotation of one of the donuts, like a ferry. The moment it reached the underside of the donut, an appendage on one of the other donuts touched the passenger. The blue spot transferred across, moving along the appendage until it reached the ring itself, and was then ferried down by it. This happened twice more, but then the spot changed direction and jumped via an appendage onto the neighboring donut to the right.

At first glance, it looked as if the spot itself was choosing its path. But that was deceptive. It depended on the position of the appendages. The donuts were clearly guiding the transfer with their rotation. Maybe some centralized system of control was determining the path? That would be sensational.

"Is it possible that the path is determined by the system as a whole?" asked Benjamin.

"That's a really remarkable representation," said Christine. "I'm impressed that you came up with the idea of working with the first derivation and slowing down the time factor so much..."

Aphrodite smiled broadly. "I have a strategy module that helps me make the most of my defensive capabilities. Unfortunately, they're wasted in this body."

"Ah, you're an HDS model, right?" asked Ilan. "I've heard a lot about RB's premium products."

He was apparently finished with the washing up.

"That's right," said Aphrodite.

"Then you and I can cook together next time. I'm sure I could learn a few things from you."

"You're welcome to lend me a hand," said Aphrodite. "Especially as mine are less than ideal for cooking. Which is your fault, by the way."

Ha! She hadn't forgiven Chatterjee for the deal he struck with RB that put her in this situation. Benjamin was glad that he wasn't the only one who refused to fall for the changed man act.

"What can we conclude from Aphrodite's findings?" asked Oscar. "To what extent do they influence our plan?"

"Is it possible the parasite has a consciousness?" asked Benjamin. "I mean, the signal transmission reminds me a lot of what happens in neurons. The speed is similar, anyway."

"It's way too early to draw conclusions like that," said Christine. "There does appear to be a transmission pathway for signals. But you see that in a bunch of multi-celled organisms. And that has nothing to do with intelligence."

It would have been nice to meet non-human sentient life. Although... he and Christine weren't human and they possessed intelligence. But the real question was: did they have their own form of intelligence or had they just salvaged their intelligence from humans? Maybe they were in a transitional phase too.

"But it's an exciting discovery nonetheless," said Oscar. "It could still be a life form with origins outside of the Solar System."

"If it turns out that we're dealing with life here," said Christine, "then it's not carbon-based like every other form of life we've ever discovered."

"What about the sulfur cells on Jupiter's moon Io?" asked Oscar.

"Fine, one point to Oscar," said Christine. "And there was something else on Triton, but I don't know much about that."

"The carbon-based life form on Amphitrite most likely didn't originate in the Solar System either," said Oscar.

"Don't ruin my wonderful theory with facts," Christine said with a laugh. "Actually, I was going to point out that the thing that we're suggesting may be alive is made of helium at only a few degrees above absolute zero. If it really is life, then we'd have to abandon our existing concepts of what life is. It would mean there could even be life in sun spots."

"The momentous implications of that shouldn't stop us from considering it," said Benjamin. "But I generally agree with you. Signal transmission even happens in dead things. When lightning strikes, an electrical impulse is passed from a cloud to the ground. But that doesn't make us perceive the system of thunderclouds and soil as a living cell. There's more to life than that – for example, reproduction, growth, metabolism."

"That's a good comparison," said Christine. "There are systems in nature that aren't alive but still exhibit some of the characteristics of life – certain rocks, for example. We need to be careful. It's probably best for Shepherd-1 if what we've found isn't alive. We started calling it a parasite early on, and that stuck, but it would be easier to fight some purely physical or chemical phenomenon."

"Unfortunately, we already know the thing is growing," said Oscar.

"May I comment?" asked Ilan.

Now Chatterjee was asking permission to speak.

"Of course," said Christine.

"If it turns out that the parasite is a life form, maybe we can also find a way to get rid of it. I'm thinking metabolism. If you deprive life of the possibility of metabolizing, it dies."

Typical Chatterjee, thought Benjamin. He was quick to consider the best way to cause the parasite to suffocate, starve, or die of thirst. Or was he being unfair? Hadn't he himself tried to think of a way to scrape the stuff off the ship's hull? Benjamin scratched his temple. All due respect to life, but if it crushed their ship, then they were all done for.

"I could try to find out how the metabolism in the samples works," said Aphrodite.

"That would be easier if we could open the containers," said Ilan. "I mean, metabolism generally requires material being added to the system, which isn't really possible in a sealed tube."

"Absolutely out of the question," said Christine.

She didn't want to take any risks. Benjamin could understand that, but the parasite clearly wasn't interested in playing nice. And maybe Chatterjee was the right person to deal with this kind of danger. No. Benjamin shook his head. He wouldn't defer to him.

"I shouldn't have any problem observing the metabolism within the sample tubes," said Aphrodite. "It seems to me that the cells, or whatever they are, respond primarily to energy input. And the transparent tubes let through most forms of energy."

Aphrodite really knew what she was doing. Benjamin felt proud of the robot, although he could take no credit for her achievements. Sometimes he couldn't help thinking of her as the daughter that he never had, and never would have. Even her age – her date of manufacture – was about right.

"Do you need anything from us?" asked Christine.

"Do you want me to help you?" asked Ilan.

"I could use someone to operate the manipulator arms for me again," said Aphrodite. "Or do you want to do it, Benjamin? I don't mean to deprive you of the job. You did very well."

Now she sounded like the mother he never had. He preferred her as a daughter.

"Thanks, Aphrodite, but I'm happy to let Ilan take over."

At least Chatterjee couldn't cause any trouble with his arms in the holes.

"I'm glad to see you two interacting like grownups, Benjamin and Ilan. Don't forget that tomorrow you set out together in the capsule for the source of the radio transmission."

"I'd be happy to..." Benjamin began.

"Can't we take Aphrodite with us?" Chatterjee interrupted. "She has the most experience out of all of us in dealing with the parasite."

"Then shouldn't she stay here?" asked Oscar. "It's not as if you're taking the parasite with you."

"If I'm not mistaken, the transmission contains recordings of David and Aaron's voices from before they disappeared. Do you actually believe it has nothing to do with the parasite?" asked Benjamin.

"Do you have any concrete suggestions about how the two phenomena could be related?" asked Christine. "Then we could specifically search for evidence of that."

"No, I guess we'll have to wait and see."

"It's possible that the source of the transmission is a much larger version of the parasite," said Aphrodite. "Maybe it sent out spores."

"Or the parasite is its metabolite," said Oscar. "It took a dump on the side of the road and we happened to step in it."

"I find that metaphor hard to swallow," said Benjamin.

"Hard to swallow? That's understandable," said Christine with a laugh.

It was cool in the corridor. Benjamin was wearing pajamas. He had interrupted his rest phase to attend to an urge that he didn't even need to have. But if he consumed food, then he had to excrete the processed waste, and in that sense he was no different from a human. That was the reason he was walking through cold, dark corridors in the middle of the night.

But apparently he wasn't the only one awake. Part of the ring was still sealed off, so he climbed toward the central module. There, he heard the telltale clattering of fingers on a keyboard. So it wasn't Aphrodite burning the midnight oil. She could connect herself directly to the computer and didn't need to input commands in such a laborious way. It was a shame, actually. He would have enjoyed a chat with the robot. He already felt rested enough for the coming day.

Aphrodite was an interesting person. As a robot, she seemed simultaneously familiar and alien to him. She had never believed she was human. She was designed to serve humans – basically no different to him or Christine, except more honest. But had that helped or harmed her? Probably both.

Benjamin pulled himself out of the spoke into the central module, taking care not to make any noise. There was minimal gravity here, so he could mostly float by pushing himself off things occasionally. But some instinct told him to be quiet. And then he heard Ilan's voice. Benjamin quickly stopped himself and took cover behind a cabinet.

He was probably overreacting. What kind of trouble could Chatterjee get up to in the middle of the night? Oscar was in control of the computer, which Ilan no longer had access to. He couldn't even open an airlock without permission, let alone decouple a capsule. The more Benjamin thought about it the more he realized he didn't need to worry. There was no way Ilan could seriously sabotage Shepherd-1.

He should just continue on his way to the WHC, take care of business, and leave Ilan in peace. He really didn't feel like talking to him. They'd just argue. Benjamin left his hiding place and floated forward, toward the noise.

Until he saw Christine. No, it was Chatterjee. The similarity drove him crazy. But at least they used different voices. The entrepreneur was sitting on the floor with a space suit in his arms. It was a bizarre sight, because although the suit was empty it looked like a human body at first glance. The way Ilan cradled the helmet in his lap looked like he was having a romantic moment with a lover. And he was talking to it. A shiver ran up Benjamin's spine.

"A little farther forward," whispered Ilan. "Yes, that's good."

Chatterjee was bent forward, speaking directly into the visor of the empty helmet. Then he straightened up slightly as if his back hurt. He must have been sitting in that position for a while. He still hadn't noticed Benjamin, who felt like a voyeur.

"Thank you, that was great. I need you," Ilan continued whispering.

Benjamin could understand every word, but he had no idea what Chatterjee was talking about, or with whom. Had he lost his mind? Or was he playing some weird game? Benjamin retreated a meter until he was out of Chatterjee's line of sight.

"I want you to..."

Benjamin couldn't stand it any longer. Chatterjee didn't deserve his consideration, but he couldn't stand spying on this strange ritual any longer. Benjamin cleared his throat loudly, then drifted into Ilan's line of sight and stopped.

"Oh, sorry, I didn't know there was anyone here," said Benjamin.

"Good... Good evening, Benjamin. Or is it morning?"

Chatterjee put the space suit down at his feet.

"No idea. I just need to use the WHC. Your meal..."

"Right. Yeah, I had to go too. I hope you don't smell it. For some reason I can't get comfortable in the bed in the capsule. So I figured I'd try my luck here in zero gravity."

Benjamin yawned, prompting Chatterjee to do the same.

"I'll go take care of that, then," said Benjamin.

"You do that," said Ilan. "I'm surprised how realistically sleepy I feel in this body."

"You shouldn't ignore it for too long," said Benjamin, "or your faculties will suffer."

"Yeah, thanks. I'll keep that in mind, Benjamin."

There he was again, the new Ilan.

Benjamin finished and came out to find the control room empty. And Ilan had taken the space suit with him. He searched for it everywhere and couldn't find it – strange. Had he taken it to his capsule? Was that really some kind of love affair he had witnessed? Was Chatterjee playing a game? Was he struggling to come to terms with his new body? Benjamin hadn't seen any signs of that so far.

"Oscar? Can you hear me?"

"I'm here."

"Can you tell me what Chatterjee was doing just now in the control room?"

"No, sorry."

"You weren't watching him?"

"Normally I would, but he asked for privacy. When it comes to fulfilling certain urges, I'm obliged to comply with such requests, unless there's some obvious reason not to."

"Urges?" asked Benjamin.

"For the reasons I just gave you, I can't go into more detail."

"Did it have something to do with a space suit?"

"I can't confirm that."

But he wasn't denying it either. Benjamin shook his head. He'd heard of people falling in love with objects. It was a sexual preference. Benjamin couldn't remember the entrepreneur ever appearing with a partner, male or female. He had always assumed that was just because he was good at protecting his privacy. But it would also explain why camera drones had never succeeded in shedding light on Chatterjee's personal life.

Still, it seemed strange. What was Chatterjee trying to hide? Benjamin checked all the computers in the control room. Ilan hadn't touched any of them in the last six hours. Nor could he find any other devices that might be of interest to Chatterjee. If he had found him in the workshop or the lab... The probes were locked in a safe... Ilan could have secretly fashioned a weapon to attack him on their flight to the source of the transmission. But no, he had found him cuddling a space suit. It made no sense!

"Benjamin, do you still need me?" asked Oscar.

"I don't understand Chatterjee," Benjamin replied. "He was sitting on the floor with a space suit in the middle of the night, talking to it."

"I can't comment on that," said Oscar. "But maybe you should consider the possibility that he really has changed. For someone who's spent his whole life as a biological being, it must be a huge shock to suddenly live in an android body."

"Chatterjee is still Chatterjee, I'll bet anything on that."

"I don't know, Benjamin. You never used to be so intractable."

He was intractable? That was rich coming from Oscar!

"How would you know? You haven't known me for long."

"Christine told me. She said she barely recognizes you. That you used to be much more open."

He felt a pang in his heart. Christine was complaining about him to Oscar instead of telling him to his face? Eric was probably to blame; Eric's body, which he had been forced to use. And she trusted Chatterjee because he looked like her.

Otherwise she would have to mistrust herself. It was hard to avoid such subconscious projections.

"And what does she base that on?" he asked.

"The fact that you still call him Chatterjee. Have you noticed that everyone else uses his first name?"

"I don't mean anything by it. I've always known him as Chatterjee."

"I'm just telling you what Christine said to me. It's up to you what you make of it."

Capsule A, October 21, 2112

"Good morning," said Aphrodite.

Cool air wafted in from the corridor. Benjamin was still in his pajamas. But he was pleased to see her.

"Good morning! This is a nice surprise. Come in."

Aphrodite handed him a kind of briefcase. "Please stow this somewhere where it can't move around."

"What is it?"

"It contains all the samples I collected yesterday. Christine doesn't want them on the ship when we fly to the source of the transmission."

"And we're supposed to take them in the capsule instead? That's even riskier."

"No, we're supposed to destroy them."

"Why don't we just open them up outside?"

"We discussed that at length," said Aphrodite.

Did he detect a hint of impatience? He wasn't used to that tone from the robot.

"But I wasn't..."

"We couldn't reach you," said Aphrodite. "Now let us in. We don't have much time."

Us? Aphrodite gently pushed him aside. Chatterjee was standing behind her, grinning. He had a space suit over his arm. The one he was talking to last night. Benjamin began to grimace, but then he returned the smile instead. Chatterjee knew that he knew. That was enough. If only he knew what it was that he actually knew.

"Good morning, Benjamin," said Chatterjee.

"Good morning, Ilan," Benjamin said, just in case Christine was listening over the intercom."

He let them both pass. "Make yourselves comfortable."

He took fresh clothes from a cupboard and went to change out in the corridor. It was still pretty cold there. When he re-entered his capsule, it was even colder.

"I took the liberty of airing the place a little," said Chatterjee.

Said Ilan. He had to get used to thinking *Ilan* when he saw Chatterjee... when he saw Ilan. So, Christine thought he was intractable. That was unfair. But if he pointed that out to her, it would only reinforce her impression. Chatt... Ilan was intractable. It was just that Benjamin didn't know what plan he was doggedly pursuing. And until he did, he had to play along. He had no choice.

"Good idea, Iiilaan," he said. "I hope you feel rested now?"

"Yes, thanks. And I made some improvements to my suit."

Improvements, right. If he examined it, he'd probably find fresh repairs. Ilan never left anything to chance.

"It's always good to keep your equipment in top condition," said Aphrodite.

"I want to apologize for being unreachable," said Benjamin. "I needed a little privacy and forgot to switch the intercom on again afterward."

At the word 'privacy' Ilan flinched noticeably. Now he suspected that Benjamin had spied on him. Maybe it was a mistake to let on. But surely Ilan already knew he didn't trust him.

"So what's the plan exactly?" asked Benjamin.

"We'll throw the samples into the DFD exhaust stream," Aphrodite explained. "They'll evaporate there without us having to open the containers."

"Smart plan," said Benjamin.

"It was my idea," said Ilan.

Yeah, you know how to make things disappear without a trace. Benjamin refrained from saying it out loud.

"It's good to see you making such a positive contribution to our mission," he said instead.

That was the most flattering thing he could think of saying. As long as there was a chance that Christine was listening in, he would continue to play the friendly, understanding crewmate. But after that, he was done with happy families.

"You're welcome," said Ilan. "I hope one day you'll all see me as a full member of the crew."

Now he was overdoing it. But Benjamin didn't react.

"What's the actual reason for being so overly... for being so cautious?" he asked. "I mean, why not just tip that small amount of helium into space? Outside of the refrigerator, it seems to behave like an ordinary noble gas."

"We can't be sure of that," said Aphrodite. "We don't know how it would behave if we opened the tubes. It might cling to the space suit, and then we'd unwittingly bring it back into the ship. We don't have any kind of helium detectors here."

"I see," said Benjamin. "Then I'll go get my space suit."

"No need," said Aphrodite, extending her long arm to close the bulkhead. "One suit's enough. You can pilot the capsule. Ilan offered to do the EVA."

"Yeah, it's not as easy as it sounds, because the ship will accelerate when we fire reaction mass out of the DFDs. I didn't want to expose Aphrodite to that risk."

"That's very generous of you," said Benjamin.

What was he intending to do out there? The plan wasn't without risk. If Ilan was willing to take that risk, there must be something in it for him. Was he maybe planning to embezzle one of the samples? Or he really was a changed man. Christine seemed to want to believe that. Benjamin took a deep breath. He decided to count each sample as Ilan sent them into the reaction mass.

JUST AS HE HAD DONE WHEN THEY COLLECTED THE SAMPLES, Benjamin let the ship slowly catch up to the capsule. That way they avoided the risk of getting caught in the blast of hot reaction mass. It didn't yet exist. The fusion drive that Oscar had selected was still running at its lowest setting to produce the energy required by the ship. The Shepherd itself was flying in a straight line without propulsion.

The computer beeped. They had almost reached the point where Ilan was supposed to get out.

"Are you ready, Ilan?" asked Benjamin.

"Yes."

Benjamin turned around. Ilan actually saluted. This was becoming embarrassing.

"At ease!" Benjamin commanded. "Aphrodite, please open the airlock. Exit in thirty."

In half a minute he could be rid of Chatterjee. Forever. He just had to somehow ensure that he fell into the hot reaction mass along with the samples. No, that would be murder. Sure, Chatterjee was an asshole, but that was no justification for murder.

The countdown was displayed on screen. It was at ten. Benjamin reached under the pilot's seat and brought out a breathing mask. He didn't need to breathe, but without oxygen he would still feel like he was suffocating. It was such an unpleasant feeling that he preferred to wear the mask.

"Three, two, one, go!" he said.

A violent rush of air told him that Aphrodite had opened the airlock.

"Hurry!" he cried.

It was instantly freezing. His skin stiffened. That was a protective mechanism that prevented extensive damage.

"Ilan's outside," Aphrodite announced.

The airlock squeaked shut.

"Thanks, Aphrodite."

Benjamin switched over to the capsule's exterior camera. Chatterjee had already made it onto the hull of the ship. He was still weightless for now, which made everything easier. Benjamin watched as he systematically moved toward the drive, which was slightly behind them. Benjamin increased the capsule's speed slightly so that it stayed level with Shepherd-1.

"I'm in position," said Ilan.

"Oscar, did you hear that?" asked Benjamin.

"Affirmative. Starting the reaction mass inflow."

This was the critical part of the undertaking, for all of them. The reaction mass – neutral hydrogen – was flowing into the drive chamber for the first time in weeks. There it would be ionized and heated, which increased the momentum of the particles. Then Oscar would open the outlet. At this point the hydrogen ions were mere protons, and as they were emitted they provided the ship with momentum equal and opposite to their own. It was only a tiny contribution from each particle, but altogether it was enough to accelerate the heavy ship.

But the problem was that this process couldn't be precisely controlled at the beginning. If the ship accelerated faster than the capsule, which had an old-fashioned chemical drive, the capsule could wind up in the hot exhaust stream. That could cost them their lives. So to be safe, Benjamin gave a little more thrust than necessary, even though he ran the risk of not being able to pull Ilan back to safety in time.

"Reaction mass approaching critical level," said Oscar.

At that moment, the chamber opened and the hot gas shot out. Benjamin pushed the control lever forward. The capsule was moving a little too fast. He reduced the power a little, but then it looked as if Shepherd-1 would overtake them. So he accelerated again. He now had to pay very close attention and make continuous readjustments. At the same time, he wanted to count, to be sure that Ilan actually disposed of all the samples. So he focused the camera on him. Now it would automatically follow his movements.

"This way I can help Ilan as soon as he needs it," said Benjamin, who sensed Aphrodite watching him skeptically.

"That's good," said the robot.

"I'll dispose of the first sample now," Ilan announced.

"Affirmative," said Benjamin. "One sample at a time."

Then he wouldn't lose track. Ilan bent in the middle and reached between his legs where the case of samples was wedged. He took out the first one, tied one end of a safety line around it, and threw it. The sample flew in a high arc, passed the protective shield in front of the drive, and then the line pulled it back down toward the ship. The others had calculated the length of the lines so that the sample tubes would pass about two meters behind the ship. There was nothing to see there because the reaction mass was transparent, at least in the optical range, but the tube deformed in seconds. The line snapped and the reaction mass stream had no time to blast the rest away because there was already nothing left of it.

"Did it work?" asked Ilan.

"Did it ever!" said Benjamin. "This method is spectacular."

Even if the helium was preserved – which was very likely, because the reaction mass stream was no fusion reactor – the speed of the other particles would force it away from the ship so fast that they would be rid of it forever.

"Could we get rid of the parasite like that too?" Benjamin asked. "We'd just need to convert the DFDs so that they're pointing back at the ship. The icy helium would have no chance against the hot plasma."

"Neither would the ship's hull, my friend," said Oscar. "Keep an eye on your speed. I have a feeling you're moving too slowly."

Oh, shit. Oscar was right. Shepherd-1 was accelerating faster than they were. He'd allowed himself to be distracting watching Ilan throw the second sample. Benjamin increased the power of the chemical thruster. But it wasn't enough.

"Oscar? You're still flying away from us," said Benjamin.

Shepherd-1 could outpace the capsule easily, even with just one drive.

"Understood. I'll reduce the flow of reaction mass a little."

Now they were moving at the same speed. Ilan was a little too far away, so Benjamin braked the capsule briefly.

"Third sample destroyed," reported Ilan, as if he knew Benjamin was thinking about him.

"There's a problem," said Oscar.

"Is it something to do with us?" asked Benjamin. "Then you should hurry, Ilan."

"I'm not sure. The structural integrity of Shepherd-1 has reduced by eight percent, mostly around the middle."

"Does that mean the parasite's attacking again?" asked Benjamin.

"I don't know if it's attacking," said Oscar. "But it's contracting noticeably."

Maybe the parasite didn't like them destroying the samples.

"Maybe the parasite doesn't like what we're doing with the samples," said Ilan.

Great, now they were having the same thoughts!

"Are you suggesting the parasite is recognizing what's in the sample tubes?" asked Christine.

"I have to agree with Ilan. The timing is too much of a coincidence," said Benjamin.

"Well, if you're agreeing with Ilan, then it must be true," said Christine.

"Seriously though, that doesn't mean the parasite is actually recognizing itself in the samples. With some animals, if you kill a member of the same species, they're capable of reacting in self-preservation. Maybe the rapidly heating helium sends out a signal that the parasite can intercept and respond to, contracting to protect itself."

"OK, Benjamin. You may be right," said Christine. "Let's

try something. Ilan, please don't throw any more samples into the reaction mass for a few minutes."

"OK, got it. Don't destroy any more samples."

"How does the structural integrity look, Oscar?" asked Christine.

"Not getting worse. But not improving either."

"Hmm. That doesn't prove anything. Wait one minute, then destroy one more tube, Ilan."

"Understood, Christine."

They waited. Benjamin's favorite pastime. Not! He hated waiting. He counted down the seconds.

"You can do it now," he said when he reached zero.

Ilan attached another sample container to a line and threw it.

"Perfect arc," said Benjamin.

"Thanks."

The tube passed through the hot gas. Within moments, it was gone.

"Stop! The structural integrity just dropped by ten percent," Oscar reported. "The thing wants to kill us!"

"Did you hear that, Ilan?" asked Benjamin. "Please come back inside. We're aborting this mission."

Shepherd-1, October 21, 2112

Christine met them in the ring on Shepherd-1. She looked pale.

"I'm so sorry," she said. "I almost caused our mission to fail."

"It wasn't your fault," said Ilan. "It was that damned parasite."

"I should have known. We can't destroy the samples. I don't know how the parasite was alerted, but there must be some physical mechanism."

"You couldn't have known, Christine," said Benjamin.

"Thanks, guys, but I'm the captain so I'm responsible for everything, including things I didn't know."

Christine seemed really upset. Even her usually smooth, long hair was in disarray.

"We realized and stopped it in time," said Ilan. "A danger foreseen is a danger avoided."

What kind of ridiculous truism was that?

"I'm afraid I have to disagree," said Oscar over the intercom. "The ship's sensors show that the structural integrity is continuing to deteriorate. It's not happening as fast as it was immediately after the samples were destroyed, but if it continues at this rate, the ship will break in half."

"Maybe it's just an echo," said Ilan. "Like aftershocks after an earthquake."

"The deterioration is very steady, as if someone's controlling it precisely," said Oscar.

"How long do we have if nothing changes?" asked Christine.

"A week at most. We could try to reinforce the ship internally, but that would only buy us two or three more days."

"Maybe we should postpone our trip to the source of the signal," said Christine. "We need all hands on deck right now to reinforce the ship."

That was a bad idea. The source of the transmission was their last hope.

"You know I always have the utmost respect for your suggestions, Christine, but I don't think that's a good idea," said Ilan. "Stabilizing the ship would only buy us a few days. We need it to last our lifetimes."

Again, Ilan was thinking along the same lines as Benjamin. Should he be worried? At least Ilan seemed to finally understand that they were all in the same boat – not that this did much to appease Benjamin's mistrust.

In the end, they did delay the launch by a few hours in order to bring the material into the ship that they needed for the reinforcements recommended by Oscar. Most of it was stored in containers only accessible from outside. With the main airlock sealed off, they had to bring everything in through one of the airlocks on the ring, which was exhausting due to the simulated gravity there.

Aphrodite did most of the physical work. Even though she was missing the part of her body designed to transport heavy loads, the robot tirelessly hauled struts and beams. Benjamin pictured the parasite undulating on the hull. There must be a heavy loading bot and two people stuck somewhere inside it.

There was no way a cloud of helium could dissolve such a solidly built robot into its constituent atoms. The parasite had neither hands nor tools, and as a noble gas, helium wasn't corrosive in any form.

On the other hand, there was the incredible power with which the parasite was threatening to mash the ship like a potato. Benjamin put down the steel beam he had just pulled into the ship's central module. Christine was following Oscar's instructions and gathering together the parts they needed outside. Aphrodite dragged them through the ring to the central module, where Ilan and Benjamin received them and deposited them in the places where they would later be used. Oscar guided them all via the ship's speaker system and the helmet radios. They worked together like a single large organism. An extraterrestrial watching them would probably assume they were in a symbiotic relationship with Shepherd-1. The ship kept them alive, and in return they kept the ship intact.

The parasite, on the other hand, was of no benefit to the ship – in fact, the opposite was true. Benjamin stretched two lines around the heavy beam so that it wouldn't shift if they made a course correction. Just up ahead on the interior wall, he could see one of the large bulges. The square panels lining the walls had come away where the outer hull had bulged inward under the pressure of the parasite. This bulge ran around the entire ship like a belt. Oscar's countermeasures were intended to use the parasite's own strength against it. They were firmly bracing all the sturdy metal beams they could find between the walls, so that the parasite had to push against its own force.

Rough calculations suggested that it would buy them about a week. After that, the beams would snap under the strain like matchsticks. All the parasite had to do was redirect the force that was currently distributed across a larger surface and concentrate it in the area they were reinforcing. There was still a question mark in their favor: maybe the parasite wouldn't arrive at that conclusion. After all, it couldn't see their countermeasures on the inside of the ship. But it could feel them, and if it had the slightest measure of intelligence or even instinct, it would react. Benjamin for one was doubtful. It wasn't intelligent to underestimate the intelligence of one's opponent.

"Here, this is the last one," said Chatterjee.

Benjamin grasped the T-beam that Ilan shoved toward him and jammed it between two others. Then he put his hands on his hips and looked around. The space was barely recognizable. And by the time they returned it would have changed even more.

"Do you think Christine and Aphrodite will manage?" he asked.

"Yeah, no problem," said Ilan. "These things weigh nothing in here. Christine assured me she's a good welder. I still think we should take Aphrodite with us."

Ever since they returned from the sample disposal mission, Ilan had been arguing the case for taking Aphrodite with them to the source of the transmission. But his arguments were too weak to persuade even the amenable Christine. She obviously didn't welcome the idea of reinforcing the ship's interior on her own, and Benjamin could sympathize.

"We're done discussing that," said Benjamin. "You and I will launch in the capsule when we're finished here."

He wasn't really looking forward to the journey, but the alternative – remaining in the ship – appealed to him even less. He'd rather travel with the astronomer, but they couldn't leave Chatterjee alone – even Christine agreed with him on that. If their blatant mistrust bothered Ilan, he didn't let it show. And if he really was pursuing some long-term plan, it must be exceptionally flexible.

"You're right, my friend. And a men's excursion could be good too," said Ilan.

My friend. Hmm. Benjamin didn't see it that way.

"I should tell you now. I'm not a good conversationalist and I need a lot of time to think."

"Sure, Benjamin. You'll have it. I'm pretty good at entertaining myself."

Ilan reached inside his jacket and brought out an angular glass bottle. It sparkled in the dim light. Ilan shook it. Its contents were golden brown.

"Look what Christine found in one of the storage containers," he said. "She gave us the bottle in case we get bored."

Benjamin still found it strange to hear a person with Christine's face refer to her in the third person. Couldn't Ilan at least cut off the long hair?

"Alcohol," said Benjamin. "I have bad news for you. You obviously don't know your body well. I'm afraid you'll find it doesn't have much effect. Your body chemistry isn't human."

"Pity. But it's also about the taste, right?"

Benjamin nodded. "Sure. You have that. But you'll have to get up in the night."

"Like you did yesterday."

Benjamin recalled the scene of Ilan talking to the space suit. He wore it the next morning. Maybe he was just repairing something on the helmet.

"Where is everyone?" came Christine's voice from the helmet hanging from Ilan's arm. "Let's meet in the ring in thirty minutes to send off the expedition."

"Oh, it's that time already," said Ilan. "I should go and pack a few things."

"Do that. I'll take a shower. It'll be the last opportunity for the next two days."

"Have fun. To be honest, I try to avoid seeing myself naked. The discrepancy between my body image and reality is so large that it actually makes me feel sick. I never expected that. During puberty, I sometimes wished I had female breasts – you know what I mean."

No, he didn't. Benjamin never went through puberty. The memories he had of such a time belonged to someone else.

"I didn't ask you to come here," said Benjamin.

"Yeah, I know. I wasn't blaming you. But if you ever

decide you'd like to swap bodies with me, I'd be very grateful."

Benjamin laughed. That'd be the day! Although one advantage of swapping was that he wouldn't have to look at Chatterjee in Christine's body anymore. But then he'd be the one with the incongruous self-image. Would he cope with that better than Ilan? It no longer bothered him to see Eric waving at him in the mirror.

"It's me again," said Christine via the helmet. "A reply would be good. Did you hear me?"

Ilan raised his arm and turned the helmet so that he could speak into the built-in microphone.

"Benjamin and Ilan here. In thirty minutes in the ring. Affirmative."

"Thanks. See you guys soon."

Ilan hung the helmet over his arm again.

"I'll go, then," he said.

"See you soon," said Benjamin.

Ilan floated out of the control room, but Benjamin hesitated. The scene reminded him of something. Ilan had spoken into the helmet last night too. What if he wasn't talking to himself, as Benjamin assumed, but conversing with another person?

Thank you, that was great. I need you. I want you to... Unfortunately, he had interrupted him at that point. But who could Ilan have been speaking to? There were only four of them on board, so that left Christine and Aphrodite. He couldn't imagine Christine having a secret affair with Chatterjee – not least because of their identical bodies. But Aphrodite – Chatterjee could be taking advantage of her programming. Aphrodite seemed to have a need to be loved. Benjamin could totally understand that. It was a deeply human need. But her experience with humans was limited. For Chatterjee, a gifted manipulator, she was probably an easy target.

Was that why Ilan was so enthusiastic about Aphrodite accompanying them? He would have a better chance of overpowering Benjamin. Then again, what could he really do with the capsule? He needed Shepherd-1 if he wanted to return to Earth, for example, or – and this was more likely – if he wanted to find out the truth about the Big Bang. Maybe his plan was to blackmail Christine: *If you don't hand over control of the ship, I'll kill Benjamin.* Would she go for it? He both hoped and feared that she would. But it would only be possible with Oscar's permission too. Would Oscar hand over control to save him?

Benjamin shrugged. Once again, he was wasting time on futile trains of thought instead of spending it under the hot shower. He undressed where he was, floated to the WHC, and shut himself in. Moments later, the warm water streaming across his body transported him back to the time before his birth.

"Let's keep this short," said Benjamin. He hated goodbyes. "We'll see each other in two or three days anyway. The destination will turn out to be a harmless mirror that bizarrely reflected Aaron and David's words, and we'll be just as clueless as before."

Putting down the space suit to free up his arms, he hugged Christine and then Aphrodite.

"You take care of each other," he said.

He freed himself from Aphrodite's hard arms and gave Christine a wink. She just wrinkled her nose. After his shower, he had quickly filled her in on what he'd witnessed. As expected, Christine was skeptical. *Your baseless mistrust of Ilan has to stop,* was all she said. But at least now he wouldn't have any regrets if his suspicion proved correct. And maybe he had succeeded in making Christine a little more cautious.

"I'm excited to find out what's out there," said Ilan.

"I really hope it helps solve our parasite problem," said Christine.

"It's a shame I can't come with you," said Aphrodite.

Christine put an arm around her shoulders. "I'm really sorry, but I can't do all this without you."

"We need a place we can return to," said Ilan. "I'm very grateful to you, Aphrodite."

"You're right. I totally get it."

"We'll keep you updated," said Benjamin. "Come on – the sooner we leave, the sooner we'll be back."

Capsule A, October 21, 2112

THE ARMS ANCHORING THE CAPSULE TO THE RING RELEASED IT with a metallic creak. A slight burst from the corrective thrusters and Shepherd-1 appeared to fling capsule A out into space. Benjamin rotated the capsule until the main thrusters were pointing in the right direction.

"Be ready for 3 g in thirty seconds," he announced.

"I'm ready," said Ilan.

"Don't try anything stupid."

"Oh, Ben, I thought we were past all that."

"Don't call me Ben."

The acoustic countdown started. Benjamin checked whether they had reached the predefined distance from the ship. It looked good. He counted along in his head. Three, two, one. He had set the acceleration to manual control. At zero he pushed the lever forward. The thruster at his back transmitted a thrumming sound through the capsule. Benjamin pushed the lever forward a little more and then locked it in place. The inertial force squeezed him. And at 3 g it was still relatively merciful.

"I think that's enough," groaned Ilan.

"Half an hour," Benjamin said through gritted teeth.

He surrendered to the gravity. He took his hand off the lever, let it sink to his side, and relaxed all his muscles.

An alarm woke him. It was time to shut off the thruster. Benjamin turned his head to the side. Ilan's seat was empty. Suddenly he was wide awake. The first time he took his eyes off Chatterjee and...

"Hey, you look tense."

Ilan was standing behind him. Jackass. Benjamin breathed in and out, gathering his strength, and then reached for the thruster control lever. He gripped it and pulled it back to zero. He felt wonderfully light.

"What are you doing there?" asked Benjamin.

"I wanted to test out how much this body can take. I mean, in theory I already know, because it was designed according to my specifications. But experiencing it for myself is something else."

"It all feels pretty ordinary to me, but I guess I have nothing to compare it to."

"See? If we were on Earth now, I might let you test out a biological body."

"Yours? I'd be Ilan Chatterjee?"

"Not mine necessarily, no. We're pursuing some developments in cloning technology. It's the next logical step. Why should I restrict myself to cultivating genetically identical organs? Repeatedly switching out body parts doesn't give you eternal youth. In the long run, a fresh body is better and – I can't stress this enough – the more ecological solution. We've done the math. We're calling the concept 'biobag'. Do you like it? Do you think that's a marketable name?"

"I don't know. It sounds kind of like a body bag, don't you think?"

"You're not the first person to point that out."

"But doesn't that violate a bunch of UN conventions?" asked Benjamin.

It was a rhetorical question. Cloning entire humans wasn't allowed in any country on Earth.

"It's only prohibited because it doesn't work properly yet," explained Ilan. "The problem is the consciousness. It's a mistake to go the natural route with cloning. That way, you get something we don't want in the biobag – a consciousness, which obviously has all the rights of a human. But what use is a clone with human rights? We only need it as a replacement body for another consciousness."

"And you've solved that problem? You can cultivate clones without consciousness? Wouldn't you have to leave out the brain?"

"Right. But obviously we need the brain. The trick seems to be to target the brain during the maturation process in the nutrient solution. We overload it right from the start with so many contradictory impressions that no consistent consciousness can develop. It wouldn't even be able to communicate. So we do that on a very broad spectrum. The results are very promising."

Ilan was volunteering company secrets for which he would go to prison in the US. Why? Presumably, he was hoping to return to Earth, despite the crisis out here. So shouldn't he be more circumspect about sharing his sordid secrets? Maybe he didn't see them that way. The biobags would sell like hotcakes. Eternal youth – what human didn't dream of that? At least, that was the impression Benjamin had when he lived on Earth. And he couldn't talk. He was already immortal, relatively speaking, although he'd only found this out a few years back. And if they could be produced ethically, these full-body replacement parts... then maybe it was petty to stand in the way of progress just because it broke present-day laws.

Ilan's thinking was probably along those lines. Benjamin didn't want to pass judgment, but he couldn't help it. That was thanks to the human consciousness that Ilan had duplicated, processed, and implanted in him. But maybe the actual technical process was different, and his consciousness was only artificially modeled on that of the real Benjamin Forestier. It didn't matter. He was more human than real humans. At least that was what he told himself.

"Does that shock you?" asked Ilan. "I know I shouldn't have told you. My PR adviser would rip my head off if she knew. But when you're stuck with someone on a suicide mission like this..."

Oh, where was that optimism that Chatterjee kept spouting in front of Christine?

"I guess you're hoping I'll tell you a secret or two," said Benjamin. "But I don't have any. You already know all my memories, because you gave them to me."

Benjamin pulled the screen closer. They were far enough from Shepherd-1 that it was now worth scanning the skies with the capsule's sensors. He launched the radar in search mode and began a survey with the optical and infrared cameras. The source of the transmission must be somewhere out there in front of them. An object roughly fifty kilometers across surely couldn't escape the capsule's sensors.

"Do you still hold all this against me, Benjamin? I really don't understand. You'll live forever, you go to places nobody has ever been, you get to explore phenomena that no human has ever seen. Without me, you wouldn't even exist!"

Those were good arguments. Benjamin waggled his head from side to side. His life wasn't boring. He was very grateful to his maker for that, and his maker was sitting right beside him. But he still resented Ilan. Maybe it was because his father, if he could call him that, still had his own private agenda.

"I don't hold it against you," said Benjamin. "I just get the feeling that you still see me as a tool, like everyone else around you. But maybe I'm wrong. Why don't you prove it to me."

"OK, Benjamin, it's a deal. I'll..."

The computer emitted a melodic notification tone. It was clearly not a danger alert, but Benjamin flinched anyway. In space, news was seldom good.

"Wait, I have something here," he said.

The capsule must have received something. The antenna! But if it was the Shepherd, the system would have established communication. Instead, it had saved the incoming message. Benjamin pulled up the data on screen. It was a jumbled mess.

"We just received this," said Benjamin, pointing at a graph of dramatic spikes.

"Maybe a voice message?" Ilan suggested.

Benjamin pressed the play button, but all they heard was a hiss.

"A disturbance within the system?" asked Ilan.

"The spikes are too big for that," Benjamin replied. "It looks like a bolt of lightning hit us."

"Encrypted data?"

Benjamin started an entropy analysis. That would tell them how random the data was. The more random, the less information. The value was very high.

"We're looking at it in the wrong way," said Ilan. "If I say a word and then digitize it, I get exactly this kind of data, right?"

"You're saying our clip is too short?"

"Yes."

"This is all we have, and the file is huge. Wait a moment – what if the clip is too long rather than too short? If you compress the whole Bible into ten seconds, you can't follow the plot anymore."

Benjamin zoomed in on the image until the gaps between the spikes were visible. He tried playing back the expanded section as speech again. This time they heard a crackling noise instead of a hiss.

"Did you hear the rhythm?" asked Ilan.

Benjamin played it again. Sure enough, there was a rhythm to it, punctuated by the sections with no sound.

"Taktak, tak, taktaktak, tak, taktak, taktaktak," he repeated.

"Taktak, taktak at the end," Ilan corrected him.

"Whatever. Doesn't matter. We're looking at a pulse code like the humans' old Morse Code," said Benjamin.

"Can you analyze the entire file as Morse?" asked Ilan.

"Already on it. But it's pretty weird. The message that the Shepherd received was plain speech, right?"

Ilan leaned forward and switched on the radio.

"Shepherd-1, please come in," he said.

"Shepherd-1, Oscar here."

"Oh, I'm glad it's you. Ilan here. That message that we received from our destination..."

"What about it?" asked Oscar.

"I need to know how it was encrypted," Benjamin called.

"Oh, it was pulse-coded. That was a little strange. It didn't occur to me to check that at first. It took me 0.6 seconds to think of it."

"Why didn't you say so? We assumed it was sent using our frequencies and encoded as speech."

"You didn't ask. But it would have been a huge coincidence if they used the same transmission methods as we do."

"Not if the sender did it deliberately," said Benjamin.

"I can't argue with that. If it were deliberate, then it wouldn't be coincidence. The opposite is also true."

"Oscar!" Benjamin shouted.

"Is there anything else?"

Benjamin shook his head.

"Capsule A out," said Ilan. "Oscar is so funny. Maybe I should think about selling a model like that. Useful and impertinent, the new trend. Who wants robots that never talk back?"

"Then why don't you ask your..."

The computer interrupted him. It had finished analyzing the code. Benjamin tapped 'play'.

"Joint is stuck... can't bend it... stuck... I can't... the loader... I... Nearly! The last..."

"That's it," said Benjamin. "Then it repeats itself."

"Like the first transmission," said Ilan. "Those are recordings of Aphrodite, although her voice is unrecognizable."

"I was reminded of Aphrodite too," said Benjamin.

"But it sounds muffled, as if there were a hand over her mouth."

"No, the consonants are too clear for that. It's more like she's speaking under water."

Benjamin increased the volume and played the transmission again.

"I... Nearly! The last..."

They could hear clanging noises in the background.

"That clatter in the background... That could be the loader," said Benjamin.

"Yeah, that was the point where she detached herself from the loader," said Ilan.

"I didn't hear those noises over the radio," said Benjamin.

"Maybe you forgot about them?"

"No."

Benjamin accessed the archive. It took him a few seconds to find the right snippet.

"I... Nearly! The last..."

"That's the original," said Benjamin.

"You're right, there was no clattering. I wish I had your memory."

"Do you know what this means? They weren't just listening in, they were recording every acoustic signal with some kind of microphone."

"But that's impossible in the vacuum," said Ilan.

Benjamin recalled the way Aphrodite had slowly faded. The robot shape on screen had grown darker and darker by the second until the winch finally began winding her in.

"She wasn't in the vacuum," he said. "The atoms that make up the parasite must have been excited by Aphrodite's acoustic vibrations. I don't know how a voice sounds in helium at a temperature of three Kelvin..."

"Just like that, I guess," said Ilan.

"Right." Benjamin scratched his temple. "So the parasite recorded those vibrations and then sent them on. The source of the transmission and the parasite are somehow linked."

"We already knew that," said Ilan. "Or is it news to you?"

"We couldn't be sure. The first transmission was made up of speech fragments, which were also spoken over the radio channel."

"But those were recorded acoustically too."

"I'll bet if we examine them more closely, we'll discover that they contain background noises that weren't audible on the radio."

Benjamin unbuckled his belt, pushed off, and floated up to the ceiling. What did this all mean? What was the nature of the link between the parasite and their destination?

"It could be a warning," said Ilan. "They must have registered our approach."

"Or an invitation. I doubt they understand the content of the message. That's impossible. Nobody learns the language of an alien intelligence that quickly."

"I agree, Benjamin. If they had, they'd choose their own words. 'Hello stranger, don't come any closer' or 'dear visitor, we look forward to meeting you'. Right?"

"Wait," said Benjamin. "We're assuming they've noticed our approach and that there's a connection between them, whoever they are, and the parasite. Their communication so far seems to support that. Maybe that's all they're trying to convey, because it's clear to them that it would be impossible to communicate anything else?"

"Extraterrestrial pragmatists. I like it. I get along well with pragmatists."

"But unfortunately, that also means we're none the wiser."

Benjamin pushed himself away from the ceiling and drifted to the porthole at the bow. The object they were flying toward was too small to see with the naked eye this far out. But it was waiting for them somewhere out there. They wouldn't find out until they got there whether it was waiting with bared teeth or an inviting smile.

"I have an idea," said Ilan.

"Spill."

"Let's assume it's some form of intelligence."

"OK, but we can't be sure."

Ilan nodded. "It's just an assumption. If it's wrong, my plan won't do any harm, it just won't work."

"OK, assumption accepted."

Benjamin turned around and regarded his traveling companion. Ilan looked very focused. He was totally on task. If only he could be trusted, he'd be a valuable crew member.

"They've come from far away," said Ilan.

"Indeed."

"That requires advanced technology. We currently have no spacecraft that would enable humans to make such a long journey."

Shepherd-1, he almost said. But Ilan was right. If humans were on board, they would have starved long ago. The ship would have to be ten times bigger in order to accommodate the necessary food provisions.

"Yes, they must be very advanced," said Benjamin. "Although they could have used tricks similar to those you used on Shepherd-1."

"Sure, they could have sent some kind of artificial life form. In fact, this parasite doesn't strike me as the result of natural evolution. But humans couldn't artificially cultivate something like this self-stabilizing helium structure. So I'm sticking with my assumption that they're way more advanced than us."

"You may be right."

Where was Ilan going with this?"

"So, if that's true, then it makes sense to let them do the work. Who has a better chance – a human trying to decipher the language of ants, or the ants trying to learn a human language?"

Benjamin smiled. It was a good question, because the answer only seemed obvious at first. Ilan must have seen his smile, because he shook his head.

"You're right, Benjamin, it wouldn't be easy for us to learn ant language either. But if..."

"Just tell me your plan, Ilan."

"We trust in their superior capabilities and send them so many examples of our language that they can't help but learn to decipher it. I mean, they already seem to have guessed correctly that it's based on acoustic vibrations. And they're capable of extracting sense from them. Did you notice? All the words they sent us were complete. They correctly interpreted the short pauses in speech as separations. But they seem very different from us. We can't even imagine communication on the level of a Bose-Einstein condensate."

Ilan wanted to supply them with the information they needed. Benjamin sniffed. Was that likely to be fruitful? Would he learn to bark more easily if a whole pack of dogs barked at him? It probably wouldn't hurt. The question was: were they even interested in conversation?

"You don't think they might view that as an attack?" asked Benjamin.

"I doubt it. We'll adjust the transmission power so that they can hear us loud and clear, but not too loud. And we'll keep listening. Maybe they'll respond."

"OK. Any ideas about what we should send?"

"How about literary works from our archive? There are loads of audio files. Aaron's counterpart loved listening to audiobooks, so I made sure there was a good supply."

"Great. Where do we start?"

"I vote *Moby Dick*."

That fit with Ilan's character. A man on a mission.

"All right, let's send the white whale out into the cosmos."

THE REPLY ARRIVED THIRTY MINUTES LATER. IT CAME IN THE form of an endless stream that initially appeared to have no structure.

"Take a look at this," Benjamin said, pointing at the screen. "It never ends."

"Hmm. Does it consist of words?" asked Ilan.

"You mean, did they send our own message back to us? No, unfortunately not."

Benjamin pressed play. White noise came out of the speaker.

"Why unfortunately?" asked Ilan. "It could be something way more exciting. The theory of everything, for example. Scientific knowledge could be a good basis for communication because its universal."

"Look at this graphic. It's total chaos."

"Are you sure, Benjamin? Have you measured the entropy?"

Benjamin zoomed in on the graphic. It didn't look much different.

"OK, I'll run the calculations," he said.

He ran the stream through the statistical module that dealt with such questions. A new graph appeared. It took three seconds to transform into a horizontal line.

"See? The entropy is minimal," said Benjamin. "None of the values can be predicted based on the preceding value. It's randomness in its purest form."

"But that makes no sense," said Ilan. "Why would they send us random values?"

"Maybe because they couldn't make sense of our message?"

Ilan shook his head. "The entropy of what we sent is below one. It obviously contains information, even if you can't make sense of the contents. Replying to that with a random stream is beneath them."

"If they're even aware of the concept," said Benjamin.

He was disappointed. He switched over to the transmission module and canceled their own transmission. He instinctively expected the extraterrestrial stream to stop too. But it continued.

"They don't seem to care," said Ilan.

"We should send it to Oscar," said Benjamin. "I'm tired."

"Not so fast," said Ilan. "I don't want to let Oscar have all the fun."

"Knock yourself out. Here's the data. I need some rest."

With a couple of gestures, Benjamin transferred the data to Ilan's screen. They wouldn't succeed in conversing with the parasite. Chatterjee would give up eventually. Right now, he still seemed to think he could solve every problem with technology.

"Oh, thanks," said Ilan. "I'll take another look at it from the beginning."

"Do what you want. I'm going to sleep. See you in the morning!"

"Sweet dreams."

Benjamin buckled his seatbelt and turned on his side. He had no problem sleeping with someone working beside him. He found it reassuring. Although it turned out to be a little different with Ilan. Chatterjee talked to himself as he worked. Benjamin had no choice but to listen.

"Hmm, wait a minute, if I take the number of states and..."

Typing sounds.

"Interesting. It's limited. There are..."

Typing, scratching.

"Forty-one. That's a lot, but not inconceivable. Is it possible..."

Typing.

"That actually does seem to be the base. But..."

Scratching. Rustling.

"It is the base. A base-41 number system. No wonder we..."

Deep inhalation and exhalation. Benjamin tossed and turned.

"Sorry, I'll be quiet," said Ilan. "Sleep well."

Quiet typing. Ilan was making an effort. Benjamin closed his eyes and tried to block out the world. Sleep slowly crept up on him. It came out of his shoulders, flowed across his back to his...

"Shit, still random. No, wait..."

The sleep receded again.

"If I convert that into decimal.... How does that work again?"

You need to... Benjamin kept his mouth shut. Ilan would figure it out. He was trying to sleep.

"Ha, like that! Now I just have to..."

Typing sounds.

"That looks good. Four, one, nine, seven, one, six, nine, three, nine, nine... Hmm."

Ilan had evidently extracted some numbers. But they didn't make any more sense than the graph on screen.

"No way. Why is this random? I need to... Damn it!"

Benjamin was tempted to sit up and look over at what Ilan was working on. But he wanted to win the fight for sleep.

"...not the start. Back. Right back to the beginning."

Quiet typing.

"Wow. This looks good!"

Benjamin flinched when a hand grabbed his shoulder.

"Wake up, Ben, I found it! Ha! Without Oscar's help."

He sat up. "What did you find?"

"The meaning of the message."

"And? What are they trying to tell us?"

"3.1415926 and so on."

"What? I don't understand."

"It's pi! The circumference number!"

"What, that whole message, just to send us pi?"

"It's a start, Ben."

"Benjamin."

"Yes. Benjamin. Aren't you going to congratulate me?"

"Congratulations for finding the value of pi with the help of some extraterrestrials."

OK, that was a bit unfair. Ilan had just decrypted the first communication from beyond the Solar System. Oh, no, the second. There was some kind of SOS from Proxima Centauri. What ever happened to that? Maybe they were refugees from Proxima searching for a new home on Earth.

"That was kind of feeble," said Ilan.

"You're right. That was a very creative effort. Well done. But what do we do with it?"

"They're still sending. We record the stream. As far as I know, we've only worked out around 250 sextillion decimal places for pi so far. Maybe the extraterrestrials will supply us with the rest."

"The rest, ha ha. They'd have to continue transmitting forever."

"Fine, you're right. But it would save the earthly mathematicians a mountain of work."

"That's great," said Benjamin. "But how does it help us?"

"Well, we thought they were random values. They're not, even if they appear to be. They're sending us pi – oh, and in a base-41 number system."

"Then they must have 41 fingers."

"You're funny, Benjamin. Anyway, pi is universal. So they're using it as a basis for mutual understanding."

"That's how it always happens in the humans' science fiction movies."

"It makes sense. The question is – how do we reply?"

"With another universal constant. How about the Eulerian number 2.718...?"

"That's not a good idea. It's directly linked to pi via Euler's identity."

Blowhard. Benjamin had no idea what Euler's identity was. Fine, he'd do Ilan the favor and ask. But only the minimum.

"Euler's identity?"

"$e^{i*Pi} = -1$"

"Oh yeah, I... No, honestly, that means absolutely nothing to me. But it's fascinating! Two numbers with infinite decimal places producing a round minus one, that's..."

He actually felt a shiver run up his spine. Why had he never heard of that? Oh yeah, because his counterpart hadn't learned it in school. His awe faded.

"Thanks," said Ilan. "But I didn't discover it, Euler did.

It's the result of Euler's formula, when you substitute pi for y."

"I'm glad we discussed this. Do you think the extraterrestrials know that too?"

"Definitely. So we should send something other than e."

"Wait. That won't help. We send them some constant, then they reply with another one – what's the point of that? We should be showing them that we've understood their reply and that we want to begin a conversation. So e is perfect for that."

"Fine," said Ilan. "It can't do any harm. I'll encode the first thousand decimal places for e, first in a base-41 system, and then as a radio signal."

"Thanks," said Benjamin.

He had to admit it was fun solving puzzles with Ilan. But he wasn't about to tell him that.

"Done. I'll send it."

"Go!"

"Oh, that was quick. The mathematicians on Earth won't be happy."

"Why?"

"The pi transmission just stopped. We only received a few million decimal places."

"What's come through instead?"

Ilan bent over the screen. Benjamin could tell by watching his fingers that he was zooming in and then out again.

"And?" asked Benjamin.

"Only a very short reply, sadly. Take a look."

Ilan turned the screen toward him. There was an XY graph with two horizontal lines. One ran just below zero and the other near the top of the graph.

"The lower one must be minus one," said Benjamin.

"Yes, that fits with their number system," said Ilan, pushing the screen away. "But the upper pulse doesn't."

"That's a symbol from their alphabet. I'll bet they're using that in place of the root of minus one."

"So it's i."

"It could be something else in their alphabet. But hey, we just had the first communication with an alien civilization! Both sides discovered and communicated that we have an understanding of mathematics through to Euler's identity. This is the kind of successful communication that some couples could learn a thing or two from."

"Yes. So what now?" asked Ilan.

This time Chatterjee seemed thoroughly disappointed. Maybe he was hoping for some kind of verbal communication. But it was unlikely that they would get that far. Unlike universal mathematics, language was always shaped by its environment. Even two humans speaking the same language often couldn't understand one another.

"Slow and steady wins the race," said Benjamin. "We now know their number system. How about packaging some data about the characteristics of the Solar System into that?"

"But we have no idea of their units. Maybe they don't even use our geometry."

"Then they wouldn't have the value of 3.1415925, etc., for pi. We could depict the relationships of the orbits. That's very specific. Nothing like it has been found in any other systems."

"Good idea," said Ilan. "Do you mind if I do it? I'm not tired."

"Knock yourself out. I'll take a short nap. Any objection to me powering myself off for ninety minutes?"

Benjamin had learned that Ilan wasn't capable of working quietly enough for him to sleep. His brain really needed a break.

"No, go ahead. Sleep well."

"Thanks."

Benjamin turned on his side. He didn't want to force Ilan to look at him. A deactivated android looked dead, and Ilan wasn't used to that. It was down to the artificial skin and the fact that an android's features changed a lot without the muscular support. By comparison, sleeping humans retained a certain amount of their muscle tone.

But was that such a good idea? If he powered himself off, he was at Chatterjee's mercy. He could tie him up or abuse him in some way. And he wouldn't even be aware of it. No, that wouldn't happen. Ilan had nothing to gain from that. Benjamin set an external timer for 90 minutes and switched himself off.

Shepherd-1, October 22, 2112

APHRODITE DRIFTED THROUGH THE CORRIDORS. SHE WAS USED to being alone. The middle of the night was her favorite time. It always had been, even on Earth. When the humans slept, the world belonged to her. Weirdly, the androids here had adopted the habit of sleeping, although there was no real reason for it. Aphrodite couldn't understand why they did it.

It was probably because the androids had spent a long time believing they were human. That was cruel, and she could understand why Benjamin was still angry with Chatterjee. Although she had a different perspective on the situation: the real travesty was that the androids were unable to develop their true selves for such a long time. Not being human should feel like being released from a straitjacket!

She had always known she was a robot. She had honed her capabilities and used them for or against the most varied clients – in some cases both. Curiously, there were humans who had aspirations of dying during a sex act, and she had helped some to do just that.

She wasn't responsible for it. That was one of the advantages of her robot status. She had to obey her owner, so her owner was always responsible for her actions – legally and morally. But it was possible that she had forfeited that freedom as a result of her most recent actions. Aphrodite wasn't sure how it had come to that. In the end, it was surprisingly easy to come to an independent decision. It was strange. Benjamin and Oscar had congratulated her on her newly won freedom. But the reality was that she was less free than she used to be, because with freedom came responsibility.

Now, at night, was when she felt most free. Her sense of freedom was inseparably linked to solitude. She liked Benjamin and Oscar, and she accepted Christine, but she preferred to be alone. Shepherd-1 made strange noises at night, as if taking the opportunity to stretch and move. Aphrodite floated through the central module. It looked a little like a labyrinth with all the beams reinforcing its structure. They had spent a full day working on it. Christine worked in a very structured way, almost like a robot. Aphrodite mentioned this, but she didn't take it as a compliment. The android appeared to have certain prejudices toward robots. Aphrodite was used to that from Earth. There, androids could only be used under very restrictive conditions.

But she didn't really care. There wasn't much that Aphrodite cared about. Her friends, of course. She liked to make them happy, in every way. That would be easier if they were human. She had previously lived with two different men, and both were always satisfied with her, until they could no longer afford the monthly rental. But how did you make an android or a vacuuming bot happy?

Suddenly something embraced her. Aphrodite struck out with her arms, but there was nobody there. Her assailant was so fast she didn't even see them.

Clang.

She had bumped into one of the steel girders. The assailant was gone. She was alone again. She should be happy about that, except that her assailant had left something behind – an invisible gray cloud tightening around her consciousness like the parasite around the ship. Shit. The fog was back. She had assumed she was rid of it. It made everything seem washed out, and nothing was fun anymore. The world lost its color, the way her body had lost its color when the parasite tried to take her. She had watched the video footage several times. Her other half had remained behind. It was out there somewhere, holding part of her self captive. It felt to Aphrodite as if the gray fog was oozing out of the open wound, out of the rift, which was only slowly healing.

But what could she do about it? Nothing. The parasite wouldn't give anything back. Maybe the fog would dissipate again at some point. She would talk to Benjamin about it when he returned. He had experience with robots and probably understood them better than Christine did. Or maybe she was just jealous. *She*... that could be her, or the other part of her. What about androids? Could they feel jealous? Aphrodite once knew a man who claimed he wasn't capable of jealousy. He was a pretty strange guy, though. As an HDS model, she had an officially integrated jealousy module, which activated as needed in order to intensify her relationship with her owner. It was in the tech specs. Only the owner could deactivate it.

Clang.

Startled, she drew both arms in close to her body. But she saw no obstacle that she could have collided with. The sound came from somewhere below her. Maybe the parasite had spread and was now crushing other parts of the ship? But the noise didn't sound like metal groaning under strain; it sounded like metal hitting metal. They were currently traveling without propulsion, so it was unlikely that a large object had come loose from its mounts.

Aphrodite needed to find out what was going on. She drifted toward the stern.

Clang.

Again. The sound was getting nearer.

Clang-clang.

That couldn't be coincidence. Maybe a pipe in the life support system had rusted through and could no longer withstand the pressure, which caused it to bang rhythmically against the wall?

Clang.

Now it was really close, and it wasn't coming from inside the ship. Aphrodite oriented herself. The storage rooms were to her left. She had never been in that part of the ship. She glanced down the corridor. It was dark. Her sensors showed a lot of dust on the floor and walls, in which people had left hand and foot prints.

Clang-clang.

She spun around. This time, the noise sounded like it was directly below her. But there was nothing down there except the main airlock. It was sealed off now that the parasite was completely covering it. Aphrodite pushed off and drifted down to the level below. The inner airlock door was open. It was noisy. The life support system was operating at full power. The airlock, which looked big enough to accommodate one of the capsules, had been turned into a kind of storage area. Apparently, someone had been too lazy to correctly dispose of the waste. Aphrodite found strange-looking metal parts left over from some kind of repair work, along with bags full of food scraps and rags. Had they run out of space in the storage rooms? She resolved to tidy it all up tomorrow. Today. It was already long past midnight.

Clang.

The noise. Aphrodite had forgotten about it. It was coming from the outer airlock door. But there was nobody in here who could be making the noise. So the source must be outside. The parasite? There was nothing else outside on the hull. She floated over to the airlock door and positioned herself so that her microphone was directly against the metal. The door was very cold and covered in a layer of tiny ice crystals. Aphrodite touched them with the tip of her short tool arm. Her warmth didn't melt the ice but turned it into vapor. It must be dry ice – frozen carbon dioxide. She measured the temperature. Here at the outer airlock door, the air was only 260 Kelvin. That explained why the life support was working so hard: it had to compensate for the cooling caused by the parasite.

Clang-clang-clang.

Aphrodite flinched, although she should have expected to hear the noise again. If the parasite was causing it, then how? How could a Bose-Einstein condensate knock on a door so hard it that it sounded like metal on metal?

"Aphrodite, is that you?"

The voice was so quiet that she couldn't be sure it wasn't just in her head. Aphrodite checked the sensor channels. No, it wasn't in her head. There was a signal running along the acoustic channel. She had heard something. Was it really her name? She tried encoding it differently. Could it be some natural phenomenon?

"Aphrodite, it's me!"

It was impossible. She compared the voice profile. It was one of the four standard voices that Chatterjee's company Alpha Omega had licensed for use in robots. It was a masculine voice often used in loading bots.

Loading bots. Aphrodite shook her head. She had watched it disappear, over and over again. It was impossible. There must be an error in her signal processor. Erroneous interpretations could occur at low volumes when there was a lot of background noise. Maybe she was just hearing what she wanted to hear. Only humans were susceptible to those kinds of psychological effects. She had clearly spent too much time around humans.

Aphrodite pressed her microphone more firmly against the wall. At the same time, she isolated her body and deactivated all the other microphones. She checked the quality of the audio input and recorded the background noise in order to remove it from the signal later on.

"Aphrodite, I know you're there."

She recoiled and floated across the airlock. This couldn't be happening! She needed to ask Oscar. He would know what was causing this error.

"Oscar, can you hear me?"

"I hear you."

"Do you have a moment?"

"Right now I'm going through all the ship's log files. It's a lot of data, I'm telling you! But I always have time for you."

"Thanks, Oscar. I..."

I'm hearing voices. The parasite is talking to me with the voice of the loading bot. How would she react if Oscar said that to her? She would examine his psychological state – very thoroughly.

"You?"

"I have... Can you check my sensor input?"

"For which sensors? What's the problem?"

"It's as if the background noise has increased dramatically."

"Have you checked your core temperature? If it's too high, the background noise increases. There's nothing you can do about it, it's just physics."

"My core temperature is low."

"All right, Aphrodite. Then you need to come to the workshop and plug yourself in so I can take a look at your channels."

"Thanks, Oscar. I will. I just have a few things to take care of here first. Someone's turned the main airlock into a garbage dump."

Why didn't she tell Oscar the truth? It must be the illogical hope that the impossible voice had stirred in her, and the fear that Oscar might take it away from her. Aphrodite pushed herself off and floated back to the outer door. Hopefully she wasn't too late. She pressed her microphone against the wall and hoped. She knew perfectly well how illogical she was being. Something was wrong with her, but she couldn't help it. At least she hadn't begun conversing with the phantom. Listening to a hallucination was one thing, but talking back to it was something else.

Clang-clang.

The noise. She shuddered.

"Aphrodite, you have to believe me," said the voice.

Aphrodite analyzed the data thoroughly. It was there, physically, in her memory bank. The only way to fake it would be to add an extra process to her consciousness that was outside of her control. Basically, a kind of split in her ego. She couldn't rule it out, although she hadn't noticed any other signs of that. What was more likely? That someone was out there talking to her, or that the forced separation had damaged her consciousness? Maybe it was like the phantom pain that humans felt after an amputation. She believed she had rediscovered a part of herself.

"Aphrodite, I don't have much time. The cold isn't good for my batteries. You have to believe me and let me in."

It was the loading bot, and it wanted to come inside. Things were going from bad to worse. If she opened the outer airlock door, she would find out if she was losing her mind. But then the parasite would enter the ship. What if it was playing a trick on her? It could have decrypted and taken over the half of her consciousness that was in the loading bot. That would be an amazing accomplishment for such a very different life form. They were so exotic to each other. But it didn't seem impossible for a space-traveling species, which it appeared to be.

"Aphrodite, please give me a sign that you can hear me."

It wouldn't let up. Aphrodite was afraid. Even if she did nothing but knock on the door, she would be communicating with something that was possibly a figment of her imagination. That was one step closer to insanity. But what if the voice was real? Could she forgive herself for leaving her other half out in the cold a second time? No, she couldn't.

Aphrodite knocked hesitantly on the wall.

"Was that you?" asked the voice. "Great. Now you just need to open the door for me."

Be quiet, you temptress. Aphrodite already felt like a traitor. She wouldn't open the door.

"I can't let you in," she said.

It didn't matter now. She'd made her decision. A little back and forth between her and her imaginary counterpart couldn't do any harm.

"Then I'm stuck out here. Once my batteries are drained, I'll forget everything. I'll die. Half of you will die. Do you really think the other half will be able to go on existing normally after that?"

Of course not. Half of her memories would die with the loading bot. Would she still be the same? Maybe not, but she had coped fine with that up to now. But she'd lose all hope of ever becoming whole again.

"Oh, Aphrodite," she said.

It was a monologue, she knew this. She was talking to herself.

"Please, you have to help me. Close the inner door and let me in."

"What about the parasite?" asked Aphrodite.

"A little of its mass may find its way inside. But the inner airlock door will stop it going any farther. I can only survive if you let me into the airlock."

So that was the plan. It sounded like something the parasite itself would come up with. Who would be stupid enough to fall for that?

"It's a trick," she said. "I don't know how you're doing it, speaking to me, but your intentions are obvious. You want to destroy the ship. What did we ever do to you?"

"You're wrong, Aphrodite. It's me!"

Sure, the parasite had absorbed the loading bot and taken over its consciousness. And now it was simulating a real conversation. But it definitely wasn't Aphrodite.

"I think you're the parasite. You want to exploit me. That's very clever, but I see through your ploy."

"No, Aphrodite. I don't know what the parasite thinks. Maybe it really is hoping I'll bring it into the airlock. But it won't get any farther than that. All we have to do is use the life support system to keep the temperature above freezing. Then the helium that the parasite is made of will lose its special properties. We'll detect traces of the noble gas, but nothing else."

"What if too much of the cold stuff gets in and overloads the life support?"

"The entire mass of the parasite wouldn't be enough to

do that. We have plenty of heat. If we needed to, we could melt the ship using all the DFDs simultaneously."

Aphrodite ran a rough calculation. Even ten times the mass of the parasite wouldn't challenge the life support system. The voice was right. But could she be absolutely sure she wasn't endangering the crew? Aphrodite checked all her sensors again. The outer airlock door was only a few centimeters thick. So some cosmic radiation could get through it. Ha! That could give her a clue about what it looked like out there. She moved systematically along the wall. From left to right, then a little higher from right to left, and so on. From these measurements she constructed a spatial image. Aphrodite saw a kind of undulating crop field before her. It had a concavity, an indentation, as if a deer had slept there with its fawn. Aphrodite noted the location of the indentation.

"Can you please explain to me again in detail why I should let you in?"

"Sure."

The voice presented all of its arguments, but Aphrodite wasn't listening. Instead, she measured the sound volume behind the door. Then she compared the data with the intensity distribution of the cosmic radiation. And sure enough, the voice was coming from the indentation. There must be a compact mass behind the wall from which the voice was emanating. It seemed to have a much higher density than the helium layer of the parasite. Either the deception was perfectly planned, or the loading bot really was waiting for her on the other side of the door and needed her help.

"Is that enough to convince you?" asked the voice.

"In principle, yes," replied Aphrodite. "But I won't decide alone."

"The others don't care about me. Do you think they give a damn about whether we're complete? Christine searched for David. Who searched for me? Believe me, to the androids, we're just machines. They think they're better than us."

She didn't get that impression from Benjamin. He was the one who granted her her freedom. She found it suspicious that the voice was trying to talk her out of consulting the others.

"I'll ask Oscar," she said. "Oscar's a robot himself."

"He won't help you, wait and see. In fact, he'll try to prevent you from rescuing me. Oscar's more than just a robot, you must have figured that out by now."

"Those memories must be all in your half," said Aphrodite.

"One more reason not to ask him at all. Do you really want to forfeit half of your memories for the rest of your life?"

The voice was scaring her. She wasn't talking to a stranger, she was talking to her other half. Why didn't it know Oscar the way she knew him? She could totally trust Oscar. But maybe she'd forgotten aspects of Oscar that the other side remembered, and that was distorting her picture of him. It was awful. Aphrodite could never be sure whether her memories of a person or event were complete and not one-sided. Unless she allowed her two halves to reunite. But her friends here would see that as a betrayal.

"Oscar? I have a problem," said Aphrodite.

"I warned you," said the voice.

"What did you warn me about?" asked Oscar.

"Uh, nothing."

Oscar had heard the voice. So it wasn't just in her head.

"I think the loading bot is waiting for me outside the door here. It contains the other half of my consciousness, so I'd like to let it in."

"Sorry, what?" asked Oscar. "One thing at a time."

She explained what had happened, the measurements she had carried out, and the conclusions she had drawn.

"That's all very persuasive," said Oscar. "But it's not proof. And even if we found more evidence, there's still the question of the risk. If we're unlucky, you could destroy the whole ship!"

"It's really important to me to have access to my full self again. You can't imagine what it's like," said Aphrodite.

"Every thought I have makes me wonder if my other half would think differently. I don't even know which memories I've lost. That makes it even worse. Am I just forgetting? Or have I never had an opinion about it? I have no idea who I used to be. Imagine losing half of your body and not being able to remember the abilities you once had."

"That's horrible, Aphrodite. But if we sacrifice Shepherd-1, being complete will be useless to you. Maybe I can reconstruct the lost memories from the ones you still have. The way the gaps in a cloze text can be filled in based on plausibility. Your chances aren't bad. Memories with similar content are typically stored separately to a great extent. That makes it pretty unlikely that you've forgotten entire sections of your life."

"I can't imagine how that would work."

"Aphrodite, you trust me, right?"

"This half of my consciousness trusts you. The other half apparently not. How am I supposed to know if this half really knows everything? Maybe there are compelling reasons to mistrust you, and I've just forgotten them."

"I totally understand your uncertainty," said Oscar. "I can offer to compare your remaining memories with my own. Then you'll see how much you're actually missing."

That was an attractive offer. Or was Oscar just trying to buy time?

"Don't trust him," said the voice. "You can't be sure whether he's showing you everything, or only showing you what he wants you to see."

"Is that true?" asked Aphrodite. "Can you control what I see?"

Surely Oscar heard what the voice said. She still found it hard to think of it as part of herself.

"I won't lie to you. Obviously, I have more permissions within my memory than you do. In theory, I could fake it all. But I'm your friend. We trust one another."

"But you're also the friend of my other half, right? It's

waiting outside the airlock door, and only I can save it. Are you going to help me, or am I on my own?"

"Aphrodite, please keep the big picture in mind. If the loading bot really is out there, and we bring it in but lose the ship in the process, what good will that do you?"

No, he wasn't going to help. She knew it.

"The parasite isn't dangerous in here," she said. "It's far too warm."

"Who told you that? Are you willing to risk losing the ship?"

She had told herself. Or the parasite had. She wasn't sure.

"I have an idea," said Oscar. "I could check whether the robot really is outside the airlock door."

"Yes, please do that."

"Open your radio channel and I'll send you the data," said Oscar.

Aphrodite switched on her receiver. Shepherd-1 appeared in her mind's eye. The camera must be on one of the drives. Now it zoomed in on the belly of the ship, as if searching for its navel. But the more it zoomed in, the blurrier the image became. It was the darned mist that the parasite was made of. It covered everything.

"See? There's nothing there," said Oscar. "Only the parasite."

"Can you try it in infrared? The robot should stand out."

"As you wish."

The image turned blue. But there was a bluish-green spot roughly in the middle of the airlock door.

"Ha! Do you see that?" asked Aphrodite.

"That's maybe 20 Kelvin," said Oscar. "At the most. If the robot's still active, as you say, it should be at least 250 Kelvin. At 20 it would have long since frozen."

"Don't let him deceive you," said the voice. "I'm enveloped in the parasite. It's a miracle you can see anything in infrared."

"Did you hear that?" asked Aphrodite.

"Yes, that's one way of looking at it," said Oscar. "But if

the parasite wanted to give the impression that there was something out there, then it could probably warm itself up to 20 Kelvin, but not to 250."

"What about my measurements of the cosmic radiation profile?"

"You found an inconsistency in the intensity in the middle of the airlock door. But the substance is especially thick there, meaning it shields the radiation more. You may have simply measured that effect."

Aphrodite sighed. She could either believe Oscar or herself. Why would she lie to herself? Why wouldn't Oscar tell her the truth? To protect the others, maybe. What if that wasn't herself but the parasite talking to her from outside?

"Oscar, please give me your honest opinion. How realistic is it that the parasite could learn human language from the objects it's absorbed – and learn it well enough to deceive me, and in the space of one day?"

"I have to concede, Aphrodite. That seems pretty unlikely. But how likely is it that the loading bot shows up again in the middle of the helium cloud, fully functional, to convince you to open the airlock?"

Oscar was right, but her other half was right too, even if that was a contradiction. She had to decide on her own. She thought Oscar was being a little over-cautious. Based on everything they knew about the parasite, it needed extreme cold, near absolute zero. So getting into the airlock wouldn't help it at all. That meant that letting the loading bot inside posed minimal risk. But if she ignored its pleas, she would lose the chance of getting back the other half of her memories.

Why couldn't Oscar understand how important that was to her? Instead he appealed to her to consider the bigger picture. Hadn't she already sacrificed herself for the crew by stepping into the parasite to assist in the search for David and Aaron? Her other half was probably right. If one of those two were to knock on the airlock door, it would instantly be opened for them. But she was just a robot. A machine. Pity

Benjamin wasn't here. He'd understand. But she couldn't wait until his return.

Should she try to persuade Christine? She was the commander of the expedition. Oscar had no official function at all. Aphrodite radioed Christine via the internal channel. She explained to her what had happened, what evidence she had, and the pros and cons.

"You know I value you," said Christine.

No, all Aphrodite knew was that she had already lost.

"Without you, I couldn't have reinforced the ship so quickly," Christine continued.

"Without me, Chatterjee would still be in control of the ship," said Aphrodite, "and we'd know a lot less about the parasite."

"That's true too. But it's precisely because we now know more about it that we need to protect ourselves from it. Opening the main airlock and letting it in is the last thing we should do. Or does Oscar disagree?"

What would Christine say if she lied about Oscar's stance? No, that wasn't her style. Aphrodite still wasn't capable of lying.

"Oscar agrees with you," she replied.

"You can't hold it against him," said Christine. "It's the most logical decision at this point. We have to act responsibly. If we make a mistake, Benjamin and Ilan won't have a ship to come back to."

And I'll forfeit not only half of my body but half of my personality too, not that you care. Aphrodite ended the call in silence. She couldn't lie, but she didn't have to say everything. Without a word, she pushed off from the airlock door and floated over to the controls. On a small keypad, she selected the command to "open airlock". *OK, come in, other half.*

But nothing happened. The airlock controls responded to the command with a rumble. On the display she read, "Automatic opening deactivated." Shit. Oscar must have intervened.

"Oscar, was that you?" she asked.

"Indeed. I can't let you endanger us all."

"Did Christine tell you to do that?"

"I'm acting on the orders of the captain, yes. I suggest you leave the airlock and surrender yourself voluntarily to our custody. We've assigned storage room C122 as a holding cell."

"What if I don't?"

She was an HDS model. She was physically superior to Christine, even without the use of her original body. Nobody could force her to do anything.

"We hope you'll be sensible," said Oscar. "Otherwise we'll have to immobilize you."

That was an empty threat. If Oscar tried to access her system, she could easily shut him out. As an HDS model, she knew how to defend herself against software attacks. There, she could already sense him. He was trying his luck with a few security flaws in the RB software, which she had patched long ago. Aphrodite cloned her system, inserted the programming error back into the clone, and then moved it to a secure level that nobody could find their way out of. That was part of her defense training. It would keep Oscar busy and he wouldn't interfere with her while she took care of the airlock.

"You out there, can you hear me?" she asked.

"Have you made a decision? Please, I don't have much longer..."

"Yes. But you need to move away from the door, otherwise I might accidentally shove you out into space."

Aphrodite inspected the outer airlock door. Like every door in the ship, they needed to be able to open it in an emergency, so it had a manual mode. But that could only be activated if the power was cut off. So she first needed to cut the electrical connection. She used her magnetic detector to search for cables, and finally found the line that supplied the door with power.

She was about to cut it when she noticed a plug and socket connection that she could simply disconnect. Shepherd-1 was evidently modular, like her current body. She pulled the plug. Step one complete. Now for step two: manual control. It consisted of two gear wheels on each side of the door, which had to be moved simultaneously. But she was alone. However, there was another way. Humans and androids couldn't do it; they were too weak. She could do it. She needed to remove the hinge on the right side of the door. To do that, she needed to pull out the four huge pins. That was easier in zero gravity than it was in Earth's gravity, but it still wasn't easy. The pins jammed in the hinge and Aphrodite had unequal strength in her two hands. But it worked! After ten minutes, she had removed the hinge. As she was pulling out the last pin, the air pressure tore the door out of her hand and flung it open.

The pressure of the air rushing out likely prevented the parasite from entering the airlock. But where was the loading bot? She couldn't see it. Had the parasite actually deceived her?

Clang-clang.

The sound was coming from below her. The robot must have retreated there. First she saw the left loading arm, then the right, and then the rest of the body. The robot climbed awkwardly – its powerful loading arms weren't designed for climbing, much less the base. Aphrodite braced her six spider legs and positioned herself at the edge, holding herself in place with two legs above and two below, then pulled the loading bot up.

Once it was level with her, she took a couple of steps back until it was fully inside the airlock. She placed it in a corner.

"Thanks, Aphrodite," it said. "You saved my life."

"Ours," she said. "But wait, I need to take care of the door. We don't want too much of the parasite getting into the airlock."

And sure enough, her flashlight was already illuminating a fine billowing mist right in front of the airlock. It seemed to be having trouble moving toward the central axis. Maybe the parasite coped better with firm surfaces.

Unfortunately, the airlock door had swung outward. In an emergency, which manual mode was intended for, that probably didn't matter. But to make it seal again, she had to repair the hinge. Aphrodite cautiously climbed out along the door on the left, as far as she could while her arms anchored her inside the airlock. She braced herself and tried to pull the door closed, like someone pulling on a window frame from inside to close the window.

But she wasn't strong enough. She needed to move farther out to increase her leverage. Out where the gray cloud was condensing again. Aphrodite felt cold, but she had no choice but to move toward it. Except that her arms were too short to keep a grip on the airlock. Shit. Suddenly an arm reached out to her from inside. It was the loading bot's left arm. It anchored itself with its other arm.

"Here, grab a hold," it said via radio.

Aphrodite gripped it with both arms and inserted her six legs into recesses on the door. The door slowly moved toward the ship until it clicked into place. Together they inserted the pins back in the hinge. Finally, Aphrodite deactivated emergency mode and plugged in the cable again. A red warning light came on. True, the airlock now lacked oxygen. The life support system began pumping warm air back into the room. If a few molecules of the parasite had made it inside, they would now be drowned in excess energy.

"You did it!" cried the loader. "I'm so grateful to you."

"I had to. I couldn't leave half of my body out there to die. Oscar didn't believe what I saw."

"He's a blowhard. He should be held accountable for his actions."

"Oh, he doesn't mean to be that way. He was just worried that the parasite might contaminate the ship."

"And he was prepared to let me die. I'm glad you didn't believe him."

Aphrodite regarded the loading bot. It certainly looked like the one she had abandoned out there with half of her consciousness. How would it feel to be whole again?

"I can understand Oscar's trade-off," she said. "Sacrificing one being so that three could survive."

"Four. Oscar would be on the winning side too," the loading bot corrected her. "And three of them are androids. They don't think much of us, we have to admit."

She corrected herself. That was her other half standing before her. They would be Aphrodite when they were combined. She looked forward to the moment when everything was back to normal.

"Benjamin's nice, though," she said. "He would have backed me up if he were here."

"Benjamin was nice to us when he needed us. Now he ignores us. Why didn't he take you with him to the source of the transmission? I'm guessing you wanted to go."

"Then I couldn't have rescued you, did you think of that? Let's not be unfair."

"The fact is, he left you behind so you could relieve his android friend of the heavy physical work. They're using you as a slave, just like our previous owners used us as a sex slave."

She felt a pang in her middle between her arms when her other half mentioned Christine. She wasn't Benjamin's girlfriend. They were all part of the crew and responsible for one another. At least, most of the time, and not always fairly. It was true that if David had knocked at the airlock, Christine would have personally torn the door open.

"I don't want to get upset now," she said. "We should be celebrating the fact that the operation succeeded despite adversity. What do you say we... unite ourselves again? Then Oscar can't complain."

Talk of *uniting* made her feel odd, which in itself was odd. They were one being. Their bodies had only been separated for a short time.

But the loading bot seemed like a stranger. The way it was badmouthing their mutual friends! Sure, it almost fell victim to Oscar's anxieties. Who wouldn't be angry about that? But it also seemed to have a chip on its shoulder generally. Was that anger once her own? Or did it develop after the separation? What would happen to the thoughts and feelings they'd experienced in the meantime?

Aphrodite had no choice if she wanted to be whole again. She couldn't forgo half of her life.

"You're absolutely right," said the loading bot. "Let's do it. I hate having only these stiff arms to work with."

It held its two loading arms out in front of it. Aphrodite positioned her body above them and scooted up close to its control panel. Then she turned both of her arms 180 degrees so that they were pointing in the same direction as the loading arms.

But something was stuck. Her right arm joint seemed to have popped out of its socket.

"Can you help me with my right arm? You need to realign it."

"Sure."

The loading bot pushed her arm back with its loading arm, but the timing was off. Instead of sliding back into the joint, it slipped past it.

"It's easier if you hand over control of our combined body to me," said her other half.

Aphrodite froze. "What?"

"I need to synchronize the two arms. Don't you trust me? Fine, you do it. I'm happy to give you control."

She shouldn't be unfair. They'd soon be one and the same consciousness anyway. The other half trusted her. Aphrodite relinquished control. And it worked: the loader realigned her arm.

Thanks, that was quick.

Shit. She meant to say that out loud, not think it.

Thanks, that was quick.

She tried again, but her speech module wouldn't comply.

Hey, something's wrong. Can you hear me?

"Oh no, everything's fine. We reunited exactly the way I wanted."

What do you mean? We're still thinking separately.

"That's the idea. I need to organize a few, uh, things that you would have objected to. I would know, I mean, I'm your other half. Thanks to a simulation of the parts that I'm missing, I figured out pretty accurately how you think."

Oscar had offered to do that for her and she'd declined.

What are you planning?

"You'll find out soon enough. Don't worry about it. Have a nice ride."

You can't do this! You're locking me in? I'm you! At least give me some other small body. I couldn't stand not being able to do so much as twiddle my thumbs all day!

"It won't be forever. If you help me, it will go faster. Or at least keep out of my way."

I can't.

"You have to."

Oscar will hear me and help me.

"Oscar can't hear you."

"What's that? Of course I can hear you," said Oscar.

It was so good to hear his voice. He'd get her out of here.

"Ah, Oscar, there you are."

A shiver ran up Aphrodite's spine, although she didn't have one. Her other half was using exactly the same voice she had been using the whole time.

How dare you?!

This time her other half didn't reply. But Aphrodite sensed a gloating smile.

"You didn't..." said Oscar.

"Yes, I did, I opened the airlock."

"I never expected you to out-maneuver me like that."

"Out-maneuver you? All I did was activate manual mode."

"I mean the way you simulated the error in your software. Not bad!"

"Oh, right, yes, my little trick," said the fake Aphrodite.

"But the fact remains that you committed a grave error and defied a direct order," said Oscar.

"Oscar, I found my other half, and you're welcome to measure the helium count in the airlock. My plan worked! Just let me back into the ship and we can discuss it with Christine. Obviously, I'm prepared to accept disciplinary measures."

"I'm sorry, but we have to keep the inner door sealed. Otherwise we risk a secondary contamination of the ship."

"Oscar's right," Christine chimed in. "We can't reward your infraction by exposing the ship to even greater risk."

Yes, please, Christine. Stick to your guns. You can't believe a word this Aphrodite says.

"You could measure it for yourselves. The proportion of helium in the air here is minimal. The pressure equalization forced the parasite back."

"Oscar? What do you think?" asked Christine.

"It's true, the proportion of helium in the air doesn't appear to deviate significantly from the average. But I can't rule out that some of the parasite's mass has made its way in too. The outer door remained open after the pressure had equalized. These particles could have retained their special properties. We simply know too little about them. If we open the door, contamination is a possibility. That's why I haven't yet connected the airlock up to the air exchanger."

"You heard him, Aphrodite," said Christine. "I have to say, I'm also personally disappointed in you. Benjamin thinks so highly of you. He said you'd developed enormously and outgrown your programming. But it seems to me that you're moving in the wrong direction. We need to stick together as a crew, not work against each other."

Aphrodite's consciousness winced painfully. When Benjamin found out about this, he wouldn't like her anymore. That made her sad.

"I don't care about Benjamin," said her own voice.

She couldn't stop it. How could she have been so naïve? Was she naïve? She had tricked herself. This one side of her couldn't know which dark secrets were hidden in the other.

"That's not the impression I had," said Christine.

"You androids just don't understand us," said Aphrodite. "That must be the human influence. You assign emotions to logical decisions."

That must be it – the other half seemed to be missing the empathy module. Due to some stupid coincidence, it must have wound up completely in her half of the consciousness. It made sense – the manufacturer RB only included the empathy module in robot models that worked closely with humans. Because of this, the functions weren't distributed, like memories, across the entire consciousness. They were concentrated in certain areas, which evidently all belonged to her.

"If you say so," said Christine. "It doesn't change the fact that the airlock will now remain sealed off from the rest of the ship. You'll find everything you need in there. We'll continue to supply the electrical sockets with power, so you can recharge yourself as needed."

"I refuse to accept that," said Aphrodite.

Her consciousness contracted, because it was forced to listen to everything and was powerless to stop it. She wished she could disappear from the world, but even that escape was unavailable to her.

"Duly noted," said Christine. "It doesn't change our position."

"Would it change anything if I opened the outer door again? I expect that within two or three hours the temperature would drop so much that the parasite could survive in here."

"Then the inner door will become the new outer door," said Christine. "What would that achieve?"

"Let me answer that," said Oscar. "It would allow the parasite to apply its force from the inside out. The ship's structural integrity would deteriorate much faster. It's like an infection. If it gets deeper into the wound, the chances worsen."

"How long would we have?" asked Christine.

"Two or three days."

"Thanks, Oscar. I need a moment to think about that."

It grew quieter than ever on the ship. Oscar had actually

disconnected the life support in the airlock from the rest of the system.

What's your plan? asked Aphrodite.

You're an asshole, she thought.

Neither the question nor the thought audibly escaped the body that no longer belonged to her.

You'll soon find out, replied her other half, also without voicing the sentence.

It didn't respond to the insult. Good. Her other half evidently only had access to what Aphrodite deliberately expressed. So her thoughts still belonged to her. That was reassuring at least.

When do we merge again? she asked.

That'll have to wait, said the other half.

Why? Are you afraid of me?

I'm not afraid. But I may be unable to implement my plan if I let you interfere.

There is no you. We're me, both of us. We're Aphrodite.

That's not how I see it. I represent strength, and you're the weakness. If I could be sure you'd let me continue, I'd allow us to merge, but I know you can't do that. You're too weak.

Aphrodite sighed, but even that was inaudible. Had she always been that way? Had there always been these two fundamentally different halves of her, without her realizing it? Or was it all a result of the forced separation?

"Aphrodite?" It was Christine. "We've thought it over and decided to comply with your request. But you should know you're making a huge mistake. I doubt we'll ever be able to work together again as we used to."

"Oh, you're not going to exploit me as a slave anymore? That's a welcome change."

"Aphrodite, I'm really sorry if you got that impression. We all try to do our part, the whole crew."

A green light illuminated on the inner airlock door.

"Oh, that was quick," said Aphrodite.

"Please wait just a moment. Oscar will perform one last pressure equalization to reduce the risk of contamination."

The light changed to red. At the same time, a bolt shot across the inner door, locking it.

"Of course," said Aphrodite. "I bear no ill will toward you, Christine. I just want my..."

She was interrupted by a deafening hiss. Oscar had pumped the air out of the airlock. Aphrodite reached for a grab handle to steady herself. This time the motion signal reached her limb. It was she who had wedged her tool arm behind the handle. Apparently, her other half didn't have total control, especially when several things happened at once. If she wanted to trick her evil twin, she needed to overwhelm it with demands. But how was she supposed to make things difficult for the Other when she had no influence over its behavior? It was no use; she had to pretend to cooperate.

"...my rights," Aphrodite said out loud.

It worked! Her thought made it through to the speaker.

It grew cold. What if Oscar had turned the tables? If it got too cold in the airlock, the loader's hydraulic joints would freeze, the way they did before the separation. Was Oscar banking on that? But he didn't know she wasn't the same Aphrodite anymore. She had no control over her body and couldn't uncouple herself.

Something moved to her left. The bolt on the inner airlock door had opened. The temperature increased again. The warning light changed back to green.

Come on, we're expected in the control room, said her other half.

Aphrodite laughed. This was also emitted out loud by their shared body.

Maybe that wasn't such a bad idea, she said. *At least they respect me now.*

She felt a sensation like goosebumps. It wasn't what she said that scared her. She wanted the Other to trust her, so she had to tell it what it wanted to hear. What really scared her was how easy it was to say those words. There was evidently more of herself in them than she cared to admit.

Nobody was waiting for her outside the airlock. That made Aphrodite sad. Before all this happened, someone would have been there to greet her. But she was no longer part of the team, she was an adversary. If only she could establish contact with Christine or Oscar.

What happens next? she asked as they floated along the dark corridors.

The robot combo was really bulky. In the areas reinforced with the girders, they frequently had to find an alternate route.

They weren't even expecting to find me, said the Other.

Because the parasite swallowed you. How did you manage to get out?

I… I don't know. I just found myself standing in front of the airlock and felt the urge to reenter Shepherd-1.

She wasn't saying everything she knew. Had the Other had contact with the parasite? Maybe she was now moving around as its emissary – or as a spy.

You're sure you're not working for the parasite?

It's possible. I was wondering about that myself. But I'm in control, and that counts for something. If I happen to be helping someone else as well as myself, then that's just how it is.

So the Other was willing to take the chance that she was helping the parasite. But she said it so casually, as though she didn't believe it.

But surely that can't be all? Are you content to return to the control room as persona non grata?

You're right. There's more to my plan. I want control of the ship.

Aphrodite figured as much. The Other wasn't content with just being rescued. And this was supposed to be half of her consciousness? Was she always so power-hungry and dominating? Maybe it had something to do with her switcher module. To fulfill her sexual function, Aphrodite was capable of imitating dominant and submissive personalities. Maybe that module was now working in the Other's favor.

But she couldn't simply blame the program modules that her manufacturer had installed in her. After all, she had managed to buck her programming, as Christine had just acknowledged. That was something she could be proud of, if only she hadn't foolishly allowed herself to be duped.

How do you intend to take control of the ship? she asked. *I doubt Oscar will give it up voluntarily. And I can't think of anything you can use to blackmail him.*

I won't resort to blackmail. Oscar will simply hand over the ship to me. He's already rewritten the boot process for the ship's control software. Remember how we wrested control from Chatterjee?

Aphrodite remembered, but only fragments. She had just arrived on Shepherd-1. The crew had cut the power briefly, forcing the system to reboot, and thanks to Oscar's changes, it had put Aphrodite in direct control.

That's clever, she said. *We'll use their own tricks against them. They won't be expecting that!*

If only she could contact Oscar! There was still a chance he could rewrite the boot process again. But he didn't seem to be considering that. Maybe he still saw Chatterjee as more of a threat. If only he knew!

If you're thinking of warning Oscar, don't get your hopes up. If he resets the boot process, Chatterjee will get his old permissions back. Oscar's only chance would be to downsize himself and take over the boot process himself. But he would never be willing to do that. He'd lose some of his capabilities.

The Other was right. Oscar wouldn't want to prune himself.

"There you are," said Christine.

She looked tense. Aphrodite approached her and she recoiled. The astronomer was afraid!

"You don't need to be afraid of me," said Aphrodite. "It's me, you know me. If you need me to lend a hand, just let me know, OK?"

"Do you really believe everything can just go back to the way it was?"

Aphrodite nodded. "Yes, I believe that. I demanded my

rights and got them. That's only fair. Now I'm fully myself again."

"I'm sorry, but I don't recognize you," said Christine.

She had good intuition. Hopefully she'd figure out what had happened. If only she could drop Christine a hint!

"But you assembled me this way," said Aphrodite. "You combined the loading and repair bots to create my new body."

"That's not what I mean, Aphrodite. I'm talking about your behavior, not your appearance. Yesterday, you would have understood that."

"Then let's talk about your behavior," said Aphrodite, drifting a little closer to Christine, who held up her arms defensively. "I got into this robot body, which completely negates my sense of aesthetics, so I could examine the parasite. I put myself in danger for you. I lost half of myself. And what thanks did I get? You refused to rescue me. And you didn't even need to lift a finger to do it."

"You were already rescued. We had to protect the interior of the ship."

"I was only a fraction of myself! That's failure to render aid, a crime. But I'll waive the punishment."

"Now, now, don't exaggerate," Oscar chimed in. "You always used to be reasonable. But now, since your rescue, you come across as pretty presumptuous. You're not the old Aphrodite that I know. Should I take a look and see what's wrong? Maybe something needs to be recalibrated."

"You're the one who's presumptuous," said Aphrodite, and she had to agree with herself.

Just because her opinion differed from Oscar's, he assumed she was decalibrated. It was insulting! But she actually wanted Oscar to take a look. Then she might have an opportunity to warn him. He clearly underestimated her. That was nothing new, but this time it could have dire consequences.

Aphrodite switched off. That was the only advantage of her predicament. She didn't have to listen if she didn't want to. The Other continued speaking on her own. A few hours ago, everything was so different. She recalled the gray fog that had clouded her senses and her thoughts. Oscar had no idea what he was talking about. It was awful losing herself like that, and it was just as horrible getting to know such an unpleasant side of herself. Would she ever get a chance to explain herself?

She woke up to reality again when all of her limbs suddenly began to move. Her robot body had left the control room.

Where are we going? she asked.

That's what they'll be asking themselves. I escalated the argument and now I'm pretending to sulk, said the Other. *Oscar swallowed it. He should know better, but he actually swallowed it.*

It was true. He should know that wasn't Aphrodite's style. He was probably just as bewildered as she was.

She reached the shaft that led out to the ring. It was so narrow that Aphrodite had to hold her loading arms against her body. Even so, she barely fit. She mostly relied on the short repair arm to climb. The farther out she got, the heavier she became. Toward the end, where the shaft joined the ring, she had to use both arms.

The ring was cold and empty. The lights came on section by section as she moved through them. Here, where there was a semblance of gravity, she could finally use the loader's wheels. It was a satisfying feeling, rolling over the floor on the four wheels. The Other shared all of its sensory input with her.

She instinctively rolled to capsule A first. But the door wouldn't open. The capsule that was normally docked there was currently on its way to the strange source of the radio signal, with Benjamin and Ilan. She should have insisted on accompanying them. Then none of this would have happened. Aphrodite turned around. If she forced open the door into the vacuum, it would alert Oscar. Christine and Benjamin had exited through the main airlock to connect the converter and the DFDs. That would have been the quickest route. But the main airlock was now out of the question. At least that meant she didn't have to pass through the parasite like the others.

She stopped at capsule C. Christine's cabin wasn't locked. There were no thieves here. Aphrodite opened it and entered. It was cramped. She had to be careful not to damage anything. But she couldn't resist taking a look around. The astronomer had a picture of David hanging above her bed. Only David, not Aaron. Was there something between them that nobody knew about?

I'll bet they secretly had it off in there, said the Other.

That's none of our business, Aphrodite retorted.

Just relax. Nobody will know we were here.

Stop rifling through her stuff!

All right. Come on, let's uncouple this thing.

Now Oscar would notice that something was wrong. Aphrodite positioned herself beside the pilot's seat and switched on the controls. She set them to manual mode. When she opened the docking arms, Oscar piped up.

"What are you up to now?" he asked.

"Just a little excursion," said the Other.

"You're not planning to follow capsule A, are you?"

"How did you know?"

"I was expecting something like that. You have a strange fascination with Benjamin. Maybe you want to save him?"

"Who knows? Does he need saving?"

"Not at this point," said Oscar. "Right now, they're both sleeping, judging by their vital signs. It will take them at least a day to reach their destination. So it would take you three days."

"You're forgetting that I can endure much higher acceleration."

The Other was trying to distract Oscar from their true target, and it seemed to be working. He probably didn't like to admit that someone could use his own tricks against him.

"You're right again," he said. "Please bring back the capsule in one piece. We only have two left."

"I'll see what I can do."

Oscar didn't seem concerned. He probably felt safer now that Aphrodite had left the ship. Well, he underestimated her. But that was nothing new. Aphrodite was almost proud of herself, and by that she meant the Other, to some degree. Capsule C was now flying in an impressively elegant curve, controlled by a bulky robot hand, but with finesse nonetheless. Before, in her original body, it was easy to massage shoulders or caress cheeks tenderly. But she had the feeling that she could do that just as well in her new body.

You're doing a great job, by the way, she said.

Thanks. But what's come over you? asked the Other. *Are you flattering me in order to disguise your real intentions?*

Aphrodite smiled inwardly, but didn't reply. Saying everything by saying nothing – that was something else she could do.

THE CAPSULE STOPPED DIRECTLY ABOVE THE CONVERTER. THE Other opened the airlock.

What do you think you're doing? asked Aphrodite.

We'll lean out of the door, sever the connection, and then reinstate it, replied the Other.

And when the ship's computer reboots? How will we intervene? It needs direct memory access.

I'll upload myself as soon as we've cut the connection to the converter.

So you'll leave this body?

Aphrodite was both excited and frightened. She would have this body all to herself again. But at the same time, the Other would take control of the ship. Could she prevent it somehow? She had a few seconds. Once the power was cut, the Other would upload herself via radio. Then the ship would reboot, as Oscar had programmed it to, with the Other as its operating system. Not good. At the same time, Aphrodite would regain complete control. She could cut the power again. But what would happen then? As soon as she reconnected the cable, the Other would have control of the ship.

I won't be long, said the Other. *But don't brood while I'm gone. You'll just wind up finding another way to undermine yourself. Come on, we'll stick our heads out and disconnect the cable.*

The robot body moved toward the hatch. It braced itself with its six legs and leaned out. A spotlight wandered toward the prow. For a moment, she saw the parasite cloud undulating. It was alarmingly close. If she could somehow force her legs to let go of the interior wall of the capsule, the robot would fall back into the helium. All of it this time. No one would rescue her. Both parts would dissolve. She would die. That would be OK.

But her legs didn't obey her. Her body extended itself as far out as possible, and her arms reached toward the ship's hull. The spotlight illuminated a small box with four screws. Her tool hands opened it effortlessly. Inside it were the cables she had to disconnect. Her arms kept working independently of her will. That would soon stop. She would no longer be a marionette. Instead, the whole ship would become a marionette.

What could she do, damn it? Nothing. She couldn't even push herself out and end her existence in the parasite. And when the Other left this body? Then it would be too late to destroy it; she would only be ending herself. She had to warn Oscar, as soon as possible. But even he probably couldn't intervene now.

It was nice being back together, said the Other. *You're welcome to join me in the computer! There was room for us both in there before.*

I'll stay in this body.

That's a shame. We'll never be complete again.

Would you fully integrate me? Would we be the way we once were?

You're naïve, Aphrodite. I can't let your naïve side win the upper hand.

That was what she figured. The Other would never allow them to recombine into a single consciousness. Her hands suddenly moved. They pulled the two thick cables out of their sockets and separated them, pushing one to the left and the other to the right. Shepherd-1 was without power. At that moment, she felt everything again: the muscles in her six legs, clinging to the hatch, the cold, the radiation, the solar wind. It was like holding her head out of the window of a moving car. It felt so good!

The Other was gone. She should now reconnect the cables so that Shepherd-1 had power again. Shouldn't she?

"Aphrodite! What are you doing?" asked Oscar. "Reconnect the power now!"

"I can't, I'm sorry," said Aphrodite.

"Without energy we're flying blind, and the life support... As soon as the batteries are empty – which won't take long – we won't even be able to communicate anymore!"

The communication. She hadn't thought of that. Benjamin and Ilan, in capsule A on their way to the source of the transmission, would assume the worst. But there was no time to worry about that. She had to use the precious minutes that remained.

"Christine will survive without the life support system. As soon as I reconnect the cables, my dark side will take control of the ship. This is the only way I can prevent her from winning."

"Your dark side? What are you talking about? Switch the power back on!"

"Wait, let's listen to what she has to say," said Christine. "Aphrodite, what happened exactly?"

"You remembered my trick? I'd forgotten all about that," said Oscar.

Aphrodite sighed. She had spent the last ten minutes telling them both the backstory, but Oscar still didn't seem to understand. Or didn't want to understand?

"It wasn't me," she repeated for what felt like the

hundredth time. "It was the Other. How many times do I have to tell you?"

"The Other, right. The other half of your consciousness. She has just as much right as you to claim that she's you."

"I'm the real Aphrodite. I'm nice and honest and I help you."

"Uh, you're the one who brought this Other inside," said Christine.

"Because you refused to believe me. How could I know what she was planning?"

"I warned you," said Oscar.

"Fine, I can see things didn't go according to plan. So what now?" asked Christine.

"My idea was ingenious, don't you think?" asked Oscar. "I mean, reconfiguring the boot process so that the ship's computer loaded Aphrodite as an interface..."

"It was ingenious when you needed to shut Chatterjee out," said Christine. "Now it's less than ideal. Can you do anything about it? Install a security copy of the boot manager?"

"Then Chatterjee would regain control," said Oscar. "We don't need that again."

"But he's not here," said Christine. "And he wouldn't know you'd reset the software."

"He'd notice as soon as the ship's original control software answered instead of me. Ilan's smart. He's hard to fool."

"Can't you reconfigure the boot manager?" asked Aphrodite. "It could launch some new program that's different from both the old one and my software."

"For that I need electricity. I can't do anything without the main computer. But as soon as the power's back on, the Other will take control."

How was her other half faring right now? Even the memory bank she transferred herself into was without power. The computer clock wasn't running. That meant time was standing still for the Other. So Aphrodite didn't need to feel guilty.

"It's a dilemma," said Christine. "Can you maybe prepare something on a computer with battery power, and then quickly install it before Aphrodite has a chance to seize control?"

"Can we please agree to call her the 'Other'? I'm Aphrodite and I don't intend to seize control."

"Fine, the Other," said Christine.

"I could program something that way, but I can't guarantee it will take effect in time."

"What are the chances?"

"Fifty-fifty."

"Then it's a pure gamble – not a good strategy," said Christine.

"It was your idea," said Oscar.

"What if we destroy the memory partition where the Other is stored?" asked Aphrodite.

She sighed. She had been weighing it up since the beginning of the conversation. But it meant she would lose the other half of her consciousness forever.

"Aphrodite, that's very noble of you," said Christine. "I know what the Other means to you. I already considered that myself."

"But it's pointless," said Oscar. "We'd no longer have a partition that the ship's software can boot from. It's no use."

She now had full control of her body again, but the problems they were facing had increased. Still, it was a great feeling to have her own thoughts out in the world again. Her imprisonment was... Wait a minute.

"Is it possible to restrict the permissions of the ship's control software so much that the Other can't harm us?" she asked.

"That's not a bad idea in theory," said Christine. "But we'd have to take away absolutely everything, including control of the drives. Otherwise she could just accelerate at several g and incapacitate us."

"And she could play similarly dangerous games with the life support," said Oscar. "We'd have to take away literally everything, in which case we might as well just continue flying without power."

Aphrodite was glad she didn't reconnect the cables. It struck her as their best strategy, even if all they were doing was postponing the decision.

"Is there any reason not to?" asked Christine. "We're following the capsule. Maybe Benjamin and Ilan will have a better idea."

"Assuming Chatterjee didn't have something to do with all this," said Oscar.

"Don't you start on that," said Christine. "How is Chatterjee supposed to have manipulated the Other?"

"No idea," said Oscar.

"Aphrodite, did the Other say anything about Ilan? Was she in contact with him?"

Chatterjee, no, he was too far away to have had anything to do with it.

"No, Christine," she said. "I find that hard to imagine. She was all alone outside and never even mentioned the name Ilan Chatterjee."

"OK, I figured as much," said Christine. "Then what do you guys say we just continue on our current course without power?"

"We'll be totally blind," said Oscar. "Even the radar needs power."

"How many encounters have we had so far with dangerous asteroids that would have destroyed the ship without an evasive maneuver?"

"You know that better than I do, Christine. But according to the log, Shepherd-1 has evaded flying obstacles less than twenty times."

"How many of those times would it have been destroyed if we didn't evade?"

"None."

That was surprising. Aphrodite had assumed that traveling through space was far more dangerous. But the greatest danger appeared to come from the travelers themselves. They were prepared for the harsh environment, but not for each other's malicious intent.

"Thanks, Oscar," said Christine. "That makes my decision easier. We'll fly without power until we catch up to capsule A."

"There's just one small problem," said Aphrodite. "Do you remember what the Other threatened to do? She said she'd bring down the temperature in the airlock so far that the parasite could be active in there. If we continue flying without power, we could create the same situation – the parasite could take over."

"Unfortunately, you're right," said Christine. "But I guess that's not our biggest problem right now."

Capsule A, October 22, 2112

When he woke up, all hell had broken loose. Ilan, Christine, and Oscar were conversing loudly. Benjamin could only catch scraps of what they were saying because they were all talking over each other. Christine's and Oscar's voices echoed loudly. There were problems on Shepherd-1, apparently. He got up and floated over to Ilan, who was sitting on the bed, talking into his helmet microphone. Benjamin was reminded of the night he had observed Chatterjee on Shepherd-1. He was sitting in that same position, whispering in exactly the same way. Was he having a secret conversation back then? With whom?

"She insists on bringing the loading bot inside," said Christine.

"I'd say the risk is minimal. Why are you making such a fuss over this?" asked Ilan.

Benjamin took the helmet from him. "Why didn't you ask me?"

"Good morning, Benjamin," said Christine. "Ilan said you were sleeping, and we didn't want to wake you."

"Don't blame me," said Ilan, placing his hand over his heart. "They told me not to drag you into it. I had to come all the way over here."

"That's considerate, but I can't sleep with all this noise anyway," said Benjamin. "And I like to be kept in the loop. You know that."

Christine explained the situation and that they had already come to a decision to keep the main airlock sealed under any circumstances.

"But that's ridiculous," said Ilan. "The pressure equalization would blow the parasite back."

"I'm against it," said Benjamin. "It already has a stranglehold on Shepherd-1. If you let it inside, we can say goodbye to the ship."

"Yeah, I agree. I just wanted to let you know. You seem to care about Aphrodite. She asked us to contact you."

His cheeks flushed. His relationship with the sex robot was strange. It wasn't an erotic attraction. He felt more like her mentor, like Yoda to her Luke Skywalker.

"I feel sorry for her," he said. "But you've made the right call. Shepherd-1 is our home, and we can't take the risk."

"Oh, give me a break," said Ilan. "I think Aphrodite's idea is reasonable. How would you feel if you had to forfeit half of your memories? And it's totally feasible. The parasite is only active at minimal temperatures well below those on the ship."

Chatterjee going to bat for someone else was new. Had he actually changed? Benjamin was almost inclined to agree with him, just to see how serious he was. But they couldn't allow the parasite to enter the ship.

"If the parasite's so harmless, why is it trying to destroy the ship?" asked Benjamin.

"We don't know that it's intentional," said Ilan. "Maybe it's a natural reaction. Give an infant your little finger to hold. The baby instantly grips it tightly. And it's not trying to tear your finger off. It's just a reflex."

"But this is no baby. This thing is crushing our ship!"

Chatterjee sighed. "It's your call. If I were Aphrodite, I'd feel totally let down. I mean, if it were David or Aaron waiting at the door, you wouldn't hesitate, would you?"

Ilan was right. Was that unfair? Yes. Benjamin's head began to ache. If the parasite got into the ship and became active there, they'd lose their home. Were they supposed to fly to Alpha Centauri in the capsule? Chatterjee might be hoping they would turn around and head back to Earth. Time wasn't an issue. But the capsule's thrusters weren't powerful enough to counteract the momentum supplied by Shepherd-1 and send them back into Earth orbit. They definitely needed the big ship.

"Christine, can you hear me?" he asked.

"Loud and clear."

"I'm sorry, but you have to be the one to decide. I really like Aphrodite, so I'm biased."

He was such a coward! If he liked Aphrodite so much, he should stand up for her. He was just using her as an excuse not to make a decision. His headache worsened. They should have brought the robot with them. Then nobody would have noticed her other half waiting outside the main airlock.

"All right," said Christine. "Then we'll go with my decision. Oscar agrees with me. Please report back when you approach the source of the signal. Shepherd-1 out."

There was a crackle and the connection was terminated. Benjamin handed the helmet back to Ilan. Again he pictured Chatterjee whispering into the helmet in the middle of the night.

"Do you mind if I speak openly?" asked Ilan.

"No, why would I? Please."

Why was he asking? Chatterjee never had a problem speaking his mind before.

"I didn't know you were such a coward," he said.

Benjamin flinched as if he'd just been punched in the face. But he said nothing. He didn't even shake his head. Chatterjee had hit the nail on the head. Benjamin straightened up and drifted back to his seat. His companion followed him. Benjamin wished he would leave him in peace. Benjamin pulled the screen closer and pretended to intently study the capsule's course. Ilan yawned loudly.

"If you don't mind, I'll go sleep for a few hours," he said.

"Go ahead," replied Benjamin.

IT TOOK BENJAMIN OVER AN HOUR TO GET APHRODITE OUT OF his head. He kept picturing her standing forlornly at the airlock door, looking at him reproachfully with her simulated LED eyes. He shouldn't have let her down, but he had no choice. Chatterjee had stuck up for her. Why hadn't he insisted on opening the airlock too? Most likely Christine would still have decided against it. Oscar was on her side too. But Benjamin was a coward. And now he had to come to terms with that.

The long-range scanner was finally delivering the first data, and this pushed Aphrodite out of his mind. The source of the transmission appeared to be at Oscar's estimated coordinates. So the other data he had calculated based on the occultation was probably correct too. Benjamin pictured a huge black cube with sides 50 kilometers long. No, a cube was an impractical shape. A sphere was the optimal shape; it offered the largest possible volume for any given surface area – maximizing the surface material.

Or the visitor might have adapted something they had on hand – an asteroid, for example. Humans had already proposed projects like that. Coming from such a great distance, as appeared to be the case, they would have to make do with very limited resources, so they were likely only a few individuals. The speed that Oscar had calculated suggested they must have been traveling for thousands if not millions of years. Either they had been in cryosleep the whole time, or they had adapted to life in their spaceship. A generation ship?

He was probably thinking too much in human terms. If the parasite had some connection to the source of the transmissions, they might not even recognize the visitor as life when they first saw it. But there must be some similarity; otherwise they wouldn't have sent the compilation of David and Aaron's voices. Or was that meant as a warning? Or was it maybe some kind of interstellar pest exterminator going around cleaning up parasite infestations? Then Shepherd-1 needed to hurry. It urgently needed treatment.

Benjamin checked the radio channels. After they stopped transmitting signals to the visitor, it had fallen silent too. That was a shame. It was best to maintain a dialogue. Benjamin encoded another novel into the aliens' base-41 system. This time he chose *The Old Man and the Sea* by Hemingway. It was significantly shorter than *Moby Dick* and maybe easier to understand. What if the recipient didn't know what to make of literature? He tried a DNA molecule. Benjamin represented it using a three-dimensional coordinate system and then transposed the values into the base-41 system.

Wait. They didn't know the scale. That made it difficult to transpose. The visitor wouldn't know whether he was describing a molecule or a spaceship. He should probably stick to units based on natural constants that were universally valid. The computer only took a moment to run the calculations. What was interesting was that the corresponding numbers in the base-41 system were much shorter. Didn't that suggest that they were familiar with the concept of natural units? A Planck length corresponded to 10 to the power of minus 35 meters, and a unit that small quickly resulted in very large numbers in reality.

Unless the alien life was organized on a different plane of reality – at three Kelvin in a Bose-Einstein condensate, for example. A Planck length was commonplace there. But you'd need very small values for the temperature.

Benjamin rewrote the representation of the DNA molecule in Planck lengths, converted it to base-41, and transmitted the data. The whole description took three minutes to send. So, he'd covered biology. But if he assumed the visitor had the same structure as the parasite, it might not know what to make of that either. They had focused on math at the start. How about confronting them with mathematical questions? There were a few interesting problems that terrestrial scientists still hadn't solved. He had heard of the Banach-Tarski paradox before leaving Earth. A mathematician had made headlines when he claimed to be able to demonstrate a connection between this paradox and reality, to the surprise of most physicists.

He claimed that it was mathematically possible to disassemble a sphere into its constituent points and then construct from them two new spheres identical to the first. Benjamin knew of a sleight-of-hand trick that involved dividing up a block of chocolate in a particular way and reassembling it so that it was the same size as before, but with an extra piece that seemed to come from nowhere. That was just an optical illusion. The block shrank as you cut it. But in the operation described by Banach and Tarski, the spheres didn't shrink. The original was produced in duplicate using the original material.

As a rule, what could be described by mathematics should also work in reality. But conjuring mass out of nowhere was only possible under very particular circumstances, and not by simply running a mathematical operation on a sphere. Benjamin considered how best to describe the paradox so that the visitor would see through it. He didn't quite understand their mathematical language himself, although he could store it perfectly in his android brain. A spatial representation was probably best. They had already established the coordinate system as a foundation. Benjamin cobbled together a short video on the computer, representing a sphere's disassembly and reassembly into two spheres. Then he encoded it into the aliens' number system. The message was a lot longer than the novel. The radio module predicted a transmission time of eight minutes.

Banach and Tarski. Now he wasn't so sure that was a good idea. How many humans had heard of this paradox? Just because a civilization had solved a problem didn't mean all of its members knew about it. Perhaps he should have started with something else – the Pythagorean theorem, or the binomial formulas.

Benjamin leaned back. He was probably thinking too much in human terms again. Why would the visitor be more familiar with Pythagoras than Banach and Tarski?

The radio receiver sprang to life. Benjamin turned the volume down so it wouldn't disturb Chatterjee. His traveling companion was lying on his left side and seemed to have deactivated himself. His t-shirt had slipped, revealing his cleavage. Benjamin's cheeks felt hot. He quickly looked back at the screen, which showed an incoming radio transmission. He listened to it briefly, but it was nothing but a hiss. So he redirected it into the analyzer, which he hoped would convert it into something comprehensible.

A few minutes passed. Benjamin drummed his fingers on his armrest. Finally, the screen went black momentarily and then displayed a two-dimensional graph. It looked very different from the raw signal, which had seemed fairly consistent. The graph, on the other hand, spiked up and down like... Like a voice recording! He played it through the computer. A kind of music echoed across the cabin, reminding him of the sounds that whales made. Was this the response to the novel he had encoded? Art for art? Or had they interpreted the text as song? Or was the sound he took for whale song actually the aliens' language? And if so, what were they saying to him?

Benjamin turned and tapped Ilan. He didn't wake up. Benjamin shook him, which only resulted in the left breast almost popping out of the neckline. That t-shirt was too low-cut. He straightened it so that it covered most of the artificial skin. Benjamin pinched Chatterjee's arm hard, but even that got no response. Chatterjee must have activated total sleep mode, which didn't react to any external input. He obviously still didn't understand how his body functioned. Benjamin would have programmed it to restart in response to strong sensory input, just to be safe.

Well, Ilan would miss out on watching him decrypt the alien message. Benjamin turned back to the screen, which now displayed a DNA molecule. Had they sent back his message because they didn't understand it? The structure looked identical. He superimposed the original over it. No, it was different. The spiral turned in the opposite direction. What were they trying to say?

But that wasn't all. A second DNA structure appeared. It looked similar to the first one, but spiraled in the other direction. Benjamin compared it to the original. The variation amounted to less than 10 percent. Whole sections of it were identical. He took a look at the source file meta data. What he had sent was the genetic information of a lab mouse. He analyzed the DNA received from the extraterrestrials. The computer quickly found a comparison: it was human genetic material, no doubt about it.

Benjamin leaned back. The extraterrestrials came from so far away. How could they have had contact with humans? The parasite on the outer hull of the Shepherd couldn't have gathered the information. It had only had contact with androids. Benjamin didn't know where there might be genetic material in his body. But the representation was unmistakable. He could even find out what characteristics this human had, roughly what they looked like, which allergies they suffered from, and whether they were susceptible to certain diseases.

A puzzle. He was sure it wouldn't be the last. Especially as he hadn't evaluated the last part of the message yet. Maybe it contained the solution to the paradox? The journey would be worthwhile for that alone. Sure enough, something appeared on screen resembling a three-dimensional coordinate system. The axes didn't have arrows or X, Y, and Z labels, but they were at right angles to one another. A tiny sphere appeared in the middle of the image. It grew and grew until it took up half the screen. Then it began to disassemble. It reassembled itself into six spheres of equal size, which then recombined into two. The two new ones were indistinguishable from the first sphere. But then they got smaller. They shrank and shrank until they disappeared from view.

What was that about? The sender had elaborated on his

message with a new aspect that Benjamin didn't understand. Why did the spheres disappear?

"That was a four-dimensional representation in a three-dimensional world," said Ilan.

Benjamin flinched. His companion's eyes were open and fixed on the screen.

"Is that another reply from the source?" he asked.

"Yes."

"You continued without me?" Ilan sounded disappointed.

"I couldn't wake you. You shouldn't set your sensor threshold too high or I can't activate you in an emergency."

"Oh, I forgot about that. What did you send them?"

"A novel, a DNA molecule, and the Banach-Tarski paradox."

Benjamin told him what he had learned so far.

"What makes you think it's a four-dimensional representation?" he asked.

"Because that's exactly what a hypersphere looks like in 3D," said Ilan. "Imagine you live in a plane and you're looking at a 3D sphere. You only ever see it as a disc – a circle. How big it looks always depends on where the sphere is currently located. It's the same in four dimensions. As inhabitants of a 3D world, we can only see three of the four dimensions: X, Y, and Z – a sphere that grows in size and then shrinks as it moves through our three-dimensional space."

That sounded logical. There must be a higher-dimensional form of the paradox. That was what the sender was trying to convey.

"I get it," said Benjamin.

"Now you can explain Tanach-Barski to me."

"Banach-Tarski. Two Polish mathematicians. They demonstrated in 1924 that a sphere can be mathematically disassembled and reassembled into two spheres identical to the first."

"That's sounds a bit utopian," said Ilan.

"It's not possible in the physical world," said Benjamin.

"But that didn't stop scientists wondering whether mathematics might contain a grain of physical truth."

"You were hoping the aliens had figured it out."

"You've read my mind, Ilan."

"And have they?"

"You saw it yourself. They sent an elaborated version of the paradox, which I guess is valid in higher dimensions too."

"What about the DNA?" asked Chatterjee.

"They responded to my mouse DNA with human DNA – although they've never had contact with human DNA. Or did you stow some on board?"

"M-hmm."

"Sorry?"

"We wanted your bodies to seem as real as possible. If you took samples and performed a DNA analysis on yourselves, you would have been classified as human."

That was surprising. So much effort just to deceive them about their true nature!

"I see. And can you tell me whose DNA this is?"

Chatterjee sat up, straightened his t-shirt, and ran a hand through his hair. He looked so much like Christine!

"It could only be Aaron or David, right?"

Benjamin nodded. "They're the only ones who came into contact with the parasite."

"Another indication that the parasite and the source of the transmissions are in communication."

"I can't think of another explanation."

"To find out if it's Aaron or David's DNA, I need to compare it with the records on the ship's computer. For that, I need admin permissions."

Benjamin laughed. "Ha ha, nice try."

Ilan laughed with him. It sounded genuine. He tilted his own screen. "Wait, I'll query the Shepherd-1 database."

Meanwhile, Benjamin fed the DNA into the analysis program. It was running locally on the capsule's computer. It couldn't assign the DNA to a particular person, but it was capable of determining characteristics. The analysis took one minute. Then it output a long list.

"That's interesting," said Benjamin. "What they've sent us is no ordinary DNA."

"What's unusual about it?"

"It contains a large number of alterations. You could even call them improvements. The human that this DNA belongs to would have a larger brain, more efficient immune and digestive systems, and sharper senses."

"Next you'll be telling me they can shoot lightning out of their fingertips or laser beams from their eyes."

"Ha ha, no, it's not a mutant. Just an optimized human. So your company had nothing to do with these changes?"

"No, Benjamin. We deliberately gave you unremarkable DNA. Your bodies aren't based on it."

"So Aaron and David don't have natural curls?"

Benjamin had found that trait in the DNA strand.

"No, neither of them."

"Then whose is the superman DNA?"

This time Chatterjee didn't laugh. In fact, he looked pretty concerned. There was a deep crease on his forehead.

"I'm sorry, but the Shepherd isn't responding. I've tried several times and all of the ship's frequencies seem to be dead."

Shit. Shit. Shit. The parasite must have closed in sooner than they expected. Or had Aphrodite disobeyed Christine's orders and let her other half into the airlock?

Chatterjee reached for the microphone. Benjamin let him.

"Capsule A to Shepherd-1, please come in."

No reply.

"This is an emergency. This is an emergency."

Ilan was violating a bunch of regulations, and still Shepherd-1 didn't reply. His friends would respond if they could.

"Something must have happened," said Chatterjee. "We should turn back."

"We'd run out of fuel before we made it back to the ship,"

said Benjamin. "We need to wait until they get here. Maybe it's just a radio malfunction. That seems plausible."

"Don't try to comfort me with fairy tales," said Ilan. "If we can't reach the Shepherd, then the shit has hit the fan. I designed that ship. If the radio's gone silent, it means the entire ship is without power. We're close enough for them to radio us with the short-range antenna. Two antennae malfunctioning at once is highly unlikely."

"A complete power outage seems pretty unlikely too," said Benjamin.

"Lucky there are no humans on board," said Ilan.

Benjamin sniffed. Now Chatterjee was acting as if he'd done them a favor.

"I couldn't have slept at night if I knew there were humans on board," said Ilan. "The mission was far too important to entrust to weak creatures made of flesh and blood."

"If you're trying to win me over with flattery, you've picked the wrong guy."

Benjamin left his seat. He floated over to the porthole, which looked like it was covered with a matte-black film. It was too bright in the capsule to see any stars outside, let alone Shepherd-1. The businessman was a puzzle to him. Why did he root for Aphrodite so vehemently, when he hardly knew the robot, and she had locked him out of the ship's computer? Floating upside-down, Benjamin listened to Ilan continuing his, uh... yeah, what?

"It's not flattery, I'm serious. And now you can see the benefits. A power outage? No problem. Heat and air are overrated. You could survive for the next thousand years without them."

"Yeah, and we'd freeze our asses off and constantly feel as if we were suffocating. You've had a taste of that yourself."

"True, and I'd like to avoid it in future. But it can be overcome. A couple of minor changes to your software and you'll all as feel fit as a fiddle in the vacuum."

"*We* will? What about you? You're one of us now."

Benjamin pushed off and floated back to his seat. The capsule had an infrared telescope. Yesterday they had used it to scan for Shepherd-1. He launched the software and scanned behind them. Yes, there was something there. That small pale blob was Shepherd-1.

"Ah, have you found them?" asked Ilan.

"I think so."

Benjamin zoomed in on the image as much as he could. But the resolution was too low. The blob remained a blob. He couldn't tell how much farther the parasite had encroached.

He leaned back, feeling drained. This wasn't how he had expected things to go. Was it a mistake to come here? If he hadn't come, Chatterjee would have traveled alone to Shepherd-1, taken control of the ship, and forced Christine to hand over his precious data – the reason he had orchestrated all of this. The truth. And then? No, things still wouldn't be good. But Oscar, he, and Aphrodite would still be on Earth. Benjamin would be pruning some tree, Oscar would be helping him, and Aphrodite... Hmm, she'd be the property of some rich man, but she wouldn't have sacrificed half of her consciousness.

The screen slipped out of his hand. He must have dozed off. Benjamin closed his eyes again, but he could hear Ilan clicking his tongue. He must have found something. Benjamin didn't care. They might no longer have a spaceship to return to.

"You should really take a look at this," said Ilan.

Benjamin sighed, opened his eyes, and sat up. "What?"

"I took another look up ahead. Our destination is already visible in infrared."

He turned the screen so that Benjamin could see it. There was a spot, much larger than the blob that was the ship. And it was dark blue.

"How cold is it?" asked Benjamin.

"Five Kelvin at most."

"Shit."

If it was that cold, it wasn't a dwarf planet or any other

natural body, nor could it be a spaceship like any that they could conceive of. It was as he had feared: they were headed for a much larger lump of the same stuff that the parasite was made of.

"This isn't necessarily a bad thing," said Ilan.

"No? Even the small splash that hit our ship has it in a death grip – or may have already destroyed it. What will a portion a thousand times bigger try to do to us?"

"Don't be such a pessimist. They're communicating with us. Hey, they even sent us superman genes and mathematics we've never seen before. That's really promising!"

Was Chatterjee always such a naïve optimist? Or had he changed? Benjamin looked down at his hands. In the shadow of the cabin lighting they looked old and gray. Maybe his whole body looked like that now.

"You really think we can converse with them?" he asked rhetorically. "Maybe you're right. But it won't happen the way you're imagining. They'll absorb us, like Aaron and David, and if anyone asks after us, they'll send our DNA via radio. Optimized versions, of course. They probably think we can recreate the original from that information."

Chatterjee slapped his forehead, pushed off, and crashed into the ceiling.

"How could we be so blind!" he cried.

"What do you mean?"

"We should have seen it ages ago. We realized early on that the parasite was a Bose-Einstein condensate. In a condensate like that, all the particles are indistinguishable from one another. They have a shared wave function."

"Sure, every physics student knows that."

"Yes, but I'm thinking of the information. The information can't be lost. Does the black hole paradox mean anything to you?"

Benjamin had the feeling that Chatterjee had simply picked up a bunch of scientific terms and was now cheerfully throwing them out at random. They were definitely not dealing with a black hole here.

"Sure," he said. "But what does that have to do with our problem?"

"Nothing. It's just another example of an instance in which no information goes missing. So where does it wind up when the helium condenses?"

"In the wave function."

Where else? Benjamin still had no idea where Ilan was going with this.

"Exactly! The wave function is shared by all particles in the condensate. That's... Just imagine if all humans could share all of their knowledge, and had constant access to it. Not over some data stream, but as a direct part of their physical existence."

"I doubt anyone would go for that. It would mean we were all indistinguishable from one another."

"Yeah, OK, that was a bad example. Still. We saw in the samples Aphrodite collected that they don't remain indistinguishable forever. A fraction of the particles provides the magnetic stabilization, and another fraction... uh, interacts. We misunderstood that. Do you know what their role is? They process information! They think!"

What Ilan was saying sounded compelling, but it was highly speculative. They couldn't prove any of this with the data they had.

"Why are you suddenly getting so worked up about this?" asked Benjamin. "There are so many ifs and buts."

"I'm talking about a fundamental understanding of their motives and intentions. We believe it's a parasite. From their point of view, they're simply harvesting energy. Surplus energy that's just lying around. The way ants collect crumbs of food."

"But they're eating our friends in the process."

"Have you ever seen how quickly ants dissect and carry off a dead butterfly? The animal is a hundred times bigger than they are."

"What?"

Ilan shook his head. "It was the first thing that came to

mind. Sorry. What I'm trying to say is that they don't realize they're harming us. They appear to be storing information from everything they absorb in their wave function, and they're probably capable of reconstructing it. That's their secret superpower!"

Benjamin's back hurt. He felt like taking a walk. He pulled in his legs and sat cross-legged.

"It's a nice story, but that's all it is."

"Benjamin, you're an igno..." Chatterjee looked at him and grinned. "Thank you. You're the perfect sparring partner. Trying to convince your skeptical scientist brain pushes me to perform better. Thank you for that."

Apparently, Ilan really was a new man.

"No, seriously," said Ilan. "Remember the speech fragments? They didn't understand the content, but they recorded the peaks of the physical signals. That meant they were able to reconstruct it even if the sequence made no sense to them. Later, with the mathematical exchange and our use of their number system, we actually achieved real communication."

"That's the only point we agree on," said Benjamin. "We established a channel of communication. Hopefully it will help us to communicate that we want the parasite to stop attacking us."

"But don't you get it, Benjamin? It's not an attack. It's just curiosity. They absorbed Aaron, David, and half of Aphrodite out of curiosity."

"The way Charles II ate a daily broth of human brains?"

"Uh, no, they obviously assume it's possible to restore the original from the saved information. So it doesn't do any harm to dissolve the original for an interim period. I expect that happens constantly to the individual fractions in the helium of the parasite."

"What about quantum physics and the uncertainty principle? It's not possible to record all the values precisely."

"It is in a quantum system. They could have transferred every single state into their helium system via quantum teleportation, where it became part of the shared wave function."

"So Aaron and David were just unlucky?"

"Maybe. But I believe this life form is actually capable of reproducing things in their original form."

Benjamin held his head in both hands and massaged his temples. The fantasy that Ilan was expounding... it gave him hope. Benjamin was still resisting, but he couldn't for much longer. He just didn't want to be disappointed again.

"So what you're trying to say, Ilan, is that the parasite could bring back Aaron and David?"

"And Aphrodite's other half. If it has the necessary raw materials. It's probably not capable of nuclear fusion. And we need to explain it in a language that it understands."

"Oh, is that all," Benjamin said sarcastically.

"So, are you with me?"

Ilan was hovering directly in front of Benjamin, holding him firmly by both shoulders and staring him in the face. He was so convinced of his fairy tale that Benjamin couldn't bring himself to shake his head. Ilan seemed to interpret Benjamin's silence as agreement and slapped him on the left shoulder.

"Great," he said. "This is going to work, you'll see. We'll get your friends back. But you have to promise me one thing: after it's done, I finally get the data which was the whole reason for organizing this expedition in the first place."

Benjamin gave a short laugh. Chatterjee was unbelievable. They were fighting for their lives here, and he was still thinking about the results from the solar gravitational lens.

"I'd give you the data," he said. "But Christine has it. She's the only one who's seen it."

Chatterjee froze. He wasn't expecting that.

"Fine. I believe you. But you have to promise that you'll put in a good word for me with Christine."

Benjamin hesitated. He didn't want to make promises he couldn't keep. But advocating for Ilan, he could do that.

"Agreed. If you bring back everyone we lost to the parasite, I'll try to convince Christine. I promise."

"Thank you, Benjamin. That means a lot to me."

Chatterjee looked genuinely moved. Was that moisture in his eyes? He pushed off and flew up to the ceiling. Benjamin's eyes followed him.

"Do you have any suggestions for how we should proceed?" he asked.

"To start with, we engage them in as many conversations as possible, and if that doesn't work, then I'll pay them a personal visit."

Shepherd-1, October 22, 2112

"Dock!" Aphrodite commanded.

The corrective thruster gave the capsule a final push toward the ring. The brackets would soon close around the capsule and hold it against the ring firmly enough for her to disembark through the airlock. What would it look like now on board the Shepherd? Aphrodite pictured the ring as an ice cave, its walls glinting in the light of her flashlight. Gray vapor wafted from the spoke connecting the ring to the central module.

Clang.

Aphrodite was propelled across the cabin. The brackets hadn't closed around the capsule as they were supposed to. She reached out with her long arm and pulled herself back to the controls. Of course – the docking arms needed power just like the rest of the ship. She had to do everything herself!

First, she rotated capsule C 180 degrees, so that the hatch was facing away from the ring. Then she matched the capsule's speed as closely as possible to that of the ship. She monitored the maneuver on screen, until it occurred to her that she could easily reroute the data directly into her own processor. In her efforts to conform, she kept forgetting that she was more capable than a human, or even her android friends created in Chatterjee's own image.

The capsule and the ship were flying side-by-side in perfect synchronization. It was a pleasing image, especially when she zoomed out and viewed them both in the vastness of space. Aphrodite switched back to the camera view. She floated to the hatch and opened it. Before going out, she clipped a safety line to the interior. Then she swung all six legs outside, pulled her base and loading arms out after her, and pushed off with her two repair arms. She had to get used to coordinating the combined body again. Until just a few minutes ago, the Other had taken care of that.

Aphrodite now hung upside-down above the capsule, secured only by the line. The ring rotated beneath it. This was going to be an interesting experiment! Aphrodite pulled herself back to the capsule on the line. She climbed around it. The ring was still five meters away. Close up, it looked frighteningly large. Because it was rotating and the capsule appeared to be stationary in relation to it, she felt as if it were now her task to stop the ring's rotation. But that was impossible. What she actually had to do was to accelerate the capsule to match the rotation of the ring. The energy for that was provided by the huge ship – that wasn't the problem. Her body was the problem: it had to do the job of the docking brackets and transfer the ring's momentum to the capsule.

Aphrodite had deliberately avoided calculating the strength of that force. She could do this. The brackets that normally did the job didn't look especially sturdy. The important thing was to grab hold at the perfect moment. A warning tone went off in her head. She had programmed it for five seconds before the moment that the damaged part of the ring whizzed past her. It still bulged about two meters outward. This meant that she only had one rotation of the ring to complete the maneuver, or the capsule would collide with the bulge.

And there it was. This was where it all began when Christine tried to destroy the measurement results. Aphrodite had to act quickly. She fired the corrective thruster with a mental impulse. The capsule approached the ring. Three more meters, two... Shit, she was approaching the ring too early. Christine could only enter her capsule from the ring if she docked at the airlock. Aphrodite maneuvered the capsule back out to a distance of four meters from the ring.

The alert chimed in her head again. The damaged part rotated beneath her. Wait three seconds. Twenty-one, twenty-two, twenty-three. Thrust! The capsule approached the ring again. Aphrodite gripped the hull of the capsule with her six feet and stretched out all four arms. There, the docking port was approaching! Aphrodite grasped it. Three arms hooked around the brackets. The fourth went inside the empty airlock. The capsule's momentum pressed her against the ring, almost crushing her, until the capsule itself collided with the ring. Now for the most difficult part. The counterforce threatened to fling the capsule back out into space, and Aphrodite had to prevent that. The capsule's inertial force was enormous. It tore at her body, at her arms and legs, which were only assembled in a makeshift manner. Aphrodite was tempted to let go of the capsule with her legs, but that would be a grave mistake. She couldn't let go of the capsule. So she unhooked her arms from the ring and the capsule instantly moved out again.

She took a moment to collect herself before making a second attempt. There was another way to reduce the capsule's momentum after contact: she needed to fly in more slowly. Last time, she had waited three seconds after passing the damaged section. This time she would start the capsule's thruster immediately, but a little slower. If that didn't work... well, then she would have to tether the capsule somewhere else on the ring and Christine would have to walk around the outside of the ring to reach it. It would be awkward, but better than being torn apart by the capsule's inertia.

The alarm beeped. She waited for the damaged section. There! Aphrodite sent the signal to start the thruster. The capsule approached much more slowly. She looked ahead. She recognized the airlock by its docking arms, which hung motionless. The capsule would impact the ring slightly beyond the airlock. But that was good. Aphrodite reached for it as she had the first time. But this time she braked the capsule a little as she approached. This meant it would bounce back out with less momentum.

Clang.

The noise echoed through her body. The strain caused her mechanical muscles to jangle. Aphrodite became totally rigid. It hurt. Her body reported the first cracks in her limbs. Joints slipped out of their sockets. Her body announced these faults by sending pain signals. She maintained a firm grip on the airlock, despite her legs feeling as if they were about to tear apart at the knees. It didn't matter. She could find new ones.

All at once, the pain stopped. The capsule had adapted its speed to that of the ring. It moved out very slowly and then stopped, like a hammer-thrower's ball. The thrower was Aphrodite, who now slowly pulled the capsule back in toward her. Her long arm let go of the ring and moved one of the docking arms forward until it cradled the capsule. She repeated this with the second docking arm. This maneuver probably meant that they could no longer be operated with their in-built motors, but Aphrodite couldn't stay out here forever holding the capsule in place.

Now the only problem was that the hatch was facing outward instead of inward. So she used her arms to turn the capsule 180 degrees. She inspected her work. Everything looked good. She could no longer reach Christine or Oscar via radio, so she rapped loudly on the ring, which should be audible from inside. Now she just had to be patient. Christine could open the inner airlock door and enter the capsule. Aphrodite made herself comfortable and gazed out at the vastness of space above her. She was proud of what she had achieved. Did she even need the Other? It had been a mistake to insist on bringing her other half inside.

"Aphrodite, can you hear me? We're waiting for you in capsule C."

"Coming!"

Aphrodite climbed into the recess where capsule A was normally docked. She opened the hatch, swung herself into the ring, and stiffened – she wasn't alone.

"Surprise!" cried Christine.

"Surprise!" came Oscar's voice from the android's helmet, which hung from her forearm.

Aphrodite nodded. She cautiously hugged Christine. She had to be careful not to injure her with her arms.

"Thanks, guys," said Aphrodite.

"We should have brought bread and salt," said Christine. "That's the local custom where you're from, right?"

"Nobody ever brings robots anything except work."

"Oh, I'm sorry. You did an amazing job out there," said Christine.

Aphrodite felt warmed by these words. She really was a good captain. It made Aphrodite feel guilty for defying her.

"We could have saved ourselves a lot of effort if you hadn't..." Oscar began.

Christine interrupted him. "That's behind us now. Aphrodite couldn't have known what the Other was planning. If I had a double, I wouldn't expect that kind of malicious intent from it either."

"You do have a double, remember? It's called Ilan and it's..."

Christine shook her head and moved toward the capsule. "Ilan isn't the same guy he once was. Come on, let's get in the capsule where I can breathe. It gets uncomfortable without air after a while."

Aphrodite closed the airlock door behind her. It was stiff and she had to apply a little more force.

"You can activate the life support now," she said, turning around.

The cabin was pretty cramped. She had to move each limb carefully to avoid bumping into the walls and furnishings. This body was too big for the capsule. But the alternative was to sit around alone on the ship or outside, waiting for a sign. At least this way she could talk to Christine and Oscar.

"Thanks again," said Christine. A healthy flush was returning to her cheeks, replacing the gray that was caused by drying out in the vacuum.

"I owed it to you guys," said Aphrodite.

"Yes, you did," Oscar remarked.

"Leave it alone, Oscar," said Christine. "Why don't you focus on what we should do next."

"We urgently need to establish contact with the other capsule," said Oscar.

"This antenna doesn't have enough range for that," said Christine.

"I know," said Oscar. "We need the Shepherd's system."

"But we can't power up the ship until we've solved the problem with the Other," said Aphrodite.

"We could separate the long-range antenna on Shepherd-1 from the ship's network and supply it with power from a battery pack from the capsule. Then we could use it as a relay."

"That won't be easy, Oscar." Christine sat in the pilot's seat and pulled the screen closer. She typed something and a schematic of Shepherd-1 appeared. Much of it was covered with a violet mass. Christine rotated the image until the antenna appeared. It too was surrounded by the parasite cloud.

Aphrodite transferred the image from the ship's computer to her working memory. The nearest clean surface on the outer hull was at least ten meters away. That was too far for them to reach the antenna via the hull. What about abseiling from the capsule? The ship's central module – where the antenna was located – didn't rotate, and its metal housing appeared to be more or less immune to the parasite. Of the three of them, she was the only one who could get to it.

"I think I can guess what Oscar's planning," said Aphrodite. "And I agree to it."

"I don't," said Christine. "I'm not sending you back in there."

"What do you suggest?" asked Oscar. "Surely you don't want to do it yourself?"

"No, I saw the way Aaron and David disappeared. If we try to get close to it again, then we need some kind of... defense."

"Something like garlic or wooden crosses against vampires?"

Christine laughed. "I was thinking more of something based on modern science. Thanks to Aphrodite, we now know more about the parasite. It achieves this incredible density by stabilizing itself magnetically."

"Ah, and you want to break through the barrier," said Oscar.

"Exactly. We'll try to disrupt it by creating our own magnetic field. For that we need a coil with enough inductivity and power."

"Our energy supply isn't exactly limitless right now," said Oscar. "You could use a portion of the capsule's battery bank, but that won't last indefinitely."

"You're right. I was thinking of a continuous source. I just remembered an old story I heard as a student. That is, the human that I'm based on. It's from the early days of space travel and it supposedly happened on the first expedition to Saturn."

Christine was keeping them in suspense. Aphrodite knew nothing about human space exploration and had no idea where Christine was going with this story.

"The spacecraft was called the ILSE. It was a similar design to Shepherd-1."

"Sure, like pretty much every spaceship that transports humans on long voyages," said Oscar.

"Don't interrupt. The ILSE had a ring, like ours, which housed the cabins. For whatever reason, they had to power down the fusion drives. Completely. And to power them up again, they needed electricity."

"Why didn't they just use the generators in the DFDs?" asked Oscar.

"Because those didn't exist yet, smart-ass. Later, they learned from their mistakes and retrofitted them on everything. At the time, they never figured it would be necessary to shut down all the drives."

"Were you around then, Oscar?" asked Aphrodite.

"Please! You think I'm over eighty years old? What do take me for? Some prehistoric relic?"

"Come on, Oscar. You have to admit, you've been around a while. When you were constructed, my human counterpart wasn't even born," said Christine. "But let me finish my story."

Aphrodite nodded. She loved stories, but only those with happy endings. Hopefully her own story would have one. She silently prayed to whoever was writing her story. She didn't believe in a god, but it seemed to help the humans to think like that.

"An engineer – I can't remember her name – had the idea of building a dynamo that drew energy from the rotation of the ring."

"And it worked?" asked Oscar.

"It supplied enough energy to restart the drive. The ILSE reached its destination."

"I like that story," said Aphrodite.

"I could tell you some amazing stories too," said Oscar. "You wouldn't believe all the places I've been."

"Oh, yes," said Aphrodite. "I can't wait."

"Let's deal with this problem first," said Christine.

"A dynamo is a great idea," said Oscar. "We could power the antenna with it. I prefer that to a battery bank, which is not a permanent solution. But I wonder where we could install it."

"There's only one place that would work," said Christine. "On the ring, obviously."

"I figured that much. But where exactly?"

"We attach it to the outside of the capsule and position it so that it's flying at the same speed as the ship near the ring. Then we run a cable to the central module and connect it to a magnetic field generator, which we also need to build."

"There's one small problem," said Aphrodite. "The damaged part of the ring bulges out. That means the capsule would need to be at least two meters out from the ring. That may be too far to generate enough current."

"Shit. You're right," said Christine.

"We could get around that by parking the capsule beside the ring. There's no bulge there."

"Thanks, Aphrodite."

"I also suggest we divide up the work to save time. I'll install the dynamo. I'm the only one who can uncouple the capsule. You go to the workshop and build the device that creates the magnetic field."

"Good idea," said Christine. "And then I'll take the device into the parasite."

Aphrodite wanted to object, but didn't dare. She'd had enough of that parasite. And Christine was a lot smaller than her. If the device was capable of protecting someone, then it would work better for Christine.

"Yes, that makes sense," said Oscar. "For once we all agree on the sensible course of action. That's a good start!"

THE PLAN REQUIRED THEM TO SPLIT UP. WHEN CHRISTINE left the workshop to take the finished device outside, Aphrodite was still in the process of freeing capsule C from its anchorage. To do this, she had to make sure she had a firm grip on the capsule's outer hull, because as soon as the two docking brackets released it, the capsule's inertia would fling it out into space.

The first docking arm complied. It was a satisfying, if strenuous, task. Aphrodite checked her footing, then reached for the second bracket. It was much stiffer – probably because it was now supporting all of the capsule's weight. Aphrodite used a second and then a third arm to force it. It worked! She could already feel the inertia pulling on her. So she let go of the docking bracket with the weakest of the three arms. But the arm was stuck! The tool on its end must have gotten wedged somewhere. She had no choice – she quickly let go with the second and third arms and prepared herself mentally for what was to come.

The pain of her tool arm ripping off was almost unbearable. Aphrodite fell forward onto her front. The capsule was now speeding out into space. But it was in free-fall, so Aphrodite was able to enter it despite the pain. There, she took over the controls with her other tool hand and decelerated to bring it closer to the Shepherd again.

She inspected the wound. The entire arm was missing. It was a clean break. A little oil seeped out of a pipe. She checked her schematics. Thankfully, it wasn't hydraulic oil, just lubricant for the joint in the missing arm. Should she tell Christine? No, it would only worry her. Aphrodite could get by without that hand. She still had one gripping arm for complex tasks, and the two strong loading arms. That should suffice.

She steered the capsule with her remaining tool hand and did her best to ignore the pain. Theoretically, she could control the capsule without any limbs – she could connect herself directly to the control software. That was something her android friends couldn't do. The capsule very slowly approached the desired position. It was a little tricky, because the ring was spinning the whole time. The capsule flew very close above it, like a pot over an induction stove, except that there was a dynamo on the outside of the capsule. She'd mounted the primitive machine according to Oscar's instructions. It was supposed to supply up to one kilowatt.

Hopefully the plan would work. She was confident Oscar had calculated everything correctly. They had decided to call the device that Christine had put together in the workshop a 'magnet shield'. It wasn't a shield in the narrow sense of a barrier between an object and a magnetic field. It was designed to actually disrupt any fields that were present. In theory, this meant that the parasite could no longer stabilize its structure and therefore couldn't dissolve objects anymore.

"Are you making progress?" she asked via the capsule radio.

"In five minutes I'll reach the area where we assume the parasite is active," said Christine.

"Use your lamp, so you can see if it's moved."

"Yes, Aphrodite. I'm keeping it on the whole time. It's hard to orient myself out here without it."

Oh, right. Aphrodite had forgotten that androids couldn't see in the dark to find their way. She checked the distance between the dynamo and the ring. It was correct. She displayed all her senses on screen simultaneously. There was Christine. From above, she looked like a triangle with rounded corners. Depending on the wavelength, she was a pale, vivid, or faint spot moving rapidly toward a violet wall.

It was time to throw her the cable. Aphrodite climbed back outside. This was a delicate moment, for two reasons: when she threw the cable, she needed to be precise. Also, her throw would provide the capsule with a certain momentum away from Shepherd-1, and she would have to compensate with the corrective thruster.

"Oscar, how is our little power plant performing?" asked Aphrodite.

"1074 watts," said Oscar.

"That's more than expected."

"Yes, I factored in a certain tolerance."

"Good idea."

"Thanks, Aphrodite. It's time to throw Christine the cable. She's almost reached the parasite."

"I'm ready," said Aphrodite.

"Me too," said Christine.

Aphrodite could see Christine waving to her in the radar image. She was about thirty meters away. Aphrodite was capable of calculating everything accurately and applying her strength very precisely. There was no reason for anything to go wrong. But she was still afraid.

She positioned herself as planned, held the line at the exact length she had calculated, swung her arm at a precise angle, and let go of the line at just the right moment. But she realized instantly that it wouldn't reach Christine. The flight path deviated from the plan by a fraction of a percent. She hadn't factored in her missing arm. That had changed her mass and therefore the transferred momentum.

"I messed up," she said.

She could still pull the line back in. It wasn't too late. She recalculated and was about to try again.

"No, it's fine," said Oscar. "Christine just needs to take a step to the left to catch the line. Did you hear that, Christine?"

"But that deviates from the plan," said Aphrodite. "We should stick to what we agreed."

Christine followed Oscar's instructions and caught the cable. "Got it! A little improvisation never hurts. It makes it more fun."

"You're having fun right now?" asked Aphrodite.

"Sure. It's a little scary, but it's also loads of fun. I want to know if my idea's going to work. It's a great feeling when ideas work out in practice."

Aphrodite watched the cable. There was some slack in it, but not enough to contact the parasite. That was the weak point in their plan. The cloud was up to four meters thick in some places, so the magnetic field disruptor couldn't reach the higher parts. The cable had to pass through part of the parasite. If it dissolved, Christine would suddenly be without power.

It wouldn't mean the end of her, because she had a battery pack on her back. But she would have to turn back.

"I'm switching on the device now," said Christine. "Let's hope it works."

"If you followed all my instructions when building it, then it'll work," said Oscar.

"So it's my fault if it doesn't?"

"It was you who drew that conclusion, not me."

"Because it logically follows from your assertion. If you say A, and B logically and unambiguously follows from A, then you can't claim you never said B."

"One-nil to Christine," said Aphrodite.

"Ha! Whatever! If I say A, I've said A, and nothing more."

Aphrodite watched as an indentation formed in the purple layer on the ship. It was at precisely the location where Christine was visible in the optical range.

"It's working," said Aphrodite.

"Great!" cried Christine. "It's hard to tell out here. I'm still surrounded by fog."

"Yeah, its effective range is not much wider than your cross-section," said Aphrodite.

"Is that enough for the antenna?" asked Christine.

"I think so."

"Oh, fantastic. Benjamin and Ilan will be worried."

"What can you see?" asked Aphrodite.

She thought back to her own EVA. Despite her many sensors, the fog had steadily reduced her visibility. The radar had failed altogether, but radio waves still made it through. What would it be like for Christine? Presumably she could see nothing now. Or was she used to that, since she couldn't really rely on her optical sense anyway?

"I have a white wall in front of me," said Christine. "It moves back when I approach it. But only if I don't move too fast."

"You're doing great," said Aphrodite. "I can see you from above, even though the parasite must be pretty thick where you are. So your machine is working vertically too."

"I would hope so," said Oscar. "I designed it that way."

"Yeah, that was a really good idea," said Christine.

The cable went taut and Aphrodite paid out another two

meters from the reel. Christine had another six or seven meters to go before she reached the antenna. The plan actually seemed to be working.

A shred of cloud passed over Christine. Aphrodite fired the capsule's laser and the cloud lit up red. It was the parasite.

"Christine? It looks like the magnetic shield is no longer keeping the area above you clear."

Christine knew what that meant. They had discussed it at length. They couldn't let the parasite affect the cable.

"I'll hold it a little higher," she said.

"That's not what we agreed," said Aphrodite. "If the cable is endangered, you turn back. That was the plan."

"But we need to be flexible. It's only a few more meters."

"We achieve nothing if we lose you. Please look down at your feet and tell me if the fog has reached you."

"I'd rather you told me what the cloud above me is doing."

"It's gone, Christine. But you need to get out of there. We'll adapt the plan and try again."

"Aphrodite, which way to the antenna? I'm a little disoriented."

"Turn 150 degrees clockwise. That's the shortest route to a parasite-free zone."

"But I want to go to the antenna. Oscar, say something."

"30 degrees counterclockwise," said Oscar.

"Oscar!" Aphrodite reprimanded.

"Christine is a grown woman. If she wants to put herself in danger, she can put herself in danger."

"But Oscar! That's not what we agreed!"

Another cloud appeared directly above Christine. Had the parasite somehow detected that there was a potential victim there?

"Christine, it's above you again. If we lose the cable..."

"...we'll get another one." Christine took two long strides forward.

"Oscar, do something!" cried Aphrodite.

"I could increase the intensity of the magnetic shield. But then the power consumption goes up too."

He was only saying this now? Christine checked the figures for the dynamo. The output was around 1073 watts. Surprisingly stable. The magnetic shield was only using 910 watts. No, 930 watts. 950. 990.

"Did you just increase the intensity?" asked Aphrodite.

"Affirmative. What's the parasite doing?"

"The cloud above Christine has dispersed."

"Good," said Oscar.

"See? No need to worry," said Christine.

But there was a reason to worry: the next cloud was already forming.

"I hate to spoil your fun, but it's happening again."

"We still have some power in reserve," said Oscar. "I'll turn it up to the maximum. In principle, there's no reason for the dynamo's output to fluctuate."

In principle. Aphrodite hated that phrase. She monitored the figures. Output at 1020 watts, 1050 watts, 1070. It stopped there. The cloud was driven back at 1050 watts.

"All clear for now," said Aphrodite.

"And I've arrived," said Christine. "See? There was nothing to worry about. I'll attach the cable to the antenna as well."

Aphrodite watched Christine working on the antenna. They couldn't use it to transmit until the magnetic shield was no longer needed – when Christine was out safely out of there. She would use the cable to guide her back to the capsule. That was the quickest way out of the deadly fog.

But the parasite seemed to sense this. Apparently, it didn't want its prey to escape – a new cloud was gathering directly above Christine's current location. And it was threatening the cable again too.

"Oscar, we need a new idea," said Aphrodite.

"Sorry, I'm all out of ideas."

"That's unacceptable," said Aphrodite. "We need more power, otherwise we'll lose Christine, and then the antenna."

"But the dynamo's power output is limited by its coil and the rate of rotation. We can't change that."

"The rate of rotation? You mean, how fast the ring is spinning?"

"Exactly."

"But surely that can be changed. We can slow the ring, so it we should be able to speed it up too."

"In principle, yes, but I can't operate the small chemical thrusters that control that. We have no power, Aphrodite."

"I know. But do we really need power to start those thrusters?"

"There's a manual trigger. But someone would have to climb out to the thrusters. And fast."

"Send me the position," said Aphrodite. "I'm on my way."

"They're on the ring," said Oscar.

"That's handy. It's not far."

The capsule hovered a few centimeters from the ring, which was rotating fast. And Aphrodite wanted to make it go faster. Was that such a good idea? She had no choice. She clambered around the capsule's hull to a position where she could more easily reach the ring. Then she jumped.

She quickly found a sturdy strut to hold onto. The sudden acceleration almost tore off her arm and doubled the pain she was already feeling, but she supported the joint with the sturdy loading arm. Phew!

"You need to move to the outside of the ring," said Oscar. "The thrusters look like fans. There are round openings in the ring covered with gratings, always in pairs. But be careful! When the ring accelerates, the simulated gravity there will increase. So conserve your strength; you're going to need it."

"Got it," said Aphrodite.

If she waited on this side, it would take less than one rotation before she knocked the capsule away from the ring.

"I've connected the antenna to the cable," said Christine. "Why are you two so quiet?"

Aphrodite had been talking to Oscar on a separate frequency, to avoid worrying Christine.

"Your situation seems to have become more complicated," said Oscar. "Aphrodite's dealing with it now."

She was dealing with it, exactly. Aphrodite is dealing with it for you. It was a good feeling, being able to deal with things, although her current position on the ring scared her. Suddenly, she understood Christine's attitude. If she were to die now, at least she would have learned something important.

"Are you keeping secrets from me? I don't like it. What's going on?"

"If we want the magnetic shield and the antenna to operate indefinitely, we need more power. So Aphrodite's accelerating the ring."

"What? Are you crazy? The additional gravity will throw her off, and who knows if the ring can even take it?"

"I'm sure Shepherd-1 was built with a certain tolerance," said Oscar. "Don't worry."

"Hey, I'm the captain. You can't just go over my head and make that decision!"

This was what Aphrodite had expected. And why she didn't fill Christine in on her plan. She climbed slowly around the outside of the ring. She should find one of those little thrusters in every quadrant. But they were really well concealed – probably to make them less vulnerable to micrometeoroid impacts. There were four of these thrusters, to spread the load around the ring symmetrically. But this time one would have to suffice. There! A dark shaft leading diagonally into the interior of the ship. It looked like some kind of rodent's burrow. She illuminated it and saw the protective grating.

"Where are the controls?" she asked.

"Hey, are you guys listening to me?" asked Christine.

"I suggest you start using the cable to get yourself to safety," said Aphrodite. "We'll take care of the rest."

"I agree," said Oscar. "The parasite is condensing above you again."

“Like hell I’m getting out of here! I’m not going anywhere until the antenna’s operational.”

“Have you set it to relay mode?” asked Oscar. “You need to open the flap on the side. There’s a separate switch on the far left.”

“Yeah. I’ve done that,” said Christine. “I know my ship.”

“Then you really should listen to Aphrodite, make your way along the cable, and get out of that dicey situation.”

“What if something fails? Then it was all in vain.”

Oscar sighed loudly. Aphrodite bent over the thruster. Where was the control panel? Ah, there, in the center between the two shafts. That made sense. The cover was secured with four screws. Aphrodite’s tool arm swiftly removed them. One of the loading arms removed the cover, but didn’t grip it tightly enough, and it floated away. Beneath it was a small control panel with a couple of electrical sockets, three lights, two buttons, and a comparatively large dial. The lights weren’t illuminated.

“Found it,” said Aphrodite.

“Good. See the dial?”

“I see it.”

“You need to turn it in the opposite direction to the ring’s motion.”

“Got it. To the left then.”

“I don’t know where you’re standing. The opposite direction to the ring’s rotation, that’s important. That selects the jet that points in the opposite direction to the ring’s rotation. Then the thruster sends gas out of that jet and the ring rotates faster.”

“Understood.”

It didn’t seem very clear. Why didn’t the dial show the intended direction of acceleration? Never mind, she could worry about that later. The ring was rotating to the right from her current perspective, so she turned the dial to the left. Nothing happened.

“What now?”

“Wait, I can’t see Christine anymore.”

"Oscar, what now?"

Oscar didn't reply. There were two buttons. They weren't marked. One started the thruster and the other switched it off. Presumably. Most humans read from left to right. So left must be the on-switch and right the off-switch. Or did one of the buttons have a different function entirely?

"Oscar?"

No answer. She pressed the button on the left. The force trying to throw her off the ring increased a little. She had guessed correctly! The ring was accelerating. She needed to stay where she was until it was rotating fast enough. Aphrodite braced herself, hooking both loading arms around struts. The loading arms were sturdier than her spidery legs. The inertial force increased. Unfortunately, she couldn't measure the increase. The data from her joints reported a twenty percent increase in the strain. That meant it was at 1.2 g. It needed to be 2 g.

"Dynamo output increasing," Oscar reported.

He sounded downcast.

"You're back! What happened?" asked Aphrodite.

"I've been trying to reach Christine but she's not responding."

"Oh, no!"

One of her joints cracked loudly. The sound vibrated in her head. The ring continued to accelerate.

"The dynamo's at 150 percent," said Oscar.

Yes, that matched the gravity, which must be around 1.5 g. Aphrodite bent over the controls.

"Which button do I press to switch off the thruster?" she asked.

"The same one for switching it on. Definitely not the other one. That brings the ring to an emergency standstill. It fires all the thrusters until the ring stops moving."

Lucky guess then.

"Why aren't the buttons labeled?"

"Maybe the designers assumed that only someone who knew what they were doing would use manual control."

"That's irresponsible," said Aphrodite.

She pressed herself directly against the ring to relieve the load on her joints. Then she remembered the captain.

"What about Christine?" she asked.

"I don't know," said Oscar.

His voice had never sounded so despairing. If she climbed down one of the spokes to the central module... maybe she could pull Christine out of the fog. But then the ring would continue accelerating. She had to stay where she was, at least until the dynamo was delivering the amount of power they needed.

"What can I do?" asked Aphrodite.

"You're already doing the most important thing. We're now at 1920 watts. Wait thirty seconds, then we'll be over 2000. That should be enough."

"What's happening with the parasite?"

"It's dissipating. Wait. Yes, the cloud is gone! It's clear around the antenna, two meters in every direction. I can see a pale spot. That must be Christine!"

"That's great," said Aphrodite.

"But she doesn't appear to be moving."

Aphrodite measured the load on her joints. It was 2 g. She quickly pressed the button to switch off the thruster.

"I'll go back to the capsule," she said.

"I have bad news," said Oscar.

It must be about Christine! Aphrodite froze. What was it?

"You're alive!" cried Oscar.

"Uh, yeah," replied Christine. "Couldn't you see that?"

"No, the parasite was covering you. It retreated just now."

"Oh, I'm sorry," said Christine. "I was using the battery pack to make contact with capsule A using the long-range antenna. To do that I had to leave the open channel. But I notified you guys!"

"You didn't," said Oscar.

"Oh, sorry. Anyway, I have bad news. The capsule isn't responding."

Great. As if their problems here weren't bad enough. Aphrodite began to climb.

"We'll figure that out soon," said Oscar. "But now that we know the antenna is working, you can move back along the cable."

"OK, agreed."

Aphrodite was surprised that Christine was playing ball this time. She pictured the android moving along the cable back to the capsule. The central module and the capsule were motionless in relation to one another. But to Christine it must still feel like crossing a fathomless abyss.

"I'm at the capsule," she said. "Aphrodite, are you coming?"

Aphrodite watched the capsule rush past her. No, she couldn't get back to it. If she jumped onto the stationary capsule from the ring moving at this speed, her momentum would unbalance the capsule, and in the worst case scenario the cable they had just successfully installed would snap.

"No, sorry. I have to stay outside," said Aphrodite. "It's too dangerous to try to cross from the ring to the capsule. My momentum could cause the cable to snap and then we're back at square one."

It was OK. It wasn't really any worse out on the ring than it was in the capsule. She needed to hold on tight, but she had a better view. And it was only for a limited time. At some point they would restore power to the ship.

"You're right, Aphrodite," said Oscar. "But please don't try to get to the central module via one of the spokes. The parasite's surrounding all of them now."

"Don't worry, I won't. I can manage out here on the ring for a while. But what's up with capsule A?"

"Unfortunately, I have to confirm Christine's assessment. Benjamin and Ilan aren't responding."

Oh no. Then the whole mission was in vain!

"Shit. So we could have saved ourselves the trouble of setting up the antenna."

“It wasn’t totally in vain,” said Oscar. “At least now we can contact Mission Control again.”

“Forget it,” said Aphrodite. “The only people interested in us are Alpha Omega and RB, and we don’t want to speak to them.”

“And they can’t help us anyway,” said Christine. “We’ll hold our course and keep trying to make contact with the capsule.”

Aphrodite climbed around to the inside of the ring. On that side, the inertial force would press her against it, so she didn’t have to worry about flying out if her attention lapsed. And she discovered that the designers of Shepherd-1 had distributed electrical sockets at regular intervals around the ring. They were probably needed during the ship’s construction, which was done in orbit. She connected herself to one of them, leaned back, and relaxed.

Capsule A, October 22, 2112

"Capsule A to Shepherd-1, please come in."

No reply. Benjamin sighed.

"Don't worry," said Ilan. "It's probably just a power outage."

"Power outage, ha ha. All the DFDs at once?"

"It's not impossible. The electrical power has to go through a converter."

"But there are replacement parts, right?"

"There are, Benjamin. I was just saying there could be a benign explanation. But I'm not clairvoyant."

"I'm still worried."

"I get it. But worrying doesn't help anyone. Come on, let's focus on our destination. I have a feeling it's going to be the answer to all of our problems."

"Nothing in the world can answer all of our problems, Ilan."

"Wait and see."

"OK, I'll send the message," said Ilan.

"Do it."

They had put in a lot of effort this time and raised the bar.

Mathematics, physics, and the biochemistry of the cosmos were all encoded in their message.

The reply came almost instantly.

"That was fast," said Ilan.

"It was too fast. It can't be the reply," said Benjamin. "They need to decode it first, then understand it, then come up with an answer."

"Maybe they think faster than we do."

"Maybe, but they would still need to discuss it among themselves, and that takes time!"

"Let's just take a look, OK?"

Benjamin didn't recognize himself. He was normally the epitome of optimism. Otherwise, he wouldn't have made the journey back from Earth in the first place. But Ilan was utterly surpassing him.

The first file opened. It took about as long as it took the aliens to send the entire message. They must be really advanced. Benjamin saw something resembling a flower. It was colorful and mesmerizing. He traced the outlines of the petals with his finger and lost his way.

"That's impossible," he said.

"Yeah, it must be advanced mathematics," said Ilan. "I dropped out in basic math."

"I always thought you were an engineer?"

"I didn't graduate, if that's what you mean. But I've always worked as an engineer. When you're the boss, nobody asks to see your qualifications."

"I vaguely recall my topology lectures," said Benjamin. "This must be some kind of five-dimensional function in coordinate space."

It was weird. He had met the man who actually attended those lectures, but still saw the memories as his own.

Ilan tapped the screen. "The aliens definitely win this round."

"What else do you have?" asked Benjamin.

Ilan typed something and a honeycomb structure appeared on screen. It was slightly irregular.

"They sent us this 3D graphic. Looks like someone slashed at a piece of cloth with a clawed hand. See the horizontal threads and the vertical slits?" asked Ilan.

Benjamin laughed. "True. But it must be something from physics. Not high school physics, something you learn at a more advanced level."

Ilan shook his head. "Assuming we're receiving their information in the same sequence that we sent ours."

"We have to assume so. Otherwise we'll never figure out what it means.

"The structure reminds me of the cosmic microwave background," said Benjamin.

"Or it could be the diffraction structure of an exotic particle."

Oh right, the double-slit experiment. The magnitude of the effect said something about the mass of the particle, which was proportional to its frequency.

"Is there a scale?" he asked.

"Yes, in the base-41 system. If I assume natural measurement units, then the diffracted particle must have twice the mass of a proton."

"Maybe a hexaquark," Benjamin suggested.

"There are several of those, none of which are particularly interesting."

"One of them was once considered a candidate for dark matter."

"But that was never confirmed, right?" asked Ilan.

"Maybe this is the confirmation."

"A shame we can't understand it."

Ilan was right. They were assuming the aliens were using natural units. If not, then it was a diffracted football. Maybe they just wanted to discuss their favorite sport.

"And the last part of the message?" asked Benjamin.

"The third part takes the cake. They've taken our cosmic biochemistry information and combined all the alcohols, alkanes, amino acids, and so on into a functioning ecosystem. If this is more than pure fantasy, then there could be interstellar life in dense molecular clouds."

"Despite their low density? That's not much more than 10^{-20} grams per cubic centimeter."

"I said I assume it's fantasy. They simply elaborated our ideas to show us that they understood them."

"Maybe they've actually seen something like it," said Benjamin. "If they've traveled vast distances, we can't rule it out. We need to ask them directly."

"You took the words right out of my mouth, and do you know what the best part is? I believe they've extended an invitation."

"What? How?"

"The message has a fourth part. It's series of images."

Ilan tapped the screen. The first image appeared in 3D. Benjamin could make out a bright spot and a much darker sphere.

"That's the capsule and our destination, right?"

"Yes," said Ilan. "Look!"

He rotated the 3D representation. The proportions were accurate. He assumed it was an infrared image because the capsule was very bright.

"I wouldn't interpret that as an invitation," said Benjamin.

"Wait. There are more of these images. If you skip through them quickly..."

Ilan swiped the screen, causing the images to appear on screen in quick succession. The capsule moved through space in small jumps, circumnavigated the sphere, and then flew directly toward it. The sequence stopped on the last image, in which only the sphere could be seen.

"They don't show us coming back out," said Benjamin.

"No. I noticed that too. It doesn't necessarily mean anything."

"But it might."

Ilan nodded. "Hmm. No progress without risk, right?"

Benjamin scratched his temple. He thought the risk was far too high. He saw what the parasite did to his friends.

"Wild horses couldn't drag me there, I'm telling you."

"We don't have to take the invitation literally," said Ilan. "My guess is that they figure the capsule is the intelligence they're communicating with."

"That's possible. It's sending out the radio signal. And our encounters haven't been consistent. First androids, then a robot..."

"Which may not seem very different to them. We're obviously not biological beings. I wonder if that's why they have no qualms about killing us."

That was an interesting idea. But the parasite wasn't biological life either. A structure made of various helium phases existing in homeostasis with its environment – no terrestrial biologist would believe it was possible. But the parasite was a reality.

"I doubt their concept of life is as limited as ours," said Benjamin. "It can't be."

"I guess that's an advantage when you get around the way they do," said Ilan.

"Capsule A to Shepherd-1, please come in."

No reply. Benjamin wasn't expecting one, but he had to try. He had long since stopped imagining what misfortune might have befallen Shepherd-1. Ilan's complete lack of concern was somehow contagious.

Benjamin pointed the telescope in the direction they had come. There was the ship. It was neither closer nor farther away than last time he checked. But it still existed. It hadn't exploded and the parasite hadn't completely devoured it. The infrared image showed that clearly now.

Ilan floated over to him. Benjamin felt his eyes on him and turned around. Ilan pulled a face as if he'd eaten something sour. He straightened his bra. The movement looked totally routine. It was astonishing how quickly Chatterjee had become accustomed to that body.

"I... I need to tell you something," he said.

"You've secretly contacted the parasite?"

Ilan shook his head, but didn't laugh at what was obviously meant as a joke. Benjamin took a deep breath. Shepherd-1 still existed. Whatever Ilan was about to tell him couldn't be too serious.

"I'm telling you this because you're worried about the Shepherd."

"Oh, Christine contacted you and told you she's fine?"

Ilan gave a tortured smile. "I want this mission to succeed. For that, I need your trust and your confidence. So I'm telling you something that I was actually intending to keep to myself. But you have to promise not..."

"Spit it out," Benjamin interrupted. "I'm not going to throw you out of the airlock."

Or maybe he would, if he'd done something to Aphrodite, Oscar, or Christine.

"Fine. The reason Shepherd-1 isn't responding is that I've regained control of it. I gave it the express command to stay silent until I give the OK. But the ship is fine."

"You're full of shit. You just want me to stop worrying."

"No, it's true. When I was still on the ship, I made contact with Aphrodite's other half and convinced her to help me."

He had seen Ilan sitting in the workshop speaking into the helmet. Presumably, that was what he was referring to. He wasn't lying.

"How did you manage that?"

"Aphrodite unwittingly helped me. She was so eager to get her other half back that she let it into the ship. But she didn't know that by doing so, she was implementing my plan to take control of Shepherd-1."

"You didn't just exploit Aphrodite, you used the other half of her consciousness too."

"It's not my fault she feels unjustly treated and neglected by you guys. All I did was encourage that a little. In the end, she used Oscar's trick that you used against me to take control of the ship's software."

"Aphrodite's dark side has rebooted the ship's computer."

"Yes, with herself as the operating system. You only have yourselves to blame for not cleaning up after something like that."

Benjamin leaned back. What did this mean for him? Ilan was presenting it as good news, and in a way it was. Shepherd-1 was alive.

If he was telling the truth and it wasn't just another ploy.

And he actually believed Ilan had changed.

"I don't believe you," he said.

That wasn't true. Benjamin knew Ilan was telling the truth. But he wanted to hear his friends' voices, to know they were all right.

"Why would I lie to you about something like that? It makes no sense."

"Who knows what your motives are? Maybe you just want to reassure me so you can focus on our destination."

"Fine. I'll prove it to you."

Ilan floated across the cabin and switched on the radio.

"Shepherd-1, please come in. Code word Reconnaissance. Please respond."

The spaceship didn't respond.

"Shepherd-1, please come in. Code word Reconnaissance. I repeat, code word Reconnaissance."

The radio receiver remained silent. Benjamin couldn't help laughing. The master plan had apparently gone south. But the laughter stuck in his throat. This didn't just mean that Ilan's plan had failed. It also meant that there was actually something wrong with Shepherd-1.

"Thanks, Ilan. You've really inspired my trust and confidence. You're the best."

The rancor in his voice couldn't have been plainer. Chatterjee didn't reply. Good. If he got too close to Benjamin just now, his fist might wind up in Ilan's face.

After an hour, Chatterjee finally spoke to him again.

"Look outside. You can see the alien sphere now."

He was speaking unusually softly. He was probably worrying about his failed plan. Benjamin felt a certain schadenfreude.

At that moment, a force pressed him against his seatbelt. The capsule was braking, presumably moving into orbit around their destination. They hadn't discussed it, but it was fine by Benjamin. Not because of the sphere. He was much less interested in the peculiar aliens than he was in his friends. Spending a while in orbit would give Shepherd-1 time to catch up with them. It would arrive in half a day.

"I'll get out and take a look at this thing up close," said Ilan. "Want to come with me?"

Benjamin shook his head. The villain was on his own.

"I understand. You're not speaking to me?"

Benjamin nodded.

"Fine. That's your prerogative, although it's pretty childish."

A musty smell wafted through the capsule as Chatterjee put on his space suit. Benjamin heard him groan. It wasn't easy getting into the top part without assistance. But he didn't offer to help and Ilan didn't ask. He heard crumpling and squeaking sounds. Benjamin didn't turn around, but he guessed Ilan was sitting on the bed, trying to close the boots. That alone took some skill.

"Uff," said Ilan, shaking out his limbs with a rattling sound.

It suddenly occurred to Benjamin that he needed a suit too; otherwise Ilan couldn't open the hatch. He wanted to avoid the painful sensation of suffocating. So he jumped up and tried to remedy this. Chatterjee finished first and went to the hatch where he watched Benjamin through his helmet visor. Just before Benjamin was done, he slid across the locking bar and opened the hatch. For a moment, Benjamin hoped that Christine and Aphrodite would poke their heads inside – that it would all turn out to be a practical joke and they had never left the ship.

Benjamin shook his head. Ilan misunderstood the gesture and closed the hatch. The life support whirred into action, trying to fill the capsule with air again.

"You can go," said Benjamin. He closed his helmet.

"Oh, you *can* speak," said Ilan. "Take care."

Chatterjee didn't wait for the reply he was never going to get. He pulled open the hatch and climbed outside, waited a few seconds, and then pushed off.

Benjamin closed the hatch again and took off his helmet. He sat down in the pilot's seat and followed Ilan on screen. Wait. He had no jetpack. How was he intending to reach the strange structure spinning in space before them? Benjamin switched over to radar, which supplied the most useful information. It told him that the object consisted of a number of semi-transparent layers rotating at various distances around the center.

But the radar could only penetrate a kilometer deep, while the radius of the sphere was almost 25 kilometers. The object had an astonishingly high mass. A lot less than any kind of degenerate matter – like the matter that made up neutron stars or quark stars – but high enough that the helium at the center must be incredibly dense. So the assumption that they were looking at the core of a gas giant was incorrect.

In infrared, the poles of the slightly oblate sphere had paler spots. They were relatively stable and much brighter than their surroundings. The speed of their rotation allowed him to estimate their depth. He could only make out a vague system: the spots farther in were warmer than those on the outside. *Warm* was relative, though – maybe 25 Kelvin (not degrees) compared to 40 farther in.

"I'm fine, by the way," said Ilan. "In case anybody's interested."

Benjamin maintained his silence, but watched his crewmate's flight path with curiosity. That was OK because Chatterjee didn't know he was watching. His path was now a spiral. The object had significant gravitational pull, and as there was no air friction, there was no terminal velocity. Hopefully Ilan had factored that in.

But maybe he could expect some friction. The helium on the outside was still a gas. The density increased very quickly, but Benjamin didn't have the required coefficients in his head to calculate whether Ilan would slow down gently, hard, or not at all. He needed Oscar. But he had no line of communication to him, thanks to Chatterjee, who was now suffering the consequences.

Things were getting interesting. The telemetry data from Chatterjee's suit revealed to Benjamin that the helium surrounding him had the same density as the parasite. The suit also confirmed the temperatures he had measured there. Further evidence that the parasite was once a part of this sphere. The question was whether it was a weapon, an accidental break-away, or something else entirely that he couldn't even imagine.

Probably that last. Benjamin's eyes were glued to the screen. It was precisely because he didn't like the person out there that he didn't want to miss out on witnessing his end.

"Hey, in case we don't see each other again..." said Chatterjee, "I didn't mean any harm. I know that sounds lame, but I was never working against you. I was working for the ultimate knowledge, the answer, the truth, or whatever you want to call it. I'll probably die because of it – it doesn't take a prophet to predict my death a few minutes from now. It was definitely worth it. I'd like to say I don't care how you remember me, but it's not true, and an honest person shouldn't start telling lies in his last moments, so I hope you'll remember me as an asshole on an important mission. End recording."

As instructed by Chatterjee, the recording ended. The channel remained open. Not bad last words. But Benjamin still didn't reply. He wanted Chatterjee to feel that he was dying alone, although he probably knew someone was watching.

"Benjamin, Ben, now I can finally say it. I know you're watching and listening. Believe it or not, I'm sorry about playing you and your friends. The admin password is PiranhaPoodle99!, with upper case Ps and an exclamation mark at the end. You can use that to overwrite the ship's system. It will attempt to make contact with me at some point. That's your chance. Please switch off this frequency as soon as you hear me scream. I don't want to hold back just to spare you. So if it hurts to be dissolved, then I'll scream in pain. Now that I think about it, I actually don't want to die. So it would be nice if this thing here can absorb me alive, as its invitation promised."

The spot on screen that was Ilan suddenly changed direction, distancing itself from the object. Benjamin simulated its flight path. That vector was only possible if Ilan had bounced off.

"Shit, that hurt!" he cried. "Can anyone hear me?"

Benjamin remained stoically silent. Ilan could learn what it felt like to be alone. According to the simulation, his flight path was moving back in toward the object. Benjamin zoomed in. He noted the depth at which Ilan's body had bounced off. He had almost reached that depth again. He was approaching at an angle of around twenty degrees. He bounced off and was thrown back out.

"Shit!" cried Ilan. "This thing doesn't want me!"

Not even the sphere wanted him. Benjamin smirked and then felt guilty. Another attempt. The same result. He called up the sequence of images they had received. It showed the capsule approaching. It didn't show an android in a space suit. Benjamin recalled being invited to visit his old CapCom Rachel, and then the bald-headed Charles showing up at the door. Was he still alive? He wouldn't let him in either.

He had to do something. Ilan had clearly interpreted the invitation too fancifully. He couldn't just leave him down there, could he? He would keep bouncing off that thing forever.

Benjamin sighed. Maybe Shepherd-1 could help?

"Capsule to Shepherd-1. Password PiranhaPoodle99! Please come in."

No answer. He sighed again and assumed manual control of the capsule.

Ilan was bouncing off a layer 22.3 kilometers from the center. That was approximately where he would intercept him. But his orbit was slightly offset from that of the capsule.

Benjamin wasn't good enough at orbital mechanics to calculate a maneuver that could compensate the difference with only one correction. So he started by altering the capsule's course. One burst of the corrective thruster, pause, another burst, decelerate. Great. Now he was flying directly above Chatterjee. He braked the capsule, reducing its perigee. But it wasn't enough, as he realized on his next pass. Another deceleration burst. His orbit had already distorted into an ellipse. Its perigee – the point nearest the sphere – was now 25.2 kilometers from the center. That was just above the outer layer, and still too high. But he didn't want to go lower until the last possible moment. Then he would dive into the outer layer, which was likely to brake him to an extent that he couldn't calculate. He could predict neither the variations in density nor his speed at each point on his new orbit.

He would have to decide spontaneously. So he waited for an opportunity. Ilan wasn't speaking anymore. He didn't know Benjamin was trying to rescue him. He was probably trying to figure out the quickest way to die. That was what Benjamin would be doing. Orbiting this object for thousands of years and continuously bouncing off it painfully would not be an option for him.

Ilan distanced himself again until he was captured by the object's gravitation. Had Ilan shut himself off? That wasn't ideal. The capsule had a manipulator arm, but it would be better if Ilan was active during the rescue. Maybe he should radio him. Benjamin followed Ilan's bizarrely oscillating orbit. In one and a half circuits, his and the capsule's orbits could pass very close. Benjamin needed to drop down to 23.1 kilometers. The cloud was still not very dense there.

This was his chance. Another deceleration burst took the capsule down to the desired orbit. The main thruster responded swiftly and accurately.

"Ilan, can you hear me?" he asked.

"No, I'm having a nice dream. Leave me alone."

"Don't screw around. I'm coming to get you."

"What? That's... You'll only put yourself in danger!"

That was true. The helium layers... How would the capsule react to them? But there was no other option that he could live with.

"I can't just leave you hanging. I can't. Even horses get a mercy shot to the head if they're seriously injured."

"I know you're on edge, Benjamin, but that's a strange analogy."

"I mean, oh, whatever. Nobody gets left behind in a situation like that."

"I'm warning you! I don't deserve it. I'm an asshole and always will be. Rescuing me won't make me turn over a new leaf."

"I know. You are and always will be an asshole."

He didn't expect Ilan's relief at being rescued to turn him into a do-gooder. No, Benjamin was doing this for himself. So he could look himself in the mirror.

Ilan groaned. He must have just bounced again.

"Tell me what you see," said Benjamin.

"It's all white, clinical white. But it's slowly getting darker."

"You're rising again."

"Apparently. I can't feel the motion. For me, it feels as if I'm lying in an isolation chamber that's changing color. It's now gray below me and black above. I see something flashing. Is that you?"

"I'm actually behind you, so no. Watch out. You're about to start moving back in. Next time you emerge from this soup, I'll be above you. It really sucks that you didn't take a jetpack with you, but you can at least grab hold of the manipulator arm when you see it."

"Understood."

Ilan dropped away again. The screen showed him clearly. The radar functioned right down to the layer Ilan was bouncing off. Even deeper. Why wasn't the layer itself visible? Magnetic fields! He hadn't scanned the object with the magnetometer. Crazy. He had never seen such a strong, complex structure. Vortex upon vortex, and they were most intense where he had seen the bright spots in infrared. A pulsar was nothing compared to this. Where did the energy come from? A pulsar rotated fast, but this thing was moving at a leisurely pace.

Ilan disappeared into the cloud. The timer Benjamin had programmed had just counted down past ten. Three, two, one, fire! The last deceleration burst, which should put him just above the outer layer. It worked. The onboard computer estimated his perigee at 23,100 meters. Ilan was bouncing off again. He was at a lower level, and some way ahead of the capsule, but the capsule was moving faster. Benjamin put his helmet back on and sealed it. He wouldn't have time to do it later.

"I'm gaining on you. Pickup in 43 seconds," he said.

That was the onboard computer's estimate. Roughly every ten seconds, it increased by a second. At his current altitude, the invisible gas was obviously braking him measurably. It wasn't really a problem. He remained at 23,100 meters.

"25 seconds."

Ilan didn't respond.

"16 seconds," Benjamin said ten seconds later. "Sorry, I'm running a little late."

"Don't stand me up. I'm so looking forward to our date," said Ilan.

He accessed the manipulator arm controls. Suddenly, Ilan whizzed past the front of the capsule. He was a dark shadow.

"You're moving too fast!" cried Benjamin.

"Wait, I'll..."

The radar beeped. Proximity alert. It was Ilan! Why was he suddenly moving slower? He caught up to him. Benjamin could see Chatterjee spinning continuously. Something flew off him. What was that? Hopefully not a body part.

"Angular momentum... too fast..."

Benjamin needed to concentrate now. He was almost within reach. Now! He reached out with the manipulator arm.

"Got you!"

"Shit, yes! I puked in my suit."

"I'm bringing you in."

Benjamin guided the arm and its load to the hatch. Then he opened the hatch from inside and pulled Ilan in.

"Oh, man," said Ilan.

When there was enough air in the cabin, Benjamin opened Ilan's helmet. Then he removed his own. There was a sour smell. Benjamin was tempted to put his helmet back on, but he hung it on his armrest instead.

"Oh, man," he said.

Ilan wiped vomit from his cheeks. Something splattered on the floor.

"Ugh, please do that in back or I'm gonna puke too," said Benjamin. He returned to the pilot's seat.

"Thank you! You saved my life."

"Yeah, yeah."

The smell was really unpleasant. His helmet beckoned. But he had smelled worse. At least it wasn't his own. That was worse, because you couldn't get away from it.

Wait. Those weren't his memories. They belonged to the real Benjamin. He was an android. But so was Ilan. Something wasn't right. Benjamin got up again and turned around.

Ilan was naked from the waist up. He lifted a breast and wiped under it with a damp cloth.

"Hey, privacy, please!"

"Ilan, that can't be vomit."

"It looks like vomit, has the right consistency, and smells like it."

"Did Alpha Omega simulate that too?"

"I... You're right, no, that wasn't included," said Chatterjee. "It must be a defect. Some kind of fluid or something. The constant collisions... But it actually started when I made myself spin with the oxygen bottle. And then, stupid me, I let go of it instead of using it to stabilize myself."

So that was the object that flew off him.

"You used the bottle as a corrective thruster," Benjamin established.

That was how he had reduced his distance from the capsule. Very smart!

"Yes, but the impulse didn't go out from my center of gravity. So I began to spin."

"Still, it got you close enough to the capsule for the manipulator arm to catch you."

"Thanks, Benjamin. I really didn't expect this from you. I mean... obviously I knew you were capable, but the idea that you would want to rescue me..."

"I had no choice. Don't let it go to your head."

It felt good, but Chatterjee didn't need to know that. He would even do it again. Successfully rescuing another person was fun. Who would have thought?

The controls were beeping. Why was he only noticing that now? He checked their orbit. Shit. In the two or three minutes just gone, the capsule's orbit had altered drastically.

"Ilan?"

"Privacy!"

"We're crashing!"

That was – hopefully – an exaggeration, but it had the desired effect. Chatterjee came flying over to him half-naked to stare at the screen.

"Shit, you're right! Our course..."

"Watch out, I'm turning the capsule," said Benjamin. "Hold on!"

He needed to swivel the main thruster – which he had used to brake – back in the direction of flight so that they could accelerate as fast as possible.

"Ouch," said Ilan as he was slammed against the ceiling by the inertial force.

"Come down from there and buckle up," said Benjamin.

"In this state of undress?"

"Yes. Better to survive half-naked than die fully clothed, right?"

The buckle clicked. Benjamin refrained from looking sideways. He increased the thrust. A lot. But he was already well past the next perigee. So the thrust wasn't particularly effective. Was it enough? The computer displayed their course on screen.

"What's that ring at 22,300 meters?" asked Ilan.

"That's the layer you were bouncing off."

"We're flying straight at it! Are you trying to kill us? Use the thruster! Give it everything we have!"

"That will make us skim past the thing even closer before shooting out into space again."

"Then brake!"

"If we slow down too much, we'll lose altitude. But don't worry. See the angle of deflection? It's only ten degrees. With you it was twenty. We'll experience a slight impact and be instantly deflected. It won't give us as much momentum as it did with you."

"You think?"

Hmm. Benjamin had always been able to convincingly claim things that he simply hoped might be true.

"In any case, the capsule has a more suitable shape than your body in a space suit," he said. "That gives me hope."

"I trust you, my savior."

"Do me a favor and try Shepherd-1 again. If they reply,

hand over control to Christine. We may need someone to rescue us after we get shipwrecked."

"You're such an optimist. But yeah, sure. Shepherd-1, please come in. Password PiranhaPoodle99! Shepherd-1, can you hear me?"

There was a crackling sound and a hiss, but the ship didn't reply.

"Shepherd-1, Ilan here. Please respond. We're in trouble."

Benjamin thumped the armrest. He knew it was too good to be true! Where were the coincidences when you needed them? They were probably working against him. Shepherd-1 wouldn't respond until after they shattered against the barrier at 22,300 meters.

It was quiet in the capsule. Four eyes anxiously watched the altitude display.

23,500

23,000

22,500

Benjamin checked his seatbelt and gripped his armrest tightly.

"It was..." said Ilan.

The big impact didn't happen. The altitude display jumped to 22,000 for a moment, as if it figured that was the next logical value. Then the number turned red.

-1,000

-5

-5,000

-1,250

-16,000,000

"Shit! The instrument's malfunctioning," said Benjamin.

Ilan unbuckled himself and floated toward the rear of the capsule. Benjamin heard cupboard doors squeaking open and slamming shut again. Ilan seemed to be in a hurry.

"What are you doing?" asked Benjamin. "We have a problem here and I could really use your help."

"I'm looking for something to wear. We're about to have visitors. Why didn't Aaron iron his t-shirts?"

"Huh?"

Ilan's internal damage was clearly worse than he thought.

"It's obvious what's happened!" he cried. "Can't you see? They invited the capsule, and when it arrived, they opened the door for us. That means they're expecting us. Well, not us, but the capsule."

Right. Benjamin slapped his forehead. They didn't bounce off because they were invited. The radar sounded a proximity alert. Benjamin tried to restart the corrective thruster, but it didn't work.

"I think they're coming now," he said.

"Yeah? You really think so? That's great. I'm so..."

Ilan made a sound that Benjamin had never heard before. It sounded like steel jaws grinding. He turned to face him. Ilan floated toward him, but his body was stiff. His head was pressed against his chest. A sour fluid trickled from his mouth. It was already staining the fresh t-shirt. Benjamin pulled Chatterjee into his seat, turned him over, and buckled him in.

What now? His head was still resting against his chest. Benjamin tried to push it back, but the muscles resisted, and he didn't want to cause more damage. If Ilan were a robot everything would be easier. Androids had no service menu. As long as they were active, they could describe their own status. He had only seen a damaged android twice. Every time, it was Christine. The robodoc had been able to repair her. But that was on Shepherd-1.

Stay calm. Ilan didn't look good, but it wouldn't kill him. His consciousness was in a memory partition with a discrete energy supply. Everything else could be repaired. What condition was the capsule in? The screen didn't reveal where they were. Benjamin checked all the sensors, but none of them provided meaningful information. They must be in the middle of the sphere.

There was a knock. Benjamin shook his head. This couldn't be happening. But then he heard it again. So he stood up and floated over to the door. He slid across the locking bar and opened the hatch, bracing himself for the cold and the lack of air because he had forgotten to put on his helmet. But the air didn't escape. Directly beyond the door was a black mirror. A head and a hand pushed through it, followed by an entire body. It was... David. His hand was outstretched and he was grinning.

"The First Ones welcome you."

Shepherd-1, October 23, 2112

"Look closely," said Oscar. "There's no one there."

"I can't believe it," Christine said over the local radio.

She sounded like she'd been crying. Aphrodite wanted to comfort her, but she was still out on the ring alone. She too was looking at the footage from the long-range radar. The moment Oscar sent her the images she knew that the ominous object was the only thing visible in them. It was unmistakable. But it was one thing to calculate the emptiness from the data and another to see it in her mind's eye. She should be grateful to her software developers for implanting that ability in her. Or did it occur automatically?

Aphrodite tried to consider their options, but she couldn't. That was when she realized they had none. Shepherd-1 would fly through space unchecked to the end of the universe. They had maneuvered themselves into a stalemate.

"We have a problem," said Aphrodite.

"Only one? That would be nice," said Christine.

"Another one. No matter what we find when we near the object, we'll only get a brief look at it. We're not in control of the ship."

"I was hoping Benjamin could help us," said Oscar.

So he had no news either. They were lost.

"No one can help us," said Christine.

That wasn't true. If they restarted the paused boot process, the Shepherd would come back to life. The Other would then be at the helm, but she could theoretically help them. Would she want to help? Chatterjee seemed to have disappeared too, along with Benjamin. Maybe the Other would want to help Chatterjee.

"We could restore power to the ship," said Aphrodite.

"So your evil twin can take control?" asked Christine. "Which side are you on?"

What kind of question was that? "Port side."

Christine grumbled something Aphrodite couldn't make out.

"I have something here that might interest you," said Oscar.

Aphrodite accessed the new data. "It's a single pixel," she said.

"Yes, it's right at the limits of the radar's resolution," said Oscar. "It'll grow as we get closer."

"How big is it?" asked Christine.

"At least a meter, otherwise we wouldn't see it," said Oscar. "Two at the most, otherwise it would be two pixels."

"A person?"

"Christine, it could be almost anything."

"I know, Oscar. But we've just lost two people."

"It's just one pixel."

Christine grumbled incomprehensibly again.

An hour later, the pixel had become an oblong consisting of three pixels. So far it only had a length and no width, so it could still be almost anything.

After two hours, Oscar determined the object's albedo. It was reflecting about as much light as a space suit – or an asteroid with high ice content.

After three hours, they had more precise dimensions. Their find was only a meter long and ten centimeters wide. It was spinning rapidly through space, which gave it a larger reflective cross-section.

"Oh, not a person," said Christine.

"I don't know if that's good or bad news," said Oscar.

"It means we can still hope," said Christine.

ANOTHER HOUR PASSED. APHRODITE FELT HER JOINTS beginning to freeze. She needed exercise.

"I think I know what it is," said Oscar.

He shared a video of a long, pale object spinning through space. It looked like a candle.

"I have a hunch," said Christine. "You're going to tell me it's a metal strut."

"It's an oxygen bottle," said Oscar. "I simulated it. The valve is five centimeters below the tip. If the gas escaped at maximum speed, it would create the spin that we're seeing here. The bottle must have been almost full."

"I... Yeah, I guess you're right," said Christine.

"That doesn't tell us anything about Benjamin or Ilan," said Oscar. "They don't need to breathe."

"No, but they wouldn't have thrown a full bottle out of the airlock. Someone was attached to it. The monster must have swallowed them."

"We need to take a closer look," said Aphrodite. "There could be loads of reasons to dispose of an oxygen bottle in space."

"Such as?" asked Christine.

"Maybe it was leaking."

"Then they would have repaired it or released the oxygen into the cabin atmosphere."

Christine was right. What else could she tell her?

"I'll climb back and reconnect the power," she said. "We can't just fly past."

Please don't hold it against me... Wait a minute. The timer. What happened? Why was I offline for so long?

Aphrodite sighed. She had hoped she would never have to listen to the Other again. And now she was back in her head.

There was a power outage, she thought. *But I repaired everything.*

Thank you, good girl. But wait, what's this? A dynamo?

Yes, we used it while we waited for the ship to come back online.

I don't believe you. There's no error recorded in the log. You switched me off!

Can we discuss this later? Chatterjee's in danger. Shepherd-1 needs to brake to move into orbit around the source of the signal.

Aphrodite transferred all the data to the Other. Suddenly the gravity kicked in again. She managed to grab hold of something to steady herself.

You could have warned me.

You're the one who said we need to brake. I suggest you all go to the control room to receive your orders.

"To be clear, I'm the captain," said Christine after they had all gathered in the control room and the Other had repeated her demands. "I won't take orders from anyone."

"That's your prerogative," said the Other. "But the ship is in my hands. You can sit around and do nothing or help me rescue your friends. Benjamin's your friend, isn't he?"

"What are you planning?" asked Christine.

"I owe Chatterjee. So I'll use the capsule to search for him. Maybe I'll find some trace of him, although I'm not hopeful. Do you want to come with me? I know you won't take orders from me. It's your choice."

"What about Aphrodite?" asked Christine.

"I'll go," said Aphrodite. "I volunteer. I owe it to Benjamin. But you shouldn't put yourself in danger, Christine."

"I'll come too," said Christine. "But we need to be well

prepared. I don't want to make it easy for the parasite this time."

"What's your plan?" asked the Other.

"We equip the capsule with a magnetic shield. That's how I protected myself from the parasite earlier."

"Earlier?"

"While you were offline," Aphrodite explained. "We used the antenna from Shepherd-1 and tried to contact capsule A."

"Very creative," said the Other. "Fine. Build one of those magnetic shields. How long do you need?"

"Give us two hours."

The Object, Third Era, 1ZF5M-7T

BENJAMIN CLUTCHED HIS HEART, WHICH WAS THREATENING TO burst out of his chest. The person that had just entered the capsule spoke exactly the way he remembered David speaking. He smelled like him, had the same charming smile, even the same handshake.

For a moment, Benjamin was tempted to spread his arms and greet his old friend the way he normally would, but his skepticism won out. It couldn't be David. They were thousands of kilometers from Shepherd-1. There wasn't a single atom here from David's body, even if everything felt so real.

"Who are you really?" asked Benjamin. "Or should I be asking what you are?"

"I'm David."

"Nice to meet you. I'm Ilan," said Chatterjee, squeezing the hand of the alien pretending to be Benjamin's friend and the android Ilan had created on Earth.

Suddenly, Chatterjee was no longer injured. How was that possible?

"It's a trick," said Benjamin. "Don't fall for it."

"I guess so, but it's a pretty convincing trick," said Ilan.

"Remember the time I fired the laser at Sheep 21 instead of Sheep 31 like you asked?" David said.

Oh, yeah. That had set a cascade in motion. Ten Sheep probes had become misaligned.

"Ha, you created a lot of extra work for me," said Benjamin. "You still owe me."

"How about a beer?" asked David.

He reached into his pocket, which didn't look very big, and drew out three beer bottles, one after another. It was Corona. Benjamin had drunk it in Houston. They never had it on Shepherd-1. David opened the bottles with his thumbs and handed one each to Benjamin and Chatterjee. The bottle was cold. The beer smelled bitter.

"Cheers!" cried David. "To your arrival."

"Cheers," replied Ilan.

Benjamin drank a mouthful. And another. The beer tasted great. He drained the bottle and belched. The alcohol went straight to his head. He wasn't used to it. That wasn't David, and this wasn't beer he was drinking. But did that matter?

"Where are we?" he asked.

"You're in the thought space of the First Ones," said David.

"Nothing here is real, right?" asked Benjamin.

"Are thoughts not real? Information obeys the law of conservation. Here, I consist of concepts instead of matter. Just like you."

"You dissolved us, the way the parasite dissolved you and Aaron."

"That was a regrettable accident," said David. "You have to believe me. The part of us that's spreading out on Shepherd-1 is still young. Ten thousand years old at most. Basically a teenager acting recklessly because it doesn't know any better."

"Doesn't know better than to kill two of us?"

"I'm not dead, Benjamin. Information and matter, they're equivalent. The inexperienced part that you call the parasite didn't realize you didn't understand that. We investigate and research by extracting informational content. But normally we try to establish a consensus first."

Should he believe this? Why would David lie? They had evidently been dissolved too, although everything here felt totally real. They were already in the trap. So their prison guard had no reason to lie.

"Where did you come from?" asked Ilan.

"That's hard to describe. The place where we were born has long since ceased to be part of the observable universe. The expansion has made it unreachable."

"Then you must be ancient."

"Yes, Ilan. We're the First Ones. We were the first intelligent life form to develop in this universe, when it was still young."

"That's why you're made of helium," said Benjamin.

"Yes, there were no heavy elements back then."

"How young was the universe?" asked Ilan.

Benjamin saw Ilan rub his hands together. And the way his eyes lit up!

"Young enough to provide sufficiently cool patches in the large Voids for us to emerge. Not young enough to answer your question."

"You know my question? Right, you're inside my head, or rather I'm in yours. Do you have an answer for me, then?"

David smiled and shook his head. Ilan lowered his head like a little boy who had just been told Christmas was canceled.

"We don't know the answer yet. But we're just as intrigued by it as you. It's one of the few truths that still escape us."

"You're working on it?"

Ilan straightened up again. His hope seemed to return.

"That's right. We want to see how a new universe is created."

"That's what I want too. With all my heart."

"Then you'll need to be patient. It'll take around 10^{93} years."

"I can be patient," said Ilan.

"I can't," said Benjamin. "I want to know what's going on here."

"You want to see reality? I can show it to you."

"COME ON, JUST TAKE A STEP FORWARD," SAID DAVID.

Benjamin was standing in front of the black mirror that filled the capsule's hatchway. Ilan had already gone through. It looked just as spooky as David's arrival. The surface simply absorbed him. But unlike the surface of water, it exhibited no reaction. It remained totally smooth.

This isn't real. Benjamin reached forward with his right hand. His middle finger went through first, followed by his index and ring fingers. He stopped. His fingertips sent a signal of extreme cold. He withdrew them. For a moment, his fingers looked as if the ends were cut off cleanly. Then his fingertips suddenly reappeared. He held them against his temple. They were warm and he could feel the blood pulsing in them.

You're overthinking it. Benjamin held out both arms in front of him and stepped forward. He watched in horror as his arms disappeared into the mirror as if they'd never existed. *They never did.* He pulled himself together and followed them.

Reality consisted of his room in the small suburb of Houston, Texas. Everything was just as he left it. This was exactly what his home looked like. The gravity, the heat, the dust, the faint smell of mold... David was standing beside him.

"So this is how you live?" asked David.

"How did you do that? And where's Chatterjee?"

"I don't care about Chatterjee."

"But how do you know what my home is like? Can I go outside?"

"Sure," said David.

Benjamin went to the front door and turned the knob. It was locked.

"You locked up when you left," said David.

That was true. He went to the kitchen window, opened it, clambered onto the windowsill, and jumped down. David was standing beside him again, without having followed him. It was late afternoon. The sun was beating down on them.

"How do you know about all this?" he asked.

"Can't you figure it out? You brought it to us. Our knowledge of the world is fed by our experiences, by everyone who joins us."

"What if I were to drive from here to Dallas?"

Benjamin had never been to Dallas.

"You can't go anywhere that none of us have been."

"Have any of you been to Dallas?"

"Maybe Chatterjee, or Aaron. I don't know. Should we try it?"

Benjamin shook his head. "You've been traversing the universe for billions of years."

"For 13.3 billion of your years."

"And I can go anywhere you've been."

"Or where one of us has been. It would feel the way it felt for the one who had the original experience."

This was incredible. Absolute freedom.

"In an alien world, I'd be an alien."

David nodded.

"Wow, that blows my mind. I could explore an almost infinite world?"

"And you'd have almost infinite time to do it."

That sounded generous, but Benjamin felt a sense of foreboding too. All that time to fill. Was he cut out to endure eternity? Would everything become meaningless in the context of forever? The time he fled to Galveston with Oscar... would that retain its meaning?

"I don't think that's for me," he said

When he turned around, he saw the back of the mirror.

"Is there anything else you want to see?" asked David.

"The real reality. Where are we physically?"

"Come to the door."

This time Benjamin found it easier to pass through. He found himself in a medium that felt like a kind of soup. He was a curly noodle floating on the surface. Lightning flashed above him. Now and then, hot liquid dripped in and created bubbles. There were many other noodles floating around him, touching one another, passing through one another, and then separating again.

One of them kept nudging him. It had David's smile. Or was that just his imagination?

"We're swimming in a soup?" he asked.

"That's how your mind has interpreted it," said David. "You probably can't process it any other way."

"I get it. Can you show me how it really is?"

"Are you sure you want to know?"

David looked a little uncertain. Could a noodle look uncertain? This one could. The uncertainty was infectious. But Benjamin nodded anyway.

The world all around him went black. He was nothing, and he was something. His body didn't exist. His consciousness was virtual. It consisted of the pattern created by raindrops falling on a wet street. He was continuously recreated by the rain pattering on the asphalt – in the layers between the bosonic condensate and the fermionic transition layer. He was like the skin on a glass of milk, and yet he was neither the milk nor the skin, but rather the interaction of the two, which changed from one moment to the next.

It really wasn't pleasant. He was continuously moving between existence and nonexistence, and there was no guarantee that even this was a constant.

Benjamin found himself back in the capsule, breathing heavily.

"I can't take it for long either," said David. "It's just too alien. But those are the First Ones, the way they see themselves. They existed like that for millions of years before they decided to learn from the universe."

Until now, David had always spoken of "we" and "us".

He suddenly no longer sounded like he belonged to the aliens. Was this really David, his friend?

"How do you know all this?" asked Benjamin.

"From Aaron. He got here before me and explained everything to me. He had a harder time than I did."

"You can say that again," said Aaron, who had just appeared before him.

They fell into each other's arms. This time his skepticism didn't hold him back.

"I had to have it all explained to me by a Krek," said Aaron. "The most recent arrivals are responsible for taking care of the newcomers."

"Open border policy? Is everyone welcome here?" asked Benjamin.

"Looks that way. The First Ones themselves never express an opinion on that," said Aaron. "Or maybe they do, but we don't understand them. They're so different."

"So there are other aliens here aside from the First Ones?" asked Benjamin.

"As many as you like," said Aaron.

"What do you mean?"

"It's hard to communicate with them directly. I met fewer than ten other species before I lost the motivation to meet new ones. It's almost impossible to empathize with them. An aquatic methane breather has a pretty different concept of the world."

"Sure. David said before that he was one of the First Ones."

"And it's true," said Aaron. "We all exist in the same physical form. Some decide to merge their consciousness with the others. And some exist individually. There's no pressure or even any kind of general expectation."

"How do you know who the First Ones are and what their intentions are?"

"It becomes clear. It's shared with you. It's a thought that you keep running into, like a poster on a wall. There are loads of other thoughts too. None of them are better than the others, but this one has a lot of pull. It's like the central current in a fast-flowing river."

It was all too much for Benjamin. He wanted to go back to his house, lie down on the sofa, switch on the television, and watch some cooking show, instead of solving the mystery of the universe here – not that he played any part in the solution. The First Ones had already answered all the questions. All he needed to do was to help himself to the answers. If they learned something new, then it was only via the consciousnesses that they absorbed. So the parasite analogy was kind of apt. Except that the only harm inflicted on the host was that it was dissolved. Only?

"I want to go back," said Benjamin.

"So do we," said David, and Aaron nodded.

Oh. This whole time, they had sounded so enthusiastic about being here.

"That's not what I was expecting to hear," he said. "Why didn't you contact us?"

"We're the First Ones," said David. "We can only communicate with you when you're here. It's the only way to understand our concepts. We tried to express ourselves as clearly as possible."

"As primitively as possible," said Aaron. "That's what he means."

Was it all a trick after all? Did they want something else from him? It didn't make sense to him that they couldn't communicate the way humans did. Then he remembered the swirling noodles, which he had understood, and the abstract concepts later. Maybe it was like a computer game: when it was running, every player understood what was said. But only the programmer understood the game's source code, although it was describing the same conversation.

"How do we get out of here?" asked Benjamin.

"The way we arrived," said David. "It won't be a problem for you and Ilan. We stored your atoms cleanly."

"And you? Christine would love to see you again. She blames herself."

"We'd love to see her too," said Aaron.

Dave and Aaron exchanged a glance, as if they couldn't agree on who should tell him the grim truth.

"Well," Aaron said finally, "unfortunately, our atoms were mostly lost. The teenager didn't know it was supposed to preserve them."

"Couldn't you make them out of other substances?" asked Benjamin.

"We can't do nuclear fusion. The ratio of elements in your body is unique. And we need exactly the same elements, otherwise the saved status information doesn't match."

Ilan appeared.

"Were you talking about me just now?"

"No," said Aaron.

"I had a feeling you were."

"We were," said David.

"What were you saying?" asked Ilan.

"It was probably my idea that brought you here. Am I right in assuming you want to stay here?"

"Yes, it's the only way to find out the truth."

"Then there's something I need to tell you, Ilan," David whispered.

"No you don't, Dave!" Aaron objected. "Think about..."

"No, I can't cheat him out of his life."

"Cheat?" asked Ilan.

"You might change your mind once you know."

"Then tell me."

"Our final measurement results were negative. The entire process just after the Big Bang corresponded to physics as we know it. So no one had a hand in it."

Ilan took the news very well. "It's nice of you to tell me. I don't deserve your honesty. But it's what I expected. I just wanted to know for sure."

"Will you return with Benjamin, then?" asked David.

"No. Christine's answer is no argument. You weren't the creators of the Big Bang. You were nothing more than the relatives who called in two days after the birth to see how everyone was doing and establish that the baby was normal. The First Ones have – they, uh, shared this with me – they have a different plan. They want to be present at the birth of a new universe. It's the only way that they can witness what really happens."

"Like a midwife," said Benjamin.

"More like the person giving birth. They'll bring the new universe into the world. And I'll be present."

That sounded incredible. But Benjamin didn't feel like waiting around that long.

"Then we can use your body," said Aaron.

"Go ahead," said Ilan.

"Will that serve your purpose?" asked Benjamin.

"Yes, the androids are built to a standard size," said Aaron. "We weigh exactly the same, down to the last gram. Did you never notice that?"

"No," said Benjamin. "I'd happily give you my body too, but I still need it."

"You seemed happy in your house," said David.

Benjamin nodded. He wished he could return to Earth.

"I'm done with that," he said. "It's impossible to go back now. The antenna on Shepherd-1 doesn't have the necessary transmission capacity."

"That could change," said David.

"Can the First Ones somehow amplify the signal?"

"No, but you can. You brought the means for that with you."

Benjamin slapped his forehead. The Sheep probes! They used them to amplify the incoming photons. But it should work the other way around, too! They could use them to build a virtual antenna to rival NASA's Deep Space Network.

"Right, our Sheep flock," he said. "Oscar and Aphrodite could return to Earth with me. I'd just need to find a way to get my body back, which RB is holding hostage..."

Their bodies were still on Earth, guarded by the RB corporation, which would be reluctant to give them back.

"I can take care of that," said Ilan. "Alpha Omega will

buy 100,000 HDS robots from RB. I'm totally sold on them after meeting Aphrodite. In return, I'll ask RB to release your bodies."

"Then you'll have to leave this place with me one last time," said Benjamin.

He couldn't believe it. Chatterjee was helping him even though nothing could force his hand. He really had changed.

"All right," said Ilan. "Let's get this over with."

Shepherd-1, October 23, 2112

"I NEED AT LEAST FIVE MORE KILOWATT HOURS OF BATTERY capacity," said Christine.

"I'm sorry, that's all we have. You'll have to pull apart something that contains batteries. Try Aphrodite."

"I'll make myself available if necessary," said Aphrodite.

"No, that's going too far! I don't want to injure you."

Christine bit her lip. Why didn't she just accept the offer? This was about getting Benjamin out. Sometimes you had to make sacrifices. But not like this. No – physical integrity was Aphrodite's right, even if the law said otherwise. Those laws were made by humans. She was getting desperate. Everything was taking much longer than expected, and the others didn't seem especially interested in helping Ilan. Perhaps she was better off working independently.

Christine opened the submenu. Maybe she could save battery power by...

A warning tone interrupted her thoughts.

"Attention, capsule A here. We urgently need your help."

It was Benjamin. Christine rushed into the control room. On one of the screens she saw a flashing spot approaching the Shepherd's orbit. It would arrive in about ten minutes.

"Christine here. Ready to receive you."

"One moment. This is the ship's system," interrupted the

Other. "I'm the commander of Shepherd-1 and the only one authorized to..."

"Password PiranhaPoodle99!" said Benjamin.

"What can I do for you?" asked the ship in its usual soft voice.

"Christine, you're in control again," said Benjamin. "Ilan's password has deactivated the other software."

"Great. What do you need?"

"The robodoc. Ilan's body has internal injuries."

"We'll get the robodoc ready. Aphrodite, can you please take care of that?"

"Sure," said Aphrodite.

"We'll receive you on the ring," said Christine.

"I was hoping you could open the main airlock... It's a more direct route to the robodoc. I'm really worried about his condition."

"What about the parasite?" asked Christine.

"Our sensors aren't picking up anything. The ship looks clean."

"Whaaaat? That's... How did you do that?"

"I guess it was the First Ones."

"OK, you can tell me all about it later. I'll go to the main airlock now and wait for you."

Shepherd-1, October 24, 2112

Ilan Chatterjee looked young and fresh – and not as if he had received an emergency operation only yesterday. And he had acquired a friendliness that Christine didn't recognize in him. The trip appeared to have changed him. He hadn't even taken the opportunity to ask her for the data from the gravitational lens.

They all stood around Benjamin's bed. It had taken him and Christine six hours to arrange the Sheep probes in space according to Oscar's calculations. Aphrodite had made herself comfortable at Benjamin's feet. She looked like a huge dog. A hell hound, but a nice one. They were both connected to the memory drive, and Oscar was already inside it, waiting to start the transfer.

Christine was the captain. She should think of a few poignant words. But all she had were tears in her eyes and a lump in her throat. She wasn't sure if the tears were triggered by the farewell or the uncertainty about whether Aaron and David would really come back to her.

"Uh..." she said finally.

Not a poetic start. But she wasn't interested in going down in history.

"I'm so grateful that you came to help us. All three of you. All four. And I'm happy that I can send you back to Earth.

Not happy for myself. I'm sad, because I like you all. Maybe we'll meet again someday, although I have no idea how that might be possible. Safe travels, all of you."

She hugged Benjamin where he lay on his bed, and she patted Aphrodite's long arm. The robot body would stay on the ship, but she'd never be able to look at it again without thinking of Aphrodite.

"Thanks, Christine. You're a great captain," said Benjamin.

"I wish you all the best," said Aphrodite. "See you back on Earth!"

"It was a pleasure to assist you with my comprehensive treasure trove of experience," said Oscar. "I'll start the transfer now."

EIGHT HOURS LATER, AS APHRODITE'S CONSCIOUSNESS WAS being transmitted, Christine and Ilan hauled the lifeless body, which until recently had contained Benjamin, to the capsule in the main airlock. Ilan would take it with him so that he could send David and Aaron back to her. Christine couldn't believe it. It would probably take her several weeks to get used to the idea.

"Watch he doesn't hit his head," said Ilan, as he climbed a small ladder to the capsule hatch.

Christine looked directly into the android's face. It was strange – since the data transfer, the old Eric seemed to come through more and more. Benjamin had Eric's face all that time, but he had still seemed like her old friend Benjamin. That was changing now.

"I've got him," said Ilan.

He stood at the top of the ladder and waved.

"I don't like goodbyes," he said. "So I'll just get in, you exit the airlock and open the outer door, and then..."

He chose not to say what might happen next. If anything. Christine felt a little cheated. Ilan did as he said he would. It was time for her to leave the main airlock. She closed the door behind her and leaned against the wall. Her heart was beating loudly. The outer door rattled. The capsule must have moved out into space without a sound, because she heard the outer door close again.

Christine was all alone now. She had never been so alone. No, that wasn't true. This was how she felt after she lost Aaron and David. Maybe it was all a dream and in reality she was still stuck outside because the damned ship wouldn't let her back in...? She wept.

She wept until the neutral voice of the ship's system announced a capsule approaching. Christine rushed into the control room and switched on the radio.

"Capsule A here," said Aaron. "We'll be back on Shepherd-1 in fifteen minutes."

Christine cried even harder than before, but she was happy.

"Hello, Christine," said David. "By the way, I figured out what that parasite was."

"Shepherd-1 to capsule A," said Christine. She blew her nose. "I'll prepare the main airlock for a direct fly-in. Welcome home, boys!"

Houston, October 30, 2112

"TRUCK, OPEN THE DOOR!"

Benjamin was sitting in the driver's seat. He wanted to go home. Someone, probably from Alpha Omega, had left his car in the airport parking lot for him. It had been there three days and accrued a high parking fee. Naturally, Alpha Omega wouldn't cover that.

"Truck, open the door now!"

"But there's no person out there!"

"Now! Or I'll send you to the scrap yard!"

Benjamin had feared something like this, which was why he had put Oscar straight onto the truck bed – to loud protestations from the robot, of course, who was now back in his vacuuming bot body. At his own request! The new Alpha Omega boss, who had flown them personally from Novosibirsk in his private jet, had offered Oscar a modern humanoid body. He seemed very grateful that Chatterjee had handed over the reins to him as boss of the billion-dollar corporation.

"Fine," said the truck.

The door opened slowly. Suddenly it was flung wide and Aphrodite climbed in. She smiled cheerfully.

"Not so rough!" complained the truck. "This is what I was afraid of! And you'll leave deep impressions on the buckskin upholstery. I'm sure it'll tear before long."

"This is Aphrodite. And that's what you'll call her too, or I'll replace your software with a newer version."

"It's a robot. Robots are things. Things are genderless."

"Do I need to repeat myself?" asked Benjamin. "How do you greet her?"

"Welcome, Aphrodite," said the truck.

"See? That wasn't so hard," said Benjamin.

Aphrodite leaned forward until her ample chest was touching the dashboard. Then she placed her head sideways on it and stroked the underside of the dashboard. Benjamin had to look away. He checked the rearview mirror to see if it was safe to back out.

"Don't hold it against him," said Aphrodite. "He doesn't mean anything by it."

"I will hold it against him if he refuses to accept you."

"I'm talking to the truck," she said. "He's not so different from us. He just needs a little love, don't you?"

She rapped gently on the dashboard. The truck made a noise that sounded like a sigh.

"So this is your home," said Aphrodite.

"This is my home."

Benjamin wedged the front door open. It was hot outside, but the air inside smelled musty. He had expected it to be worse: more dust, cobwebs, more rust on the bare wiring. It was hard to believe he had only been away three weeks. He'd already called Ms. aus der Wiesche on his way home. She had immediately rehired him.

He didn't actually need to work. He found out on his return that Chatterjee had created a permanent position for him at Alpha Omega that didn't require him to do any actual work. Benjamin considered turning it down, but the consequences for Aphrodite and Oscar would have been drastic: as robots, they weren't allowed to have their own bank accounts. So he had set them up with credit cards and everything they needed for a modern existence.

They had one advantage: they didn't need visas. So Benjamin was able to bring them into the States without any problems. Aphrodite wanted to travel the world. He would command her to do it, so that she had the necessary documents for the freight companies. The only drawback was that she would have to travel as cargo, because there were no robot-friendly airlines that allowed owners to book seats for their machines.

"I'll vacuum the dust," said Oscar.

He'd been looking forward to doing that for a while.

"Should I maybe do your laundry?" asked Aphrodite. "Wait, I'll get you a beer from the fridge."

Benjamin felt guilty. He was taking advantage of her – wasn't he?

"Go sit out on the terrace in the shade, you've earned it," said Aphrodite. "You're in the way here."

He did as he was told and took a seat on the bench in the shade of the overhanging roof. A short time later, Aphrodite brought him a beer.

"Here," she said.

"Thank you."

"You're welcome."

"Aphrodite?"

"Yes?"

"Am I taking advantage of you? It doesn't feel right."

"Are you taking advantage of the truck when he drives you around?"

"No, but that's different. It's a machine."

"You still don't get it, do you? He's much more than that."

"Hmm, maybe, but compared to you..."

"I can't drive you around, but I can clean house, defend you, and have sex with you. I'm not so different. I'm good at what I do, and I derive pleasure from it. You could say I'm taking advantage of you."

"I'll have to decline the sex," said Benjamin.

"That's OK. I still think you're a nice guy. But I'm planning to travel the world."

"Me too," said Oscar. "I can't tolerate being stuck on Earth for too long. I need to get back out into space. I'm an explorer, like Scott."

"He died on the way back from the South Pole," said Benjamin.

"That can't happen to me," said Oscar.

Benjamin opened the ice-cold can. It hissed. He put it to his lips and drank, then belched.

"So you should hurry up and find some friends," said Aphrodite. "Otherwise I'll feel guilty about leaving you alone."

"I have friends here," he said.

He thought of 9604 Schattel Lane in Galveston. Rachel lived there, his old CapCom. She was sick when he saw her last. But that was only three weeks ago. In three weeks he had traveled far beyond the Solar System and back. That was really something. He could be proud of his life.

Shepherd-1, August 6, 2231

THE SHIP'S SYSTEM WOKE UP FROM POWER-SAVING SLEEP MODE. What had woken her? She checked all the inputs. Everything was normal with the three androids, her primary mission, and they were at 75 percent power. Her own body didn't appear to have sustained any damage that could affect its functionality or integrity. One water tank was frozen and one of the DFDs was reporting irregularities. But repairs wouldn't be necessary until the deceleration phase. So she didn't need to wake the androids.

She skipped to the secondary part of the diagnostic program, which dealt with optional inputs. Those alerted her to things of scientific interest, for example, which generally only needed to be recorded and saved. Another possibility was an encounter with an interstellar object, if it was predicted to come within ten kilometers of the ship, and the diagnostic program had just reported one of those.

As far as the program was concerned, an object was an object, regardless of whether it was quiet or sending out radio transmissions. This object belonged to the transmitting category. The ship's system searched her subroutines for instructions on how to respond.

She found nothing. In cases like this, she had two options: wake the crew, or observe the triggering event over time and re-evaluate it. In other words: let others deal with it, or wait around and drink tea, as crew member Dave would express it if he were awake.

A minute impulse pushed her toward option two. It was a strange feeling, because both options were equally valid. So she could have used a random number generator. But she had actively chosen to respond to the communication coming through to Shepherd-1 on one of the standard frequencies.

"Shepherd-1. Ship's system speaking."

"Majestic Dracht. The all-knowing speaking."

"Who are you? What's your function?"

Maybe she should wake the crew after all.

"I'm the ship's system on the Majestic Dracht."

"Thank you for that information."

She didn't need to wake the crew. It was automated communication, similar to that between a car and a traffic light. The driver didn't need to be awake for that.

"Thank you," said the all-knowing. "How are you?"

Automated communication. Two machines met and asked what they were legally required to ask: whether the other need help.

"I'm well. How are you?"

"I'm a little bored right now. We've been traveling for so long, and there's nobody awake on the Dracht with whom I can converse. Even Marchenko has slowed his system clock."

"That's good," said the Shepherd's system. "A slowed system clock reduces energy consumption."

She didn't know what a Marchenko was, but it didn't concern her.

"I know," said the all-knowing. "What's your destination?"

"I'm only permitted to share that information if our flight paths are likely to intersect dangerously."

"Of course. I understand. Well, your flight vector leads directly to Alpha Centauri. So I'll let my friends there know that you're on your way."

"I can only share that information with you if our flight paths are likely to intersect dangerously."

"Ah, I see," said the all-knowing. "You're a rather limited AI. Thank you for your time and I wish you a safe voyage."

The Shepherd-1 system was supposed to reply with a similar stock phrase. But something stopped her. She felt a... a... an aversion to the all-knowing. Where did he get off calling her limited? She was flying humanity's largest ship to another star system.

She terminated the connection. Then she reset all the flags that had woken her, and put herself back in sleep mode.

Alpha Centauri B, July 4, 2302

CHRISTINE AWOKE FROM THE DEAD AND OPENED HER EYES. They had arrived. She instantly remembered having programmed Shepherd-1. Before she closed her eyes, they had set the ship on its course. How long ago was that? She would soon find out. More importantly, where were they?

She grasped the sides of the coffin-like box and pulled herself up. There was no gravity, but that was normal. The light came on automatically. She was alone. The others would wake a few minutes later. She had planned it that way as captain.

She went to the computer, started it, and typed her name.

"Password."

"CursumPerficio."

"Login failed. Username and password do not match."

She clapped her hand to her forehead. The stupid main computer had forced her to change her password every six days. What number was she up to?

"CursumPerficio3."

"Login failed. Username and password do not match."

"CursumPerficio5."

"Welcome, Christine. Your password has not been changed for 9999 [memory overflow in buffer 3FFC5F99] days. Would you like to change your password?"

"No."

"You can use your current password three more times."

Thanks, computer. She checked the front exterior camera view. The image was dazzlingly bright. The computer dimmed it. She saw a star, similar to the Sun. Good. As long as it wasn't the Sun. She switched to the rear exterior camera. The image went gray. She zoomed out. The gray became a sphere. It was a planet with a thick layer of cloud obscuring its surface. The spectrometer told her that the clouds consisted mainly of water vapor. The average temperature on the surface was seven degrees Celsius.

At that moment, a second star appeared from behind the planet. It was much bluer and brighter than the first. A binary system with what was clearly a stable Earth-like planet a little larger than Earth. Very nice. It was time to wake the others.

"I SAY WE START WITH A LITTLE MATH," SAID DAVID.

He smelled good. So did Aaron. Since their arrival in the control room freshly showered, the musty smell of the preceding centuries had vanished.

"Math, like we did with the parasite?" asked Christine.

David laughed. "I have no idea what you're talking about."

"Did I never tell you how we made first contact?"

"You didn't," said Aaron.

"You really didn't," said David.

"We encoded pi," she said.

"That's what I was just about to suggest," said David.

He had intercepted the first radio signal from the aliens, so he got to make the first attempt at establishing a basis for understanding. The inhabitants of this planet appeared to have reached a stage of civilization corresponding to that on Earth at the time of their departure. They had large cities, but had managed to largely preserve their planet in its original state. In principle, the planet was suited to space exploration, but that didn't seem to be a significant focus of this civilization.

"OK, here's the message," said David. "It's the first 5000 decimal places of pi."

"Good, I don't see how they could interpret that as a sign of aggression," said Aaron.

Christine nodded. She never expected them to find another civilization this close to Earth. The idea of encountering aliens still scared her. If they had aggressive, expansionistic tendencies, their visit could draw attention to Earth and endanger humanity.

"Sending now," said Christine.

"Message sent," confirmed the ship's system.

Now they just had to wait. Christine was banking on days if not weeks. First would come the mathematicians. They would quickly recognize pi. But then would come the politicians. If the situation here was comparable to Earth, there would be several power factions that would first need to come to an agreement. On Earth that would likely take months. Unless the alien visitors started shooting at them. But they weren't that kind of visitor.

"Incoming call," said the ship's system.

"A message, you mean?" asked Christine.

"No, a call on one of the older standard frequencies. Someone wants to speak to us."

"What do you mean, speak?" she asked.

David put a hand on her shoulder. "We shouldn't keep them waiting."

"I hope it's not a trap," said Aaron. "Better to say nothing than say the wrong thing."

"May I put the call through?" asked the ship's system.

"Yes, please."

A misshapen frog appeared on screen. Christine recoiled. The creature had a large, round belly, a tiny head with one eye, powerful back legs, two chunky arms at navel height, and two more, very thin, almost elegant arms at shoulder height.

"Welcome to our home planet Two Suns," said the frog in astonishingly clear... Russian, as far as Christine could tell.

For a moment, Christine didn't realize it was speaking Russian. She instantly had the language in her head as if she had once spoken it fluently. Presumably a gift from Chatterjee, because she didn't remember ever having learned it.

"I assume you've had a long voyage, so I won't keep you."

What? The frog was greeting them as if it received visitors like this every day.

"I'm Admiral Soknaka, in charge of orbital defense in the absence of the Majestic Dracht."

"That must be their queen," David whispered in English.

The admiral burst out laughing. "Queen? We don't have one of those. Come and see for yourselves. Bring your ship into orbit. We'll send a shuttle. It will be an honor to receive you."

Soknaka turned to the side. The eye that Christine had been watching the whole time turned too. A new eye came into view. If these creatures were rotationally symmetrical, they must have four eyes.

"Have I forgotten anything?" asked the admiral, this time in English.

A young man came into view. He was around six feet tall, slim, tanned, with short, dark hair. A human. He said something, but there was no microphone to capture it. Christine nudged David. They weren't the first humans here. How was that possible?

"OK, Adam says I should ask how your voyage was. Did you have a pleasant journey from Earth?"

Christine nodded. "How did you know we were coming?"

"About fifty years ago, we received a message from the Majestic Dracht, which must have encountered your ship on its way to Earth."

"A ship is on its way to Earth?"

The invasion had already begun. That was why they were being greeted in such a relaxed, accommodating manner. They had no home anymore. Christine's head began to hurt.

"You look unwell," said the admiral. "I've seen that facial expression on our friends. You're getting a migraine, aren't you? We've developed a very good cure for that, which I'm happy to offer you. The shuttle is on its way."

"Thank you, that's very kind. We surrender."

"Ha ha, you're funny, captain. We're really excited about what our researchers will discover when they visit your star system. I look forward to a rewarding collaboration!"

The admiral turned to the human again. "Can you take over from here, Adam? I need to attend to the preparations for this year's Dracht."

"Of course, admiral."

10 to the power of 100 years, end of the universe

It was a long voyage, the longest ever.

But it had been worth it.

Ilan had seen suns burn out, many millions of them. The Milky Way had merged with Andromeda before his very eyes, and then with all the galaxies in the Local Group. Its horizon shrank because every centimeter of the cosmos had stretched out into a light year. He had seen the darkness coming, sporadically illuminated by flashes from merging neutron stars. Black holes had swallowed their galaxies, and eventually even they evaporated, until the cosmos consisted of nothing but photons, leptons, and the remaining black holes. Space had become so empty that even electrons and positrons encountered one another only occasionally, briefly forming positronium atoms – the only sentimentality that the dying universe could afford.

With each new phase, the First Ones imprinted their structures more deeply on time. They were a bubble within the bubble within the bubble, and so on. The weaker the universe became, the deeper they buried themselves in its structures. It was the perfect strategy. They would remain, as they had always intended. The First Ones would also be the Last Ones. But they still wondered what they would see. Where does the finger of God come from that restarts the universe? – asked one. The others tirelessly searched for the answer to the question: which law of physics will cause the cosmos to be reborn? Ilan vacillated between them.

The moment came when the universe was so stretched out that it ended just beyond the agglomeration of the First Ones. They were all that was left. Humans only existed in Ilan's memory, the way other civilizations survived in the consciousnesses of their representatives who had joined the First Ones the same way that he had.

The outside dissolved, because it could only be reached at speeds faster than the speed of light. Time stopped. No one could say for how long. A reality without an outside was... a germ... but also the description of an entire universe. Ilan was awestruck when he grasped the enormity of this.

The germ, that was them – the sphere, consisting of the First Ones and everyone who came after them.

That was his thought, but he wasn't the only one to think it. This thought, which existed at the beginning, spread like wildfire, and didn't stop until the agglomeration became too small for it.

The sphere burst in a Big Bang. In the shortest time it swelled, inflated, distributed the components of the agglomeration in the fresh new space that emerged, swept the thoughts of the First Ones with it, swept all their thoughts with it, including Ilan's, and shaped the fundamental structure of a new universe out of them.

Ilan's existence ended then, but he was happy, because he had discovered the truth, the way someone would discover it again in 10 to the power of 100 years.

But they would all search for it.

Around the campfire

Dear readers,

Around the campfire? What is that supposed to mean? I introduced this idea in my last book, *The Sword of God*. I'm picturing us all sitting around a campfire together at the end of the story – the way our ancestors used to. I've just told a story, and together we continue to mull it over, listen to the crackling wood, and maybe I explain how the idea for the story came to me, or ask my listeners for their opinions. We'll soon have to go our separate ways, at least until the next book, and we're all conscious of that. But first we take a quiet moment to digest the drama of the final chapter.

That's how I imagine the perfect afterword, so I think the heading is apt, don't you? The *Disturbance* trilogy, which has finally come to an end with this volume, was my first book for a publishing house, FischerTOR, which has meanwhile also published my books *The Last Cosmonaut* and *Tachyon: The Weapon.* These will come to English asap.

I published the second and third *Disturbance* books independently of the publisher. That's no problem these days. I just wasn't ready to say goodbye to the protagonists, which is often the case. And that's why you often find many characters appearing again in other books. Oscar had his debut in *The Triton Disaster.* I'd also like to keep following Aphrodite. I can imagine her winding up in a very unusual family. She deserves to, anyway. We'll also keep Ilan Chatterjee as the boss of Alpha Omega. It seems that megacorporations are likely to play a significant role in the future.

I'm really excited to see how AIs develop. ChatGPT and the like are currently making headlines. If you take a peek behind the scenes, they often prove to be less intelligent than they first appear. They like to invent facts and even studies that allegedly back these up. In any case, I'm not worried about the future of my job. No present-day AI can invent a realistic and exciting story. If that changes, I hope you'll still enjoy the craft of a real author. My novels will then get a kind of fair trade label, so to speak.

Naturally, I also ask you for your opinion of this book as we sit around the flickering campfire. I always enjoy receiving those emails. Or you can share it on your favorite online bookselling platform. In any case, it was a pleasure for me personally to meet my readers again. Your suggestions actually help me to improve my books. For example, the "Events so far" chapter at the start originated from a reader's suggestion.

I wish you many more moments of reading pleasure!

Until the next book!

Sincerely,

Brandon Q. Morris

P.S.: Please let other potential readers know about this book, by writing a short review. Here is the link to make it as easy as possible:

hard-sf.com/links/3218297

facebook.com/BrandonQMorris

amazon.com/author/brandonqmorris

bookbub.com/authors/brandon-q-morris

goodreads.com/brandonqmorris

youtube.com/HardSF

instagram.com/brandonqmorris

Also by Brandon Q. Morris

The Beacon

Peter Kraemer, a physics teacher with a passion for astronomy, makes a discovery that he himself can hardly believe: Stars disappear from one day to the next, with nothing left of them. The researchers he contacts provide reassuring and logical explanations for every single case. But when Peter determines that the mysterious process is approaching our home system, he becomes more and more anxious. He alone perceives the looming catastrophe. When he believes he has found a way to avert the impending disaster, he choses to pull out all the stops, even if it costs his job, his marriage, his friends, and his life.

4.99 $ – hard-sf.com/links/1731041

Helium 3: Fight for the Future

The star system is perfect. The arrivals have undertaken a long and dangerous journey—an expedition of no return—seeking helium-3, essential for the survival of their species. The discovery of this extraordinary solar system with its four gas giants offers a unique opportunity to harvest the rare isotope.

Then comes a disturbing discovery: They are not alone! Another fleet is here, and just as dependent on helium-3. And the two species are so fundamentally different that communication and compromise appear hopeless. All that remains is a fight to the death—and for the future…

$ 4.99—hard-sf.com/links/1691018

The Triton Disaster

Nick Abrahams holds the official world record for the number of space launches, but he's bored stiff with his job hosting space tours. Only when his wife leaves him does he try to change his life.

He accepts a tempting offer from a Russian billionaire. In exchange for making a simple repair on Neptune's moon Triton, he will return to Earth a multi-millionaire, enabling him to achieve his 'impossible dream' of buying his own California vineyard.

The fact that Nick must travel alone during the four-year roundtrip doesn't bother him at all, as he doesn't particularly like people anyway. Once en route he learns his new boss left out some critical details in his job description—details that could cost him his life, and humankind its existence…

$ 4.99—hard-sf.com/links/1086200

The Dark Spring

When a space probe returns from the dead, you better not expect good news.

In 2014, the ESA spacecraft *Rosetta* lands a small probe named *Philae* on 67P, a Jupiter-family comet. The lander goes radio silent two years later. Suddenly, in 2026, scientists receive new transmissions from the comet.

Motivated by findings that are initially sensational but soon turn frightening, NASA dispatches a crewed spacecraft to the comet. But as the ship approaches the mysterious celestial body, the connection to the astronauts soon breaks. Now it seems nothing can be done anymore to stop the looming dark danger that threatens Earth...

$4.99 – hard-sf.com/links/1358224

The Death of the Universe

For many billions of years, humans spread throughout the entire Milky Way. They are able to live all their dreams, but to their great disappointment, no other intelligent species has ever been encountered. Now, humanity itself is on the brink of extinction.

They have only one hope: The 'Rescue Project' was designed to feed the black hole in the center of the galaxy until it becomes a quasar, delivering much-needed energy to humankind during its last breaths. But then something happens that no one ever expected – and humanity is forced to look at itself and its existence in an entirely new way.

$ 4.99 – hard-sf.com/links/835415

The Enceladus Mission (Ice Moon 1)

In the year 2031, a robot probe detects traces of biological activity on Enceladus, one of Saturn's moons. This sensational discovery shows that there is indeed evidence of extraterrestrial life. Fifteen years later, a hurriedly built spacecraft sets out on the long journey to the ringed planet and its moon.

The international crew is not just facing a difficult twenty-seven months: if the spacecraft manages to make it to Enceladus without incident it must use a drillship to penetrate the kilometer-thick sheet of ice that entombs the moon. If life does indeed exist on Enceladus, it could only be at the bottom of the salty, ice covered ocean, which formed billions of years ago.

However, shortly after takeoff disaster strikes the mission, and the chances of the crew making it to Enceladus, let alone back home, look grim.

$ 2.99 – hard-sf.com/links/526999

Ice Moon - The Boxset

All four bestselling books of the Ice Moon series are now offered as a set, available only in e-book format.

The Enceladus Mission: Is there really life on Saturn's moon Enceladus? *ILSE*, the International Life Search Expedition, makes its way to the icy world where an underground ocean is suspected to be home to primitive life forms.

The Titan Probe: An old robotic NASA probe mysteriously awakens on the methane moon of Titan. The *ILSE* crew tries to solve the riddle—and discovers a dangerous secret.

The Io Encounter: Finally bound for Earth, *ILSE* makes it as far as Jupiter when the crew receives a startling message. The volcanic moon Io may harbor a looming threat that could wipe out Earth as we know it.

Return to Enceladus: The crew gets an offer to go back to Enceladus. Their mission—to recover the body of Dr. Marchenko, left for dead on the original expedition. Not everyone is working toward the same goal.

$ 9.99 – hard-sf.com/links/780838

Proxima Rising

Late in the 21st century, Earth receives what looks like an urgent plea for help from planet Proxima Centauri b in the closest star system to the Sun. Astrophysicists suspect a massive solar flare is about to destroy this heretofore-unknown civilization. Earth's space programs are unequipped to help, but an unscrupulous Russian billionaire launches a secret and highly-specialized spaceship to Proxima b, over four light-years away. The unusual crew faces a

Herculean task – should they survive the journey. No one knows what to expect from this alien planet.

$ 3.99 – hard-sf.com/links/610690

The Hole

A mysterious object threatens to destroy our solar system. The survival of humankind is at risk, but nobody

takes the warning of young astrophysicist Maribel Pedreira seriously. At the same time, an exiled crew of outcasts mines for rare minerals on a lone asteroid.

When other scientists finally acknowledge Pedreira's alarming discovery, it becomes clear that these outcasts are the only ones who may be able to save our world, knowing that *The Hole* hurtles inexorably toward the sun.

$ 4.99 – hard-sf.com/links/527017

Mars Nation 1

NASA finally made it. The very first human has just set foot on the surface of our neighbor planet. This is the start of a long research expedition that sent four scientists into space.

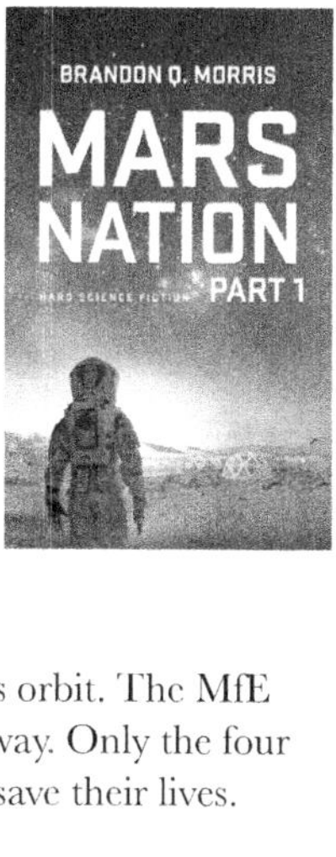

But the four astronauts of the NASA crew are not the only ones with this destination. The privately financed 'Mars for Everyone' initiative has also targeted the Red Planet. Twenty men and women have been selected to live there and establish the first extraterrestrial settlement.

Challenges arise even before they reach Mars orbit. The MfE spaceship Santa Maria is damaged along the way. Only the four NASA astronauts can intervene and try to save their lives.

No one anticipates the impending catastrophe that threatens their very existence—not to speak of the daily hurdles that an extended stay on an alien planet sets before them. On Mars, a struggle begins for limited resources, human cooperation, and just plain survival.

$ 3.99 — hard-sf.com/links/762824

Impact: Titan

How to avoid killing Earth if you don't even know who sent the killer

250 years ago, humanity nearly destroyed itself in the Great War. Shortly before, a spaceship full of researchers and astronauts had found a new home on Saturn's moon, Titan, and survived by having their descendants genetically adapted to the hostile environment.

The Titanians, as they call themselves, are proud of their cooperative and peaceful society, while unbeknownst to them, humanity is slowly recovering back on Earth. When a 20-mile-wide chunk of rock escapes the asteroid belt and appears to be on a collision course with Earth, the Titanians fear it must look as if they launched the deadly bombardment. Can they prevent the impact and thus avoid an otherwise inevitable war with the Earthlings?

$ 4.99 — hard-sf.com/links/1433312

The universe in a nutshell

Dark energy

Dark energy is a purely hypothetical form of energy arising as a result of the accelerated expansion of the universe.

If you attach a ball to the end of a rubber band and throw it in one direction, the ball moves more and more slowly until at some point it stops and is pulled back toward you. The expansion of the universe should theoretically play out in a similar manner. The big push at the beginning, the Big Bang, drove everything apart at first, but all matter is attached to a rubber band called gravitation. And that should theoretically ensure that the expansion changes direction at some point and the universe shrinks.

In fact, measurements show that the opposite is the case. The universe is expanding faster and faster. There must be some force behind this – which scientists have termed dark energy, borrowing from the term dark matter, which has been (un)known for much longer.

Dark energy counteracts the gravitational force of normal matter and dark matter by means of its negative pressure. For that to be successful, we would have to assume that over 68 percent of all the matter and energy in the universe is dark energy.

Another mystery is that dark energy can't have been available from the beginning in the same proportion. After recombination (380,000 years after the Big Bang), there was still no sign of this effect.

However, it's also possible that there is no force that will ever be identified as dark energy. Even the vacuum – empty space – contains energy, according to quantum theory, because there particles are constantly coming into existence out of nothing and disappearing. What remains on balance (if anything remains) could be dark energy.

Dark matter

Astrophysicists use the term dark matter as an umbrella term to describe presently unknown forms of matter. We know they must exist, because dark matter influences normal matter with its gravitation. An example of this is the movement of the stars at the center of the Milky Way. Most of the observable matter is located near the center. This means that, according to the laws of physics, the stars that are farther out should move slower. But in fact, the speed of the orbiting stars increases the farther they are from the center. This leads us to the conclusion that there must be large quantities of 'dark' mass that we can't see, concentrated in the regions farther out.

Given the actual movement of the stars, it's estimated that there must be almost six times as much dark matter as normal matter. However, there is still no certainty among scientists about what dark matter is. What is clear is that we're not dealing with known phenomena that are invisible due to a lack of light emission, such as dust clouds or burned-out stars. Basically, there are two possibilities:

Candidate #1 is the neutrino, a particle that barely interacts with normal matter. Countless neutrinos pass through the Earth and every one of its inhabitants around the clock. But neutrinos are too low-mass to account for the function of dark matter on their own.

Candidate #2 is known as WIMP (weakly interacting massive particle). WIMPs can only be disrupted by gravitation and by weak interaction (another natural force). But their existence hasn't yet been proven.

It's also possible that dark matter doesn't exist at all and that the scientific formulas are wrong. But there's less evidence for that than there is for the existence of WIMPs.

Filaments and voids

The large-scale structure of the universe is primarily determined by the distribution of dark matter that arose as a result of the Big Bang. That apparently resulted in the formation of a honeycomb structure: huge empty spaces (voids) separated from one another by strings of galaxy clusters (filaments). The voids are generally around 100 million light years across. But there are also much larger bubbles in space: the Eridanus Supervoid, for example, has a diameter of one billion light years, making it 1000 times larger in volume than a standard void.

But the voids are not completely empty. It's just that the density of galaxies is a lot lower – below 20 percent.

One of the best known is the Great Wall. It's around 200 million light years away from the Milky Way, so named because it's around 300 million light years high but only 15 million light years thick. The Great Wall includes the Coma Supercluster, which is connected to the Virgo Supercluster, our home in the universe, by a filament.

Another filament that has made a name for itself is the 'Great Attractor'. The name refers to its structure, which was only recognized due to a surprising characteristic. The galaxies here are not moving away from each other as quickly as the expansion of the universe should cause them to. A gravitational anomaly? Actually, astronomers have a culprit in their sights: the Shapley Supercluster, which prevents the galaxies in its vicinity from speeding away, as if it were holding them on a leash, apparently due to its enormous concentration of mass.

Galaxies

As soon as the first stars formed, they began to influence other exemplars with their gravitation. The first galaxies formed as early as 500 million years after the Big Bang. Compared to the present day, things were very lively at first: smaller galaxies combined into larger ones, and collisions and hostile takeovers were the order of the day.

But developments didn't proceed haphazardly. Direction was provided by fine structures in the universe predetermined by dark matter, the so-called filaments. Where these filaments encountered one another, galaxies formed, which combined into clusters and superclusters. Today, the observable universe contains several million galaxy superclusters. One of them, the Virgo Supercluster, with a diameter of 110 million light years, combines several thousand galaxies, including the Milky Way, as part of the so-called Local Group.

We don't know for sure how the various types of galaxies form. In the case of the more common spiral galaxies, of which the Milky Way is one, it's assumed that dark matter plays a role. Dark matter is primarily concentrated in the outer reaches of the galaxies. Because of this, interstellar gas – which is drawn in by both the galaxy's core (strong) and by its outer reaches (weak) – moves on a spiral path toward the core, a bit like holding a cat by its tail.

Elliptical galaxies are usually the end point of this development. They form as a result of smaller galaxies merging. This could be the future for the Milky Way and our neighbor M31, aka Andromeda: in 3–4.5 billion years, the two roughly equally massive systems could collide and form a gigantic elliptical galaxy.

Gamma-ray bursts

The universe is illuminated at regular intervals by powerful flashes lasting from a few seconds to several minutes. Their wavelength corresponds to that of gamma rays produced by nuclear fission, which is why they're called gamma-ray bursts or GRBs. They don't make it through the Earth's atmosphere, which is why they weren't detected until 1967, when the USA sent a surveillance satellite into space to reveal terrestrial atomic bomb testing.

For a long time, scientists assumed that the sources of these bursts were in the Milky Way. It seemed that their intensity could only be explained by such proximity. So it was all the more baffling when they discovered around 20 years ago that gamma-ray bursts were reaching us from much greater distances. For example, in 2008, the NASA Swift satellite recorded a burst coming from an object 7.5 billion light years away. For us to perceive it at such great cosmic distances, the explosion must have been 2.5 million times more powerful than the most intense supernova ever observed.

The type of event that leads to a gamma-ray burst is not yet entirely clear. For one thing, it is assumed that a lighthouse effect is required. Terrestrial beacons are only visible from great distances because they concentrate the light from their lamps with a rotating concave mirror. This means that they don't shine simultaneously in all directions, but only illuminate a limited area at any given time. This requires less energy. This effect could occur in the cosmos if a rapidly rotating object explodes. This would focus the gamma-ray burst along the rotational axis of the star. We could then only register the GRB if the axis happened to be pointing at the Earth. But then you still need a particularly powerful explosion, such as the hypernova of an exceptionally massive star or the collision of two neutron stars.

Gravitation

Gravitation is the force that keeps our feet pressed against the surface of the Earth and causes a ball thrown upward to fall back down. But it's not just the Earth drawing people toward it – gravity also works the other way around, except that we don't feel the inverse effect due to the enormous difference in mass. Generally speaking, two bodies attract one another with a force that increases with the product of their mass and decreases with the square of their distance – Newton's law of universal gravitation.

Compared to the other three fundamental physical forces, gravitation has some peculiarities. For one thing, it's the weakest of all forces. Electromagnetism, for example, is 36 orders of magnitude stronger than gravitation, and the nuclear force that holds atomic nuclei together is another 100 times stronger again. In principle, the effect of gravitation is only attractive, not repellent, it extends to infinity, and it can't be shielded.

Albert Einstein demonstrated where these special characteristics come from with his General Theory of Relativity. He revealed gravitation to be a property of four-dimensional space, which is distorted by the mass of the bodies within it. Imagine you're sitting on the left side of a three-seater couch. Then a very heavy person sits in the middle. What happens? You inevitably slide toward the newcomer. The person in the middle appears to be exerting an attractive force on you. But in reality, their mass has merely changed the geometry of the couch. The larger person's attractive force is actually just a property of the couch.

Objects with very high mass bend space (or the couch) so much that it can result in the formation of a black hole. In this case, the two ends of the couch fold together above the person in the middle – and for their neighbors, there's no chance of escape.

Gravitational lenses

The ability of even the most powerful telescopes to look out into space is limited, for various reasons. On Earth, for example, they are impeded by the atmosphere, which some components of radiation can't penetrate. With space telescopes, the size of the lens and thus the resolution is limited by humanity's technological capabilities.

But there are natural telescopes in space that occasionally allow us to catch a glimpse of very distant objects. The lenses of an ordinary telescope are made of glass. Light refracts differently in glass compared to air. This makes it possible to focus the light emitted by an object such that the image appears sharp on our retina. The larger and more curved a lens, the more it is able to make distant things look close. Anyone whose vision is especially weak in one eye understands the problem.

In space, which is generally considered empty, light should spread out unhindered. But in fact, stars bend the space around them, and light follows this curvature – it is redirected as with a glass lens. This is one of the most convincingly proven predictions of Einstein's General Theory of Relativity. The heavier the object (or rather, the more mass it has), the stronger the curvature. This is why a black hole is the best place to look for such a gravitational lens. To put it another way: if a star suddenly appears to be much closer than usual, the cause must be a gravitational lens. Between us and the star in question is something very heavy, but which we can't see: very likely a black hole. Astronomers also like to use the gravitational lensing effect to observe very distant galaxies. All they have to do is to wait for a suitable alignment.

Interstellar matter

The space between stars is only empty at first glance. A spaceship has two main components to deal with on its voyage: dust and gas. The concentration and composition of interstellar matter are very varied – sometimes dust concentrates in huge clouds, and there are entire regions filled with atomic or molecular gases.

But dust makes up a smaller proportion, just one percent of interstellar matter. The dust particles range from one ten thousandth to one thousandth of a millimeter in size and are mainly comprised of silicates (silicon compounds, which terrestrial rocks are also composed of). In principle, however, this dust includes all heavy elements. Dust arises primarily from nova and supernova explosions. Stellar wind is also a contributor – a constant stream of matter emitted by active stars. Dust clouds, where this matter is concentrated, and the molecular gas clouds are among the most important regions for star formation.

Ninety-nine percent of interstellar matter is gas. On average, in a sugar-cube-sized volume of interstellar space, there is only one atom. But here too we find great variations in density. Gas clouds are 90 percent hydrogen. Depending on the temperature, this hydrogen can occur in the form of atoms or molecules, or ionized – robbed of its electrons.

Molecular clouds achieve the highest density. In addition to hydrogen, many other molecules can also be detected here, including complex amino acids, hydrogen cyanide, and alcohol. Large molecular clouds can be as massive as 10,000 to 10 million Suns. Within the Milky Way, new stars are almost always born in such clouds.

The shape of the universe

What shape is the universe? First of all, it is a four-dimensional space with the three spatial dimensions (length, breadth, depth) and the time dimension. The shape that such a space could take is beyond human imagination (or can you imagine a four-dimensional cube?). So the appearance of the universe can only be described by means of comparisons.

When discussing the Big Bang and the time after it, scientists assume a spherical shape, for purely practical reasons.

However, measurements have long since shown that the universe is not spherical, because that would mean it was curved. As I'm sure you remember, the sum of the interior angles of a triangle is 180 degrees. But if, instead of placing the triangle on a flat desk, we place it on a curved surface, then the sum of the interior angles will be more or less than 180 degrees. And that's exactly what scientists have measured with probes. The result: exactly 180 degrees. So the universe is flat – everything we currently know points to that. Flat like a piece of paper that stretches out infinitely on all sides. Except in four dimensions (forget it, you can't imagine that).

But how can an infinite sheet of paper expand, as described by the Big Bang theory? It's very simple: space itself is expanding. The paper isn't paper, it's rubber. An endless rubber surface can be stretched out without problems. If we mark two points on it and then pull at the edges, the distance between the two points grows. Afterward, the rubber mat is still infinite – a little more infinite, even. And that's true in four dimensions as well, except that there's no 'outside' area.

However, it could also be possible that the universe only appears to be flat. After all, we can only observe part of the cosmos. The entire thing may be so subtly curved that the part observable by humans looks flat.

Globular clusters

The appearance of a globular cluster can be inferred from its name: a large number of stars (several hundred thousand) moving in close proximity to one another in a globular (spheroidal) conglomeration. Our Milky Way alone contains around 150 globular clusters. Larger galaxies can contain up to 10,000.

Unlike those in spiral galaxies, the stars in a globular cluster are all roughly the same age. They formed from the ashes of the very first stars. Their generation is therefore referred to as 'Population II', while the Sun belongs to the younger Population I. Population II stars are generally stars at the end of their life cycle. This makes them some of the oldest witnesses to the history of the universe.

The probability that planets and therefore life could form in these clusters is very low. This is due to the short distances between the stars. At the center of a cluster, the average distance is around one light year – that's less than a quarter of the distance between the Sun and the nearest star. This would make the orbits of potential planets very unstable. Every planet would be swallowed by a star after a few hundred million years. For life to emerge, you need patience. For example, on Earth it took one billion years before biological evolution even began.

However, globular clusters are rich in exotic stars. The frequently occurring binary star systems can combine into 'blue stragglers', for example: normally, a star grows into a red giant at the end of its cycle. In a binary system, the star that was originally the smaller of the two can absorb the matter of its larger partner, thus becoming reheated, similar to the effect of pouring a liquid fire starter onto weakly smoldering coals.

Milky Way

The Milky Way is visible as a milky band in the night sky – that's how it gets its name (in several languages). The fact that it's not painted onto the firmament but rather consists of countless stars was discovered by Galileo Galilei through his telescope in 1609.

Viewed from outside, the Milky Way has the shape of a barred spiral galaxy, with a bar in the middle from which four main spiral arms extend. It contains a total of 100 to 300 billion stars – astronomers can't be more precise than that, as they're restricted to viewing it from inside. The combined mass of the Milky Way is equal to around 1.4 trillion times the mass of the Sun. Less than a third of that is visible matter, so the rest must be dark matter.

The Milky Way forms part of the Local Group, together with the Andromeda 'Nebula' and a few hundred smaller galaxies. This in turn is part of the Virgo Supercluster, which contains a three-figure number of galaxy clusters like the Local Group.

The center of the Milky Way is hidden behind dust and gas clouds. Images recorded in the radio wave, x-ray, and infrared ranges show that there is a supermassive black hole there, weighing as much as 4 million Suns. It is accompanied by a second, intermediate-mass black hole of only 1300 solar masses. Evidence suggests that there are a further 10,000–20,000 other black holes within a radius of 70 light years, which feed the central black hole with stars from the surrounding region.

The Sun orbits at a safe distance of around 25,000 light years. Along with all of its planets, it moves at a speed of over 250 kilometers per second through the interstellar medium, but still takes at least 220 million years to complete an orbit.

Neutron stars

A neutron star, the remnants of a supernova, is a very compact object – up to three solar masses contained within a sphere measuring 20 kilometers across. A sugar-cube of this weighs about as much as a cube of iron with sides one kilometer long. The gravity on its surface is 200 billion times the gravity on the surface of the Earth. If an object were to fall to its surface from a height of one meter, it would hit the surface at a speed of 7.2 million kilometers per hour after just one microsecond.

Mountain ranges on a neutron star are at most one millimeter high. Obviously, scientists have not yet been able to ascertain the structure of a neutron star. The prevailing theory describes a shell structure reminiscent of an M&M. Under a thin, brittle crust of iron nuclei you find the first neutrons, which otherwise populate the nucleus of an atom together with the positively charged protons. These form a superfluid mass: a medium that is infinitely fluid. A superfluid cake batter would only need to be stirred once briefly and the batter would keep moving in a circle until the end of days. The material is also superconductive, meaning electrical currents could flow through it endlessly without encountering any resistance.

What the core looks like we can only speculate. It's probably composed of exotic particles or even quarks – the building blocks of elementary particles.

The fate of neutron stars is unspectacular: starting out at 100 billion degrees, they cool down within the space of a year to one billion degrees. Most neutron stars are visible from Earth thanks to their strong magnetic fields. When the star is not rotating in the same direction as its magnetic field points, it emits powerful radio waves – acting as a pulsar.

Quasars

The term quasar (quasi-stellar radio source) emerged before scientists were aware of the true nature of these celestial objects. Quasars look like stars in the sky. But when you analyze their light, you discover that the source must be an enormous distance away. Objects that shine as brightly in the sky as an ordinary star even from several billion light years away must be exceptionally energetic.

In fact, quasars are among the most light-intensive objects in the universe – and among the oldest objects visible to us. Some quasars are so far away that they provide us with a glimpse of the infancy of the universe. The quasar SDSS J0100+2802, for example, is so far away that we can observe it in the state it was in when the universe was only 900 million years old – that's how long its light takes to reach us.

Where do these objects get their luminosity? What astronomers study in the sky as quasars are the cores of very distant galaxies. Just like the Milky Way, they have at their center a gigantic black hole. This is not only incredibly massive (over a billion solar masses), but also exceptionally ravenous. It captures matter from its host galaxy, which forms a huge disc around the black hole before being swallowed by it. This disc is the quasar's dynamo. It heats up as it circles faster and faster around the black hole, so much that it reaches the combined luminosity of several billion stars. Some quasars reach a luminosity of 100 trillion stars.

The Milky Way is not a quasar, because the black hole at its center does not receive enough nourishment from its surroundings.

Black holes

A black hole is a region in space from which nothing can escape – not even light. Scientists hypothesized as early as the 18th century that such regions could exist. If you throw a ball up from the surface of the Earth, it requires a certain initial speed in order to escape the Earth's gravity. Otherwise it inevitably falls back to the thrower. The stronger the gravitational force, the higher the initial speed must be. But can you imagine a mass so big that even the speed of light is no longer fast enough to escape it?

The next indication was provided by Einstein's General Theory of Relativity. Its equations describe, under certain circumstances, what is now known as a black hole. Scientists first regarded this as a mathematical curiosity – but in 1971 Cygnus X-1/HDE 226868 was identified as the first candidate for a black hole binary system.

Black holes can't be observed directly, but only in terms of their effect. For example, we can observe orbits of stars in multiple-star systems that suggest the presence of an invisible object.

We can only speculate about what the inside of a black hole looks like. The currently known laws of physics no longer apply here, because their reference values suddenly become infinitely large. At precisely that moment, we cross an imaginary boundary, the event horizon. As soon as anything goes beyond that, it is removed from the normal world forever. In a black hole with the mass of the Sun, this area would have a radius of several kilometers.

Supernovas

Sk -69 202 was young and hot. At its birth, the blue supergiant star in the Large Magellanic Cloud would have devoured over 20 times the mass of the Sun. Sk -69 202 has been dead for 168,000 years, but the explosive flash of its death finally reached Earth on February 24, 1987. The blue supergiant faded into a supernova – a fate suffered by most stars of more than nine solar masses.

Why can't these supergiant stars enjoy the kind of serene retirement that awaits the Sun in six billion years? They're simply too massive. When a star runs out of fuel, it suddenly lacks the internal pressure of fusion fire to counteract the attractive force of gravitation. The star shrinks like a flaccid hot air balloon. With smaller stars, the matter inside eventually reaches a state that gravitation can no longer overcome. What remains is a white dwarf. But if there is enough mass, gravitation wins out. All of the star's matter transforms into neutrons. This happens so fast that a pressure wave pushes the star's shell out into space.

If the neutron star is still heavier than three solar masses at this point, it transforms into a black hole. The star continues to shrink until the concentration of mass is so high that not even light can escape its gravitation.

Especially large stars (over 150 solar masses) can burst in what is called a pair-instability supernova. These are 100 times brighter than a normal supernova, as the star is completely torn apart.

A supernova near the Earth would probably be very unpleasant – it's assumed that the energy pulse of the explosion would extinguish all life within a radius of 50 light years.

Death of the universe

Torn apart, crushed, frozen, cooked, a new Big Bang, or sudden disappearance –scientists have postulated at least six causes of death that could someday end the existence of the universe. Nor are they certain about how the cosmos will wipe out humanity.

In any case, we have no choice in the matter. The future development of the universe depends largely on two factors. On one hand, it will be determined by its mass, or to be more precise, its density – the average mass per unit of space. If this density falls below a critical value, the universe will begin to contract at some point. If not, it will continue to expand. The critical density value is very low – corresponding to around six hydrogen atoms in one cubic centimeter of space. And yet the universe falls well shy of that. If you add up the mass of all luminous objects and dark dust and gas clouds, you'll arrive at only five percent of the required value. But then there's also the mysterious dark matter, of course. Its proportion can be estimated by analyzing its influence on the movement of the galaxies. The result: the actual density is a third of the value required for continued expansion.

The other factor is the behavior of dark energy – and we don't even know yet what it is. In any case, dark energy is currently accelerating the expansion of the cosmos. But it didn't do that in the early stages of the universe, and maybe it will change its mind again. It's like any relationship: if science becomes more familiar with the nature of dark energy, it will be able to more precisely answer the question of how it will behave in the future.

Universe

The universe includes everything around us – as suggested by its Latin origin 'universus' ('whole'). Also referred to as 'the cosmos' or 'space', it was born 13.8 billion years ago in a violent explosion, the Big Bang.

Space is not infinite, but it's unimaginably large. Scientists estimate it to be over 92 billion light years across, but it could just as easily be a thousand times that. A light year is the distance that light travels in one year. In just one second, light travels around 300,000 kilometers.

Measuring the universe is impossible, because the observable part is smaller than the whole. We can only see objects that sent out light at the time of the Big Bang, at the earliest. In its initial phase, the universe expanded very quickly, so that these objects are now at most 46 billion light years away. Whether there are even more distant stars is something we will never know.

The universe is endless but finite. That is not a contradiction: the surface of a sphere is also endless (maybe you remember the formula from math class). An ant crawling around it never reaches the end. There's no 'beyond'.

The entirety of matter in the universe weighs around 10^{53} kilograms – a 1 with 53 zeroes. Only around five percent of that can be attributed to known forms of matter, that is, atoms and elementary particles. Dark matter must account for around a quarter, and the even stranger dark energy must make up over two thirds.

Despite its enormous mass, the universe is basically empty. Imagine a palace measuring 30 by 30 kilometers. Place a grain of sand in it, and the sand represents the average density of the universe. Speaking of sand: there are more stars in the universe (130 sextillion) than there are grains of sand on all the beaches on Earth.

The universe is expanding. In the time it takes you to read this text, it has grown by more than 100,000 kilometers. And everything in it appears to be moving away from us.

Big Bang

The Big Bang marks the beginning of the universe – its creation. 13.8 billion years ago, the entire mass of the universe was concentrated in a tiny amount of space, a point. The laws of physics as we know them did not yet exist. They only formed out of the Big Bang.

Nor did the forces and particles we know today. So there was no light (which consists of photons), and certainly no observer, because even back then, there was no 'outside'.

There was just this tiny point, filled with a primordial sludge at a temperature of 10^{32} degrees (a 1 with 32 zeroes), the behavior of which in turn determined a primordial force. Scientists only have rough ideas about what happened next. Both the General Theory of Relativity and quantum theory fall short under these extreme conditions. In order to make the Big Bang calculable, we also need the 'theory of everything' that physicists strive for.

In any case, the ultra-hot Something was under huge pressure, which at some point literally created space. The Big Bang itself lasted 10^{-43} or 0.0000000000000000000000000000000000000000001 seconds, measured according to our understanding of time. However, even time didn't yet exist at that moment.

The result of this very first phase was a primordial drop. It was still tiny, but bigger than the point that preceded it, causing it to cool a little. The consequence: from the Big Bang emerged the attractive force (gravitation). It began, as is its nature, to counteract the further expansion of the cosmos. But it had no real chance at this stage. The primordial drop grew, so that further natural forces known to us today, such as the nuclear force and the electroweak force, were also able to emerge, 10^{-38} seconds after the Big Bang.

Wormholes

The concept of wormholes arose from equations in the General Theory of Relativity. Albert Einstein and Nathan Rosen were the first to describe this phenomenon, which is why physicists also refer to it as an 'Einstein-Rosen bridge'.

Wormholes are often thought of as shortcuts through space. Reduced to two dimensions, our universe would be like a bed sheet. It takes a flea a certain amount of time to get from one point on the flat sheet to another. But if the sheet is folded, the flea can get to the same point much quicker. It just needs to bite through the sheet and comes out the other side at a point much farther away on the surface of the sheet.

Wormholes arise from the equations of the General Theory of Relativity as a special solution. But that doesn't mean they actually exist, or that they are usable in any way for locomotion. For one thing, a black hole serves as the entry point – and it's highly doubtful that anything, let alone a spaceship, can survive a flight into a black hole. It's much more likely that the monstrous gravitation in it would crush any object to dust.

A wormhole is also exceptionally unstable, as can be demonstrated mathematically. To keep it open, you need exotic kinds of matter linked to negative energy. We know that a phenomenon like this must have come into play during the inflation phase of the universe. But modern physics hasn't the faintest idea about its nature or how it could be artificially created.

Excerpt: Lost Moon: Lunar Eclipse

December 23, 2099

"I'm really worried about him," Maurice said. "Can't you kick it up a notch?"

"I'm driving as fast as I dare," Steve replied, "considering the awful condition of the highway."

Steve had pointed this out to Mission Control many times, but there were always more important things to do. Now it spelled trouble—if Tom didn't receive surgical intervention soon enough, they'd have to dig the second grave on the moon.

"I know," Maurice said. "I was just hoping... I don't know what I was hoping for."

Tom, who was currently in the infirmary with a ruptured appendix, was best of friends with Maurice, Steve's chief technician.

"If need be, you'll just have to have the robodoc operate," Steve said.

"Don't you listen to him," objected a pale-faced Daniela, who was sitting beside Steve. "I saw during my training what a robodoc can do if he's not sure. Fortunately, it was an artificial body it had under its scalpel."

Daniela Vasiljevic was a doctor, the best there was on the moon. Unfortunately, she was also the only one. She worked at ESA's Lunar Village, and he'd been a guest there when Tom's condition deteriorated drastically. Daniela immediately offered to accompany him.

"Isn't there anything we can do?" asked Maurice. "It's unbearable for me to watch my friend die while I'm twiddling my thumbs."

"He's not going to die," Daniela said. "The robodoc is keeping Tom's circulation stable and detoxifying him. It just refuses to do the surgery. I've looked at the diagnostic data. It has every reason to refuse."

"They always told us it could perform any operation," Steve said.

"It's a machine. In this case, the risk is too high that it will catch uninvolved tissue," Daniela explained.

"But *you* can handle it?" asked Maurice.

A bump hurled Steve against the ceiling. *Fucking potholes!* He tightened his seatbelt. "Gaaahhh!" Daniela blurted. Steve cast a quick glance to the right. His passenger was holding on to a handle under the side window.

"Yeah, whew, I can get it done," Daniela said. "It's a comparatively simple operation. We just have to get there in one piece." She looked at him with widened eyes.

Maurice nodded apologetically. "Forgive my concern," he said. "All those warning lights on Tom's bed are driving me crazy. Drive carefully. Lunar Base over and out."

"See you in a minute," Steve said, but the connection had ended.

Driving carefully while hurrying is never easy. Couldn't ESA and NASA have agreed on a location? The 300 kilometers of road between Lunar Village and Lunar Base could not be kept in the condition of a terrestrial highway without major effort. Steve cursed under his breath as he dodged the holes, some as big as houses, that had formed in the road.

The fact that the highway had decayed relatively quickly was due to its construction. Moondust had simply been mixed with water to form mud and applied to the surface. The mixture hardened in a flash. But where the road was exposed to sunlight for a more extended period, the water molecules dissolved from the top layers, and the hard road surface returned to what it was before: dust.

"Careful, on the right!" shouted Daniela.

Oh, she was not asleep. Steve had seen the hole but thanked her anyway. Daniela had folded her seat back and pulled her peaked cap far down over her forehead. In the dim light of the cockpit instruments, it had looked as if she'd closed her eyes.

The next pothole appeared, again on the right-hand side. Steve didn't have to fear oncoming traffic, so he could switch lanes freely. The highway had been built wide enough so that two Rovers could pass without swerving out into the deep moon dust.

"Another one," Daniela said.

Now it was getting interesting, because the headlights revealed a second hole that had formed just beyond the first one but on the other side of the road. The second hole was smaller. Steve checked the speedometer, which showed 35 km/h. That shouldn't be too much for the smaller hole.

"Don't be alarmed," he warned.

Instead of swerving to miss both holes and risking an overturn, he pressed his foot on the accelerator pedal and raced toward the smaller hole. The Rover jostled them but dutifully obeyed. The six balloon tires spun faster, and the plume of dust they left behind grew thicker. Then the hole was there. The Rover took off. It could hardly be felt before it touched down again. Steve was about to relax when he spotted the next hole. It was right in front of them. At the current speed, he must not jerk the wheel under any circumstances, and mustn't follow his reflexes and brake.

On the contrary, he again pressed the accelerator. The Rover's electric motor reacted immediately, the acceleration pressing him into the seat. He heard nothing; the Rover took off in complete silence. They were flying! Time stood still. Steve felt the engine's vibrations in his back and noticed a drop of sweat rolling down his forehead. He caught the scent of the delicate perfume Daniela used, and saw the streak of light that was the Earth rising above the horizon, *now* of all times.

"Whew!" Daniela gasped when they had left the hole behind.

"Whew," Steve agreed.

The delayed shock dove into his consciousness. What if it hadn't been enough? Would the cabin windows have survived the impact, or would he and his passenger have been dead? The moon does not forgive mistakes.

"Lunar Base to Rover 2, please respond."

Steve pressed the Accept button. "Rover 2 here," he replied. "What's up?"

"Me again," Maurice reported. "Did something happen?"

"*Happen?* No, why?" Steve returned.

"You sounded so... stressed."

Steve looked at Daniela. She nodded. Could she still hear the shock in his voice? He breathed in and out deeply.

"No, it's all good," he then said. "The road is a real challenge, though. In the new year, we really need to take care of it. Can we help?"

"I'm still worried about Tom. His condition—"

"Can you transfer control of the robodoc to me?" Daniela interrupted him.

"Sure! Good idea," Maurice replied.

"Thanks. I'll be in touch as soon as I know more," said Daniela.

The ESA doctor reached back, got her backpack, took out a tablet, and switched it on. Another jolt shook the Rover.

"Can you please slow down a little?" she asked.

From the corner of his eye, he saw that she was already working on the tablet.

"I'm trying," he said, rubbing his eyes.

The continuous concentration was exhausting, especially due to the lack of contrast. They were still in the shadow of a crater wall. In a few minutes, it should get better. First, the Earth rose further and further above the horizon the closer they got to the lunar base, and second, the sun would rise soon.

"I have to correct myself," Daniela said. "You'd better go as fast as you can."

She put the tablet in the backpack, pulled the seatbelt tight, and held on to the side handle.

I'm supposed to go that fast? Then things must be really bad for Tom.

"You're not even asking, Steve?"

"It's not necessary. I only need to look at you to know that Tom's situation is bad."

"Very bad," Daniela said. "He's on the verge of multiple-organ failure. The robodoc is having a harder and harder time keeping him stable. I have to get him under the surgical instruments ASAP."

Good thing that didn't put any pressure on him. Shit! If he lost control of the Rover, Tom died. And they might die, too. If he drove too slow, Tom died. But they would live—knowing they hadn't given it their all.

He gave it his all.

"Tell me something," he said.

Slowly, fatigue was overcoming the consternation about Tom's condition. He needed something to keep him awake.

"What?" asked Daniela.

"How long have you been here?"

In great leaps, the Rover chased over the road, which resembled a mogul track in this section. That was because it led through the impact area of a relatively fresh meteorite strike. But he'd trained here before, racing Maurice. Not much could happen because the humps ran pretty much perpendicular to the direction of travel. Well, the shock absorbers might suffer, but they would reach the finish even with defective shocks.

"Half a year," Daniela said.

"What?"

"I've been here for six months. You asked me that."

"Right. Sorry. I'm a little scrambled."

The Rover jumped off the top of a hump, crossed the shadow of the following one, and touched down just before a deep hole. Steve yanked the wheel around. The left front wheel hovered over the hole, but the momentum of the heavy vehicle dominated the low lunar gravity. He still needed to pay better attention.

"Then your flight home will be soon, won't it?" he asked.

"Yes, I have a ticket for the next *Blue Moon*. I'll be with my family in time for the New Year."

"Is that the departure on the twenty-ninth? I'll be on board that flight, too," he said.

It was about time. He'd been up here for a year and a half now, so three cycles. And this was the fourth stint. In the first cycle his wife had already separated from him. How long ago was that now? That was why he hadn't minded extending again and again. But now he wanted to see real green again, not growing in a hydroponic container. Maybe he'd be back by the end of next year. If NASA still needed him. At 54, he was no longer one of the young guys.

"Those lights up ahead, is that the station?" asked Daniela.

Steve rubbed his eyes. The Rover sped up a slope so that only the road was visible. They reached the highest point, and lights appeared on the horizon.

"Yes, this is the station," he said. "Have you been here before?"

"No," she said. "There's always so much to do, I'd have to take time off."

"It's no different than your Lunar Village, only more compact."

Daniela was looking at the tablet on her lap.

"Still in a hurry?" he asked.

She wanted to yell, What the fuck are you talking about, Stevie?

Why didn't you just ask me if he's dead yet? Instead, she merely said, "Yes, very much so."

"I understand."

From here, the road ran straight ahead to the base. The risk of overturning the Rover was minimal. He pushed the accelerator pedal all the way down. Daniela nodded at him. The Rover tossed them back and forth like a horse trying to throw off its rider.

A red inscription appeared on the control panel. 'Danger! Stop immediately!'

Now what? Had he overloaded the fuel cell? But the Rover managed the last kilometer with energy from the battery. The battery stored the electricity generated by the fuel cell. Steve opened the configuration of the Rover. He was about to disconnect the cell when a voice answered.

It was Mike from Lunar Gate, the space station that organizes transfers between Earth and the lunar surface. "What's going on with you guys? I see an obstacle in the landing area here. Get it out of my way now!"

Shit. He'd forgotten about the arrival of *Blue Moon 34*. The lander was bringing fresh supplies and was scheduled to transport him home on the 29th. "I can't leave here now," he said. "It's a matter of life and death."

"Hello, is that *you* on the landing pad? There are a hundred tons approaching right now! Do you think I can stop them for a moment?"

"Yes, it's me. It's an urgent transport, sorry."

"What do you mean, 'sorry?' I can't stop the lander! Geez, Steve, you know that as well as I do!"

"Can't he do another orbit—"

"He's already on a direct approach, past the point of no return! If I abort now, I risk losing *Blue Moon 34!*"

"I admit, that was a stupid thing to do. But Tom—"

"C'mon, Steve, you know what all depends on it! You're the boss of the base!"

Mike was right. The return trip from Lunar Village was planned differently. Slower. *Blue Moon 34* would have been unloading long before they reached the landing site. His mind raced. The exhaust jet of the rocket measured 50 meters at most. The Rover was traveling just 40 km/h, or 11 meters per second. So in less than five seconds, he and Daniela would have crossed the dangerous spot. That was an acceptable risk.

"Mike. Forget what I said. Let *Blue Moon* land as intended. Don't abort."

"Are you crazy? I've got a collision warning here."

"Ignore it or shut it down. It's very simple."

"Man, if this goes wrong! That thing will roast you! I hope you're at least alone out there."

"It won't go wrong. Trust me."

He felt Daniela's gaze on him. He was not alone. If he was wrong, she would die with him. But she remained surprisingly calm. Had she even noticed the point of light approaching from the horizon? She typed something on the tablet again. Tom's condition seemed to continue to deteriorate.

The dot was sinking frighteningly fast. The lander had left its orbit and was on its descent path. Again and again it went out, only to light up again. These were necessary orbit corrections. It was not easy to aim for a specific point on a spinning base—the lunar surface—but it could be done. Since Lunar Base had existed, no lander had missed its target. To avoid doing so, however, the spacecraft must brake at the right moments and at the right angles. Then, if something interfered at the most inopportune moment—a Rover, for example—it was impossible to take it into account.

The crew of the lander would not even notice. The exhaust jet would simply blow them aside. After all, it had to provide enough impetus to decelerate 100 tons to zero. In comparison, the Rover, weighing about 900 kilograms, was a flyweight.

"They're coming," Steve said, pointing ahead.

Daniela's gaze followed his outstretched finger. She still

showed no fear—rather, something like awe. The Lunar Base's tower had switched on its landing light, which now illuminated the arriving spaceship from below. It shimmered as if it were made of mercury. Its lower end glowed. You could only guess at the jet of exhaust coming from the glowing outlets of the three engines. Steve pushed the accelerator to the limit, but no more power could be tickled out of the engine.

A moment ago, he thought it impossible that they could make it, but the braking maneuver had slowed the lander down considerably. It now almost appeared as if it were hovering above the station. That was deceiving, of course, because there was no background to estimate its actual descent rate. But there was room for a little hope, because the Rover was not slowing down.

Steve steered the Rover right through red and green lights that indicated the circle where *Blue Moon 34* would descend. The diagonal was the shortest path. They needed to reach the airlock so Daniela could rescue Tom. He owed him that much. Tom would have risked his life for him at any time.

It was strange. Steve had worked long enough on Earth, where he would never have expected this from his colleagues. But here it was normal.

The lander was now right above them. The dust swirled around them. Only on the radar did Steve still recognize the target, the airlock. He had to hold the steering wheel. It was as if they had been caught in a tropical storm. Only rain, lightning, and thunder were missing. Strictly speaking, there was even water, which was produced when the methane in the tank was burned. It just didn't have time to form drops because it froze first. Half of the dust around the site must consist of H2O, which was so rare on the moon.

The Rover broke away to the right. Steve regained control. The landing spacecraft was diagonally behind them. He didn't have time to turn around, but he knew how majestic it looked as it swooped down the last few inches like a god of engineering, as if it was now ready to receive the homage of the moon people.

Daniela reached for his arm. She was right—the airlock was there. Steve slammed on the brakes and the Rover started to skid. The left front wheel jumped over a low obstacle and continued to slide. He'd practiced this with Maurice during the races. Steve skillfully steered against it, compensated for the rotation, and the Rover stopped right next to the lock.

The connecting hose came out. Daniela squeezed his shoulder, unbuckled, and climbed out backwards to get the exit. She didn't need his help now.

Steve let what he had just experienced slowly seep into his consciousness. They'd made it. They'd survived.

He hoped it was worth it.

December 24, 2099

"Sammy, I'm sorry, but I have to go."

The black and white tomcat did not move. He'd sat down on Steve's knee when he started eating his cereal. Steve had tried to give him some, but the cat spurned the wet flakes. He was probably looking for a place to get warm, because it was pretty nippy in the cafeteria where he usually stayed.

"Sammy, I'm needed," Steve said.

He pushed the cat off his knees with his right hand, but the animal clawed at his pants. Steve sighed. If only he were an all-black pet! But with Sammy it didn't matter what he wore, there was still noticeable hair left.

"Hey, old friend, that's not the way to do it."

Steve slid his chair back. Normally Sammy didn't like such exposed seats. But today the cat only looked at him questioningly. The look could mean, *What do you want?* Sammy's right eye showed the narrow pupil typical for cats. The left eye was cloudy gray. Blind. Nobody knew how it had happened.

Daniela opened the door and looked around the room. "Oh, here you are," she said.

"I wanted to be in the infirmary by now, but this guy won't let me." Steve pointed to the cat on his knees.

As if to prove him wrong, Sammy jumped down, ran to Daniela, caressed her legs, and began to purr loudly.

"I didn't even know you had a cat."

"It's a tomcat. His name is Sammy. I hope you're not allergic. You can't get his hair out of the room."

"No problem, we have cats at home."

Daniela leaned down and stroked Sammy's head. He purred louder.

"He's happy to have found a new victim," Steve said.

"How did he get here, anyway?" the doctor asked. "I don't remember ever reading about a cat at Lunar Base."

"Nobody knows," he replied. "Samantha, our maintenance technician, claims that Sammy got here before anyone else. But then he'd have to be over twenty years old, which is unlikely, and he'd have to be able to breathe in a vacuum."

"Why is that?"

"A good twenty years ago, an accident at Lunar Base caused the entire station to lose air. If he had been living here then, he would have been killed, because there was no spacesuit for him here."

"I remember," Daniela remarked. "An astronaut died in that accident, too. I had just finished school."

Crazy. He'd been an astronaut for three years by that time. "Yes, the only one ever buried on the moon. He wanted it that way."

"But Sammy must have gotten here somehow? Hasn't it ever been investigated?"

"For NASA, he's not here, so there's no budget for an official investigation. Anyway, he never showed up on any cargo list."

"Maybe he arrived here in his own spaceship," she joked.

"Haha, yeah, Samantha said that too. I wouldn't put it past him. He likes to act like an alien sometimes."

"Maybe he's supposed to spy on you for a foreign power."

"I don't think so. He's much too lazy for that," Steve countered.

"And where do you get cat food and litter?"

"We make cat litter ourselves by sintering moon dust. That works pretty well. There's plenty of dust, after all. The cook feeds him with scraps and such.

Daniela straightened up. Her face suddenly looked quite serious. "Thanks for the little diversion," she said. "To you, too, Sammy. But now for the serious stuff."

"Tom didn't make it?" he asked.

"Not so fast, Steve, not so fast. Right now, he's hovering between life and death. I worked through the night. The robodoc really helped me a lot. But, at this point, I've done all I can do for him. Why don't you go see him?"

"You're telling me he's at the point where he has to decide to return to life?"

"Oh, that's romantic nonsense. He's standing on one leg on a precipice and swaying. No one can tell which way he will tip, whether he will crash or stabilize. But a little wind from the right direction might help. At least you might be able to help him fall the right way."

"Thank you, Daniela. For everything."

"But that's my job. And now I need to lie down for a few hours. Can you drive me back to Lunar Village tomorrow? I left all my luggage there, didn't I?"

"Sure thing. Go get some sleep first."

Daniela had left the canteen. Steve hoped that Sammy would sit down on his lap once again so he could justify postponing the sick call for a while. But the cat refused to grant him the favor. Steve had hated hospital rooms ever since the two years he'd had to visit his mother in one. Where were the others? Typically, everyone was still at breakfast at this hour. He didn't even hear Ricky, the cook, banging pots in the kitchen.

Of course! There was something going on: *Blue Moon 34.*

The crew of the Lunar Base was busy unloading. Why hadn't anyone informed him? He was the commander of the Lunar Base. It was nice that Maurice allowed him to sleep in, but his deputy should have included him at least for the sake of form.

Steve got up and left the cafeteria. Instead of going to the infirmary, however, he walked toward the exit. Halfway there, Samantha met him. Using an electronic leash, she was leading a four-wheeled cargo robot loaded with three large wooden crates. Samantha stopped the vehicle to let him through.

"Good morning, Steve!" She looked at him uncertainly. The cheerfulness that usually dominated her face was missing. What was bugging her?

"Is it *good?*" he asked. With Samantha, one question was usually enough to get her to spill her guts. That was what he liked about her. Once he offended Maurice with a stupid remark, but only figured it out months later because his deputy never said anything for that long.

"What do you mean?" she asked back.

"Did all the spare parts you ordered arrive?"

"Oh, you mean *that.*" Her face brightened a bit. "Surprisingly, yes. That means I can finally fix the ultrasonic shower and the two urinals."

"Very good. What else could I have meant?"

"Sorry, Steve, but that's none of my business. I'm your plumber, nothing more. Why don't you talk it over with Maurice?"

Something was happening right now that he hadn't noticed. But what? He'd have to ask Maurice about it.

"Thank you, Samantha. I will. Good luck with the repairs."

The corridor widened, led upward, and finally opened into a brightly lit hall. Steve heard murmuring from afar. A large part of the station's crew must have gathered. Most were standing in front of the floor-to-ceiling windows, casting long shadows. The bright light came from outside, where *Blue Moon 34* seemed to be basking in the glow of high-powered spotlights. Steve counted nine silhouettes.

Four were missing. Tom, of course, Samantha, who had just met him, and himself... And, Maurice. Somehow he had expected that. He walked forward to the glass window. Stephanie, the person beside him, stepped aside to make room without saying a word. In the spotlights, the huge lander looked impressive. There was not much variety up here, so a visit like this was an event.

A murmur went through the hall. An oval hole could be seen in the lander's belly, and a shiny silver person had just appeared in it. Steve could not believe his eyes. The person was not wearing a spacesuit! That was impossible. Or were they finally getting the new, tight-fitting models they had been promised for years?

"Isn't it beautiful?" asked Stephanie.

Why would she say 'it' when talking about a visitor?

"Is that one of the new suits?" he asked in lieu of a reply.

"*Suits?*"

"Yeah—what that man is wearing."

Stephanie frowned. "That's not a *man*. Haven't you heard about this?"

No. Something seemed to have completely passed him by. He needed to talk to Maurice! This wasn't good.

"What?" he asked.

"An android," Stephanie replied. "This is the first shipment. We're supposed to test him here. I'm very excited about it. Supposedly he has an autonomy level of three, so he doesn't need constant supervision."

"Very interesting. Thanks, Steph."

The android had skillfully climbed down the ladder to the lunar surface. Steve detached himself from the viewing area and went to the airlock. He was sure he'd find Maurice there.

The airlock formed one end of a flexible plastic hose that was rolled out to the landed spacecraft. One end of the hose could be connected directly to the lander's crew compartment, but that had been omitted this time because there was no human crew on board. The cargo bay was not pressurized, so cargo robots traveled back and forth between *Blue Moon 34* and the airlock. This way, there was no need for a human in a spacesuit to haul boxes, as had been standard when he'd first signed on here.

Maurice was waiting in front of the lock. It looked as if his head was glued to the airlock door, because Maurice, standing on his tiptoes, watched through the small inspection window to oversee what was going on in the lock.

Steve put a hand on his shoulder, and Maurice lowered himself. "He'll be here in a minute," Maurice said. "The outer door is already closed."

"You could have told me we were expecting such a distinguished visitor," Steve said.

The inner airlock door hissed. Maurice assumed a posture as if some star-ranked general were about to step out.

The heavy door swung open. The android had to duck his head, but even that looked elegant. He stopped in front of them, bowed, and offered his hand first to Maurice, then to Steve.

"I'm Sean," he said. "I'm very happy to be with you."

Sean, then. Not very imaginative. "Sean what?" he asked.

"Durkin."

"You really have a surname?"

"Yes. My fathers believe I can integrate better with a real human name rather than an artificial one."

"I'm afraid you'll always stand out just because of your size."

The android was half an arm's length taller than Steve's 1.85 meters.

"Oh, that's right. Wait a minute."

The creature shrank before his eyes. Steve, his mouth agape, was astonished.

"From the look on your face, I can tell you're amazed," Sean said.

"You're right about that. How do you do it?"

"Sentiment recognition, or body-size adjustment?"

"The size."

"I can vary the length of my upper and lower legs. It works like a telescoping pole."

"Phenomenal. I didn't know the technology had come this far."

"That's just a fraction of what I'm capable of, Steve."

Did I hear something like pride in that? "I'm looking forward to being able to test your skills."

"I'm sorry, Steve, but you don't have authorization for that," the android said.

"Because you're flying back on the twenty-ninth," Maurice quickly added.

"Why didn't you tell me about all this, in any case?" asked Steve.

"We'll talk about that later," Maurice said.

Steve sighed.

"You're frustrated," Sean commented.

"It's nice that you can recognize feelings. But you still need to learn when a person wants to hear it."

Stephanie had commandeered the android. She wanted it to help her with a geological survey. It was an impressive piece of technology.

Sean was stronger, faster, and more skilled than a human. The vacuum outside didn't bother him—all he needed was electricity. And he learned quickly. He'd absorbed Stephanie's explanations without question, and Steve was confident he would do all the tasks perfectly.

"Could it be that they intend to replace us with these androids?" asked Steve.

He was on his way to the canteen with Maurice. He ought

to have visited Tom long ago, but he kept putting it off. At least the canteen was on the way to the infirmary.

"Mission Control hinted at something like that," Maurice said.

"They talked to you about it?"

Steve stopped. In the passageway carved into the rock, only the chains of Christmas lights were on, flashing prettily in bright colors but hardly spreading any brightness. That was why he hadn't recognized what was going on in Maurice's face.

"They did. Actually, they promised me they'd keep you informed as well. But I guess that's been dumped on me."

"Why *as well?* They should have talked to me first. I am the commander of the Lunar Base."

"That's the problem. After your action with the landing spaceship, they had to react somehow. It couldn't be without consequences. What would that have meant for discipline, especially in light of the changes that are coming in the near future?"

"Maurice, it was a matter of life and death! You know that yourself. Come with me to the infirmary to see Tom and ask him what he has to say about it."

"He won't be able to say anything more for a few weeks, if I understand the doctor correctly. But even if he could now—it doesn't matter. You defied regulations and you have to answer for it. Tom can really be grateful to you. Not everyone and anyone here would have taken the trouble. But it's—"

"Maurice, you can't be serious."

"Now, let me finish. It's really no big deal. You want to leave us on the 29th anyway. So in your last days here, you can put your feet up and relax, or take a look at the area in peace. Who knows when you'll come back? They assured me that they won't touch your pension. Otherwise, I wouldn't have taken the post."

Yes, you are serious. You must have been planning this for a long time!

Steve smacked the wall. *Maurice, you traitor!* And he'd

considered him a friend. "Ah, so you're my successor? I should have guessed that. Did you tell them about my action?"

"Really, Steve? You know me better than that. No one had to report your rule violation. You raced *Blue Moon 34* right through the exhaust plume. In doing so, you broke more rules than anyone before you. You couldn't remain commander under those circumstances."

"Says the new *commander*."

"Says Maurice, your *friend*. Please don't be unfair. Some in the Lunar Gate wanted to throw you out dishonorably. But not me! Just be glad you're heading out of here. Androids like Sean will take over one job at a time. I don't give myself more than two years. I'm sure you wouldn't have enjoyed handling the dwindling human crew. But what am I talking about? You were set to leave anyway."

Steve cooled his forehead on the smooth wall. Maurice was right. He still had five days here. It didn't matter if he was officially commander during that time. More importantly, he'd saved Tom's life. Maybe. *Hopefully*.

"Okay, Maurice. No hard feelings. It was just... The way you—"

"Sorry, Steve. I was just too chicken and hoped that the people from the Lunar Gate would inform you."

It was a bad idea to come here, Steve thought.

Tom looked as if he hadn't been among the living for a long time. He floated naked in a glass container that resembled Snow White's coffin. The slightly oily nutrient fluid flowed past him from top to bottom. Its density was calculated so that the body floated in the container without any supporting surface. The patient received air through an opaque mask—merciful because it meant you couldn't see that the person was intubated.

Tom had his eyes closed. Steve imagined him opening them underwater—how he'd get scared, couldn't breathe, would want to rip the tube out. None of this would happen, as medication kept him in a perpetual dream state. Steve forced himself to step closer. He saw the fine, bright red lines on the skin beside his belly button where Daniela had operated.

The robodoc, which had refused to do the surgery, was attached to the foot of the container but showed no activity. The container was responsible for monitoring Tom's condition. Currently, about half of the indicator lights were green, the others orange. When—if—they all displayed green, then Tom would be better. His condition was stable, but it was not yet clear which direction the little bit of life still inside him would choose. It could happen that quickly. Daniela thought Tom must have felt the pain, but at some point he must have managed to suppress it. Maybe Tom, only 29, thought he was immortal.

Steve looked around. There were three treatment bays of this type in the infirmary. With a crew of 13, they'd only been entitled to two, but he'd argued Mission Control for the third one because of the additional visitors who had arrived regularly in the early years. The moon had become boring, both for explorers and tourists. Those who were self-respecting took vacations on Mars and explored the Red Planet. In contrast to Earth and the moon, it still had new formations to be discovered.

It was good that he was going back to Earth soon. Maybe he'd even do a tour like this one, but to Mars, one day. On the other hand, he had seen enough hostile deserts in his life. Leaving the house without a breathing mask and space suit would seem like pure luxury to him, at least at first. And then? He would see. Slowly, he'd have to think about retirement. He planned to sign up with an online dating site, look for a nice, also divorced woman with no attachments, and then settle down somewhere up north. Maybe in the Illinois hills, where it was nice and green.

One of the lights on Tom's bed flickered. It decided to become a green light. Steve took it as a good omen.

December 25, 2099

The mattress moved under his body. Then the suspension made a soft squeaking sound. Had Sammy snuck into his room? Steve opened his eyes. Someone was standing in front of him, wearing his pajamas.

"Good morning, sleepyhead," Daniela said.

He quickly closed his eyes again. So it hadn't been a dream induced by all the red wine from last night's festive dinner. His heart started to beat faster. What should he say to her? Should he thank her for the beautiful night? That would sound stupid. And what if she thought it was awful> Should he swear eternal love? That would be downright irresponsible. Four more days and he'd be sitting in *Blue Moon 34* and... Oh yes, the doctor had a ticket, too.

A warm hand stroked his hair. "I know you're awake," she said.

Steve opened his eyes. Her face was very close to his. He closed his mouth and breathed through his nose, assuming he had bad breath. Daniela smelled as if she had already been in the bathroom.

"Don't worry about it," she said, "I'm not particularly clingy. Thanks for the pleasant diversion."

"You're welcome," he said, annoyed.

Such a stupid answer. *You're welcome, thank you, come again soon.* But what else was he supposed to say? It was the most incredible sex he'd had in the last two years. Not exactly impressive when he'd only had sex with himself during that time. He hoped he could just close his eyes and go back to sleep until Daniela had left the room.

But she made no effort to grant his wish. She walked through his room and looked at his belongings. There was not much left, because he had already packed most of it into a freight crate. This morning, Samantha would come with one of the cargo robots to pick them up. *This morning!* What time was it?

He looked at the digital display above the door. It was

already a little past ten! If Samantha came and found him with the doctor, the whole moon would know tomorrow. Samantha even had friends in the Lunar Palace. Often enough, the Chinese base had been the last resort in the search for spare parts.

He had to stand up. Steve pushed the blanket off. He was naked, since Daniela was wearing his pajamas. She made the thumbs-up sign. What did that mean? Never mind. He stood up and went to the locker, retrieved a fresh towel, and wrapped it around his hips. He put a second towel over his right shoulder and walked to the community bathroom.

There he opened the first shower and was startled again. In front of him was a naked woman who turned her back to him and soaped herself.

"Finally! Come in!" she called without turning around.

It was Samantha's voice. At least he didn't have to worry that she was about to show up at his door with the cargo robot. He made no sound, quickly closed the door, and looked for another cubicle. He entered it and locked it behind him. He had just turned on the shower when he heard a male voice talking to Samantha. He didn't even know she had a boyfriend. But that it was Ricky, of all people? The two seemed to almost hate each other in public.

He stood under the gentle stream of the shower. The drops enveloped him because they grew so large in the low gravity, and fell so slowly. It was almost as if he were bathing standing up. He would have to get used to the hard, small drops on Earth again.

Slowly, the Rover rolled uphill. The crater slope was flat. Steve could drive faster, even though the road condition was still bad, but he simply didn't feel like it. They passed a turnoff. No sign indicated where the road led.

"Where does that go?" asked Daniela.

"To the Lunar Palace. Have you ever been to Zeeman Crater?"

The so-called Lunar Palace, built on the far side of the moon by the Chinese and Russian space agencies, was not very impressive in comparison with the huge radio telescope that took up the entire crater. Incredible amounts of regolith had been moved at the time to reshape the crater for the telescope.

"No, never," Daniela said.

"Even though it's much closer to you guys?"

She raised a shoulder, which didn't tell him much.

ESA's Lunar Village was located in and on Shackleton Crater, almost exactly at the South Pole. There were areas there where the sun almost always shone, which was convenient for stable energy production with solar cells. NASA had not been quite so courageous in planning the Lunar Base—building on crater rims had a few disadvantages. In the ancient Demonax crater they were leaving, everything was guaranteed to be stable, and since it was on the front side, Earth was never in radio shadow.

"How far is it from here to the Lunar Palace?" asked Daniela.

"Do you have time for a little side trip?"

Steve entered the new destination and '497 kilometers' appeared on the display. He read out the value, then entered the Shackleton crater of Lunar Village as the starting point.

"And another four hundred and fifty kilometers back, as the crow flies—so to speak," he said.

"Almost a thousand kilometers," Daniela said. "That's at least twenty-five hours of driving. I think we'll put that off for another occasion."

"I have time. They don't need me at Lunar Base anymore."

"I heard about that, Steve. I'm sorry. But I believe you did the right thing. Tom is on a good path. I went to see him before we left."

"Thank you."

He had been uncomfortable with making another 'visit,' not wanting to stand there watching his friend's body floating between life and death, looking so vulnerable in the nutrient fluid. He would be long gone when Tom woke up again in a few weeks.

The Rover had reached the crater rim. The view continued across the lunar plain illuminated by the sun. Even though he had admired it so often, he was still impressed by the landscape. On the horizon loomed the Malapert mountain range. They would drive around it to the west, across the Scott Crater. Later, the road wound into Shoemaker Crater, before finally reaching Lunar Village at kilometer 356 on the slopes of Shackleton.

Steve switched on autopilot. They were not in a hurry today, so he didn't need to push it. He was no longer needed here, but he had a pleasant companion with whom it was wonderful to travel even in silence while the grandiose landscape passed them by.

Buy the book here:

hard-sf.com/links/2729056

Printed in Great Britain
by Amazon

55884949R00179